It was a Small Affair

KEN HART

This is a work of fiction. Names, characters, places, and incidents are products of the author's imagination or are used fictitiously and are not to be construed as real. Any resemblance to actual events, locations, organizations, or persons, living or dead, is entirely coincidental.

World Castle Publishing, LLC
Pensacola, Florida

Paperback ISBN: 9781629899985
eBook ISBN: 9781629899992
First Edition World Castle Publishing, LLC, October 8, 2018
http://www.worldcastlepublishing.com

Licensing Notes

Cover: Moriarty
Editor: Maxine Bringenberg

Table of Contents

Prologue

Many people considered the numerous stairs fronting the Library of Congress in Washington, D.C. a daunting trek as they made their way to the top, but a young army lieutenant easily took the stairs two at a time. When he reached the top, he looked back and smiled because he was not at all fatigued when he walked through the doors.

"Good morning. How can I help you?" the receptionist at the front desk said.

"Yes, ma'am. I'm First Lieutenant William Walker. I applied for a research card last month," he replied with an obvious southern drawl.

"May I see your identification card please?" The receptionist entered the information from his card into the computer on her desk. "Thank you for your service, Lieutenant Walker. Please go to Ms. Allen's desk." She pointed to the desk as she returned his ID card. "She's the chief librarian on duty today, and she will give you your research card."

The young soldier made his way to the head librarian's desk. "Ms. Allen? I'm First Lieutenant Walker. I've been referred to you for my research card."

"May I see your ID card? Thank you for your service, Lieutenant Walker. This is your Library of Congress Reader Identification Card. Please keep it clipped to your jacket or shirt. You may use any computer in the main public reading room, where you will have unlimited use of the computer system. Do you know how to use a computer?"

"Yes, ma'am. Doesn't everyone these days?"

"You'd be surprised by how many people come in without any computer knowledge. Some come in to use books because they enjoy the tactile feeling of a book in their hand. Others claim the words on the page of a book cannot be altered like computer records."

"It sounds like they're afraid of a government conspiracy."

"I'm not allowed to comment on that. Please follow me, and we'll log you in."

"Thank you. I have to admit, I'm awed by the immensity of this place."

"We're very proud of it. Here is a station you can use. Please have a seat and login as WWalker. Type in today's date as all numbers, 022210, then the code on the back of your research card, and…there, you're in. Most of our catalog has been scanned into the computer, but if you want specific documents or books, put your request in through the computer request form. If the document is here, in this library, it will be located and brought to you. If the document is in one of the off-site archives, it will be sent here and brought to you. It could take several minutes to a few hours to fill your request, so please be patient. If your request is restricted because of environmental concerns, or it's fragile, a special request to view the item must be made directly through me, and I'll make arrangements for you to view the item. If you have any problems, please ask any of our staff librarians, and they will be happy to help you. To help you get started, what would you like to research today?"

"I'm interested in the Civil War, and I hope to find letters, diaries, journals, anything written during the Battle of Gettysburg by General Lee and General Meade. I hope to gain some insight on their personalities, and their thoughts as leaders of their respective armies."

"To begin, I suggest you enter their names, and the search engine will give you what we have cross referenced under their names."

"It's like Google."

"Our system is faster and much more efficient. Good luck, Lieutenant Walker."

"Thank you."

***

Walker was reading an order from General Meade when he was approached by a tall, gaunt, almost ancient looking man wearing a name tag that simply read "Librarian."

"Lieutenant Walker, come with me. I will show you a document in the restricted archives you will be interested in," he said stiffly, as if he was struggling with the language.

"Am I allowed in the restricted archives?" Walker asked, intrigued by the offer.

"Restricted archives, yes."

"Should we ask Ms. Allen for permission to enter the archives?"

"Not necessary."

On the way to the archives, Walker noticed the security cameras were shrouded in a fog clinging to the ceiling.

"It looks like the air conditioning needs adjustment. There's a lot of humidity up there."

"Humidity, like a blinding cloud, yes," Librarian said, but didn't look up.

Walker was led to a secured, heavy metal door. Barely touching the dial, Librarian spun a combination lock. The door opened, and they entered an airlock leading to a controlled environment vault. At a desk, Librarian reached into a drawer and said, "Wear these." When Walker was handed a pair of white, lint free gloves, an electric arc jumped through the gloves.

"Wow, static!" Walker exclaimed, recoiling and shaking his hand.

"Static, yes. Wait here." Librarian was unaffected by the shock.

Librarian went to the end of a row of large, movable filing cabinets and operated a three-pronged wheel. The entire stack of vertical cabinets moved aside, and he disappeared into the opening. He returned with a cardboard container, placed it on the table, and opened it.

"Read."

"'A Survivors History of the Battle of the Alamo'? I can think of someone who'd be interested in this," Walker said as he read the first page of the old, handwritten document.

"Webber, yes."

"Do you know Staff Sergeant Webber?"

Librarian looked at the door and said, "There is another document. I will get it."

Walker watched as Librarian hurriedly disappeared around the row of cabinets. Shortly after, a cloud-like fog such as one from a CO2 fire extinguisher silently spilled from between the filing cabinets, then quickly dissipated.

"Lieutenant Walker! What are you doing in here?" Ms. Allen

asked.

"I was escorted by one of your staff."

"I didn't get a request for research in the restricted archives. Who escorted you?" Ms. Allen asked gruffly, looking around the archive.

"He went down that last row of cabinets."

"Who's in here?" When she looked down the row, she said, "Lieutenant Walker, will you come here please?"

"Where'd he go?" Walker asked when he looked around the corner of the cabinets.

"There's no exit from here. Did you see his name tag?"

"Yes, it said Librarian."

"Of course he was a librarian, but what's his name?"

"That's it, Librarian."

"You must've misread it, because we don't have any employees named Librarian. What did he look like?"

"He was tall, old, thin, spoke with an accent I didn't recognize; and he was odd."

"Odd?"

"Yes, ma'am. Very odd."

"We have no one by that description. I'll have to escort you out."

"Yes, ma'am. I apologize for being here."

As they were leaving, he paused at the table. "Ms. Allen, do you know anything about this document that was brought to me?"

"Since you're already here, we can look at them. These cover sheets are acid free to prevent damage. These codes tell me this document entered the archives in 1836 during John Meehan's tenure as the Fourth Librarian of Congress. In fact, the initials on this second page tell me he accepted this document himself. It was converted to microfiche in 1934 and was converted again to computer files in 2006."

"So, it's genuine?" Walker asked.

"We do not knowingly keep fraudulent documents, unless the fraudulent nature of the document has historical significance, and they are always marked as such. This one is not marked."

"When I was glancing through it, I saw something strange. Will you read the first page for me, please?"

She reached into a drawer, retrieved a pair of white gloves, and gently turned to the first page. "No, this isn't possible. This document's been in the library since 1836." She again looked at the two cover sheets, and then leaned in close to the page. "The writing was not made by quill and ink. The lines are too fine and consistent. It looks like it's been written with a ball point pen. Did you put this here?"

"Absolutely not, ma'am. Like I said, Librarian brought it to me."

"This has to be a forgery of some kind."

"How's that possible? You said it's been here since 1836."

"This will have to be investigated," Ms. Allen stated, not taking her eyes from it as she gently turned another page.

"Can I get copies of it from the computer?"

"Of course. There's a reference number on the first cover page. Write down the number and I'll take you to your station," Ms. Allen said, reluctant to tear herself from the document as she carefully scrutinized every aspect of it.

After Walker printed and retrieved the pages, he sat at a desk and began to read. After he read the first few pages, he rapidly skimmed through the remainder of the document.

***

Librarian stealthily approached Walker from behind, pressed

two buttons on his shirt, and whispered, "Return to Fort Hood. Stop Webber," then quickly stepped back.

"I've got to get back to Fort Hood!" Walker bounded out of the chair, stuffed the printed papers into his briefcase with the intent of reading them on the way, and hurriedly left the library to catch a flight back to Texas.

Seeing Lieutenant Walker leave the building, Librarian walked to the men's room and entered a stall. Fog filled the stall, followed by electrical arching that quickly dissipated. Librarian had disappeared.

From a nearby stall, someone exclaimed, "What in the hell was that?"

CHAPTER 1
TUESDAY, FEBRUARY 23, 2010

It was hot, agonizingly hot as I stood in an open field of neatly manicured bright green grass. I never saw such green in Afghanistan, or felt such heat. The field was littered with bodies of wounded soldiers, moaning, screaming. Suddenly sweeping from the sky were vampires, dozens of them, landing on the wounded soldiers, sucking life out of the screaming men. I had to help them, but I had no weapon.

"Staff Sergeant Webber?"

I was running, breathlessly running to help those men when a sudden blaze of bright light stopped the screams.

"Staff Sergeant Webber!" The company charge of quarters shouted from a safe distance next to the door, where he flipped the light switch on.

"What?" I mumbled, wiping the sweat from my face across my pillow. Blinking sleepily and fighting off another sudden headache, I rolled over to face the lunatic who had blinded me.

"We've been called up. Get your platoon on the company area behind the orderly room, packed for rapid deployment. Be on line at 0600 hours."

"Where's Sergeant First Class McFadden?"

"He's not answering his phone. You're next on the recall roster."

"I'll get the platoon up."

I glanced at my clock and saw we had less than two hours to get wired and out of the barracks. In my boxer shorts and socks, I walked around the hall and banged on all the platoon members' doors, relaying the orders to get up and get packed. Returning to my room, I pulled out my nearly packed duffle bag, and was dressing when a silent shadow walked in.

"Welcome back, Sergeant Sutter."

"Yeah, I'm back in time for another trip," he mumbled tiredly as he pulled out his equipment and began changing out of his civilian clothes.

"You know, you could've stayed on leave until we found out if this is just an exercise."

"I wasn't going to run around, trying to get ready at the last minute, if it was an emergency deployment."

"Good idea. How was your leave?"

"My mother and Oregon family argued as usual, but my dad…." Sutter stifled himself with a huge yawn. "…and my California family is fine. Time with my dad and brothers was too short, as usual."

"Time flies when you're having fun. Are you ready for war?"

"I go where they tell me. Where's our platoon sergeant?"

"The CQ said Mac's not answering his phone, so it looks like we're it."

"Great. You have control of the misfit platoon, and I'm in charge of the last chance squad," Sutter muttered sarcastically.

"Sergeant Sutter, you know that's not true. Second Platoon is not a misfit platoon."

"Yeah? Well, I heard the first sergeant tasked Mac to weed out the non-soldiers and recommend discharge for those who can't cut it in First Squad."

"You know we're not supposed to speak about that, but since it's open we'll have a quick discussion, and then it's closed; understood?"

"Understood. Why does our squad have all the misfits in the company?"

"It only seems that way. Let's start at the top with our platoon leader, First Lieutenant Walker. He's been with Second Platoon since long before we arrived, and as far as I can tell he's a good officer. Then we have Sergeant First Class McFadden, who's one hell of a good NCO. He's hard, but as fair as they come. Then there's you—"

"Did we skip someone here?" Sutter interrupted.

"You're here under a medical evaluation for your leg wound."

"I can do anything any man in the platoon can do!"

"Better in most cases. Moving on, we have Corporal Breckenridge, Private First Class Carpenter, Private First Class Ruiz, Private First Class Snyder, and Private Wallace; all good soldiers with no unusual disciplinary problems or medical conditions. Now we come to reasons why First Squad is called the last chance squad. Corporal Thompson got religious, and I won't criticize him for it, but when it interferes with his duties, something has to be done. He has applied for conscientious objector status but wishes to remain in the army and become a chaplain's assistant. Considering how long he's been in the army, I doubt he'll get away with it. Private Sanchez was a good soldier until he started running with Private Hernández. Sergeant First Class McFadden said to keep him apart from Hernández as much as possible. Private Hernández is our one true problem within the platoon. He's lazy, disobedient, and disrespectful at every opportunity he thinks he can get away with. I have no proof, but I suspect he's the one behind the problems with racist complaints at battalion legal. Ever since Sergeant First Class McFadden was summoned to battalion legal, I think he's lost patience with Hernández."

"I wouldn't want to be on Mac's bad side," Sutter commented.

"Call him Mac to his face, and you might get crushed on his bad side."

"The only problem child left is you." Sutter's broad smile was a bit annoying.

"Like you, mine's a medical evaluation."

"What kind of—?"

"Medical…evaluation. Subject closed. Move on."

"Maybe Mac's wife went into labor," Sutter said, quickly changing the subject.

"She was huge when we were at his barbecue last month. She might be having twins."

"That'd please him," Sutter commented. "It's getting late. We'd better check the platoon."

"I'm not worried about those of us living in the barracks, but those living off post had better show up on time. If not, the first sergeant will be all over them, and there'll be hell to pay. You finish up here, and I'll motivate the platoon."

I went to each shared platoon room to make sure the men were up and moving. Pride and dedication were showing in second platoon, because almost everyone was ready on the short notice. Roommates were helping those who weren't ready as they hurriedly packed their duffle bags with necessary equipment and supplies.

"Come on people; get it on the company street!" I shouted

as the squad filed past me, except for Corporal Thompson, who was on his knees beside his bed. "Come on, Reverend, move it!"

It was a few seconds before he responded with, "I'm in prayer."

"Until your request for conscientious objector is approved, you have a job to do. Get to it!"

"You're a heathen, unworthy of Heaven!" Thompson shouted after I left the room.

He was probably right, but instead of dragging his ass downstairs, I shook my head at his comment and checked the other rooms to be sure all were out. Fortunately for Thompson, he'd vacated the room before I returned. I checked to see if Sutter was still in our room, placed my duffle bag on my shoulders, and went outside. The crisp February air was a great stimulant. Not as good as coffee, but enough for now.

Rather than march everyone to the orderly room, I decided to include a bit of physical training to brighten our morning.

"Get your spacing! Quickly, people, quickly! Tighten up the heavy bags. Fall in! Right, face! Forward, march! Double time, march! Here in the army, what do they say?"

"All work, work!" the platoon responded, clapping to the cadence as we jogged to the orderly room.

"All work, hard work, that's what they say!"

"All work, work!"

"Up in the morning 'bout a quarter to four!"

"All work, work!"

"Got to get another days' pay!"

"All work, work!"

Shouting the cadence, we shuffled around the loosely forming platoons until I commanded "Quick time…march! Platoon…halt! Ground your packs, line 'em up by squad, and fall in." I noted most of our platoon's soldiers who lived off-post were already waiting. It was not surprising, because they got the calls before we did in the barracks.

When the packs were neatly grounded, everyone aligned themselves with their squad leaders in four ranks. Being without our platoon sergeant, I took the command position in front of the platoon and shouted, "Fall in! Squad leaders report."

"First Squad, two unaccounted for." Sutter said with a salute.

"Second Squad, all present or accounted for."

"Third Squad, all present."

"Fourth Squad, all present."

"Sergeant Sutter, you're missing Private Sanchez and Private Hernández." I looked at the squad to confirm his report.

"Yes, Staff Sergeant."

"Sergeant Davis, who're you missing and, where are they?"

"Sergeant Wright and Corporal Barnes. Wright is in the arms room, and Barnes is driving."

"Corporal Thompson, front and center." After he had come to attention before me, I said quietly, "The little run in full gear this morning is because of you."

"But—"

"Call me a heathen again, and we'll see just how far the whole platoon can run in full gear before *you* fall out. Or, I can take you to the captain and see what an Article 15 can do for you. I'm certain the non-judicial punishment would do wonders for your request for chaplain duty. Do you understand?"

"Yeah."

"Do you understand?" I shouted.

"Yes, Staff Sergeant!"

"Fall in," I said with a nod of my head. "At ease. It looks like we had some rain last night. Sergeant Sutter, what's the weather forecast?"

"Clearing later today with a warming trend. Tonight and tomorrow, seasonably cool for a Texas February, with no rain during the rest of the week." I nodded my agreement.

"Staff Sergeant, why is the weather forecast so important to you?" Private First Class Snyder asked.

"It should be important to everyone. Knowing the weather as far in advance as possible gives a soldier an advantage by being able to prepare himself and his equipment. During the Second World War, the Germans used weather to a great advantage when they attacked through the Ardennes Forest."

"What's the Ardennes?" someone said.

"Doesn't anyone care about military history? Sergeant Sutter, explain."

"It's known as the Battle of the Bulge. Bitter cold and snowy weather covered the Nazis' sneak attack through the Ardennes Forest. The lack of fuel, and Nazi obsession with the town of Bastogne, was met by coordinated Allied counter-attacks that caused the Germans to lose their last, best chance to win World War Two."

"I've never heard the Germans were obsessed with Bastogne. They had to take Bastogne because it was a strategic position with several roads converging on the town."

"The Germans could've left a token force surrounding Bastogne to keep the Allies trapped there while they secured fuel depots in the rear of the Allied lines. With a strategic position behind the Allied lines and the fuel they needed, they could've taken Bastogne with reserves later."

"They did leave a token force when Hitler ordered them to bypass Bastogne and take the Allied fuel reserves. The Germans almost reached the advanced fuel depots near the Meuse River, but the Allies stopped them before they could get there." I couldn't believe I'd gotten sucked into that conversation. I hoped this never got back to Lieutenant Walker. I was sure it would've started an energetic discussion between the armchair generals.

"Sarge, are we—?"

"Professionalism, Private Wallace. Say the rank of the person you're talking to first. If an officer or some hardcore NCO heard you say Sarge, they could go ugly on you."

"Too late, some of them own ugly," someone said, as stifled chuckles filtered from the platoon.

"Staff Sergeant Webber, are we going to war?" Wallace asked, nervous about the call up.

"Instead of partying, you should read the papers or watch the news. There's nothing happening in the world right now that'd warrant a quick call up. It's probably another EDRE. If we were under a unit deployment, we would've been preparing for it long before now."

The platoons had loosely formed behind the orderly room, and I was chafing at the bit with impatience as I frequently reminded myself of the army mantra, "Hurry up and wait."

It was nearly 0700 hours when the company commander and first sergeant came out of the orderly room. Everyone went quiet as they quickly aligned themselves with their squad leaders.

"Company!" Captain Ibanez shouted.

"Platoon!" the platoon sergeants responded.

"Ah...Ten...Shun!"

"Lock and load!" the four infantry platoons shouted as they snapped to attention.

"Platoon sergeants, report!"

"All present or accounted for!" the first platoon sergeant responded with a salute.

"Excellent!" The captain returned the salute.

"Three unaccounted for!" I said with a snappy salute as acting platoon sergeant.

"Thank you." The captain looked down in mock disappointment when he returned my salute.

"All present!" The third platoon sergeant shouted with his salute.

"Outstanding!" Captain Ibanez shouted, slightly leaning back, twisting back and forth before straightening up and returning the salute. I heard snickering from behind me. Some of the men within the platoons were a little too comfortable with—how dare I put it—our company commander's little eccentricities.

"All present!" the fourth platoon sergeant said with his salute.

"Outstanding!" Captain Ibanez shouted, performing his little act before acknowledging the salute. He looked slowly across the platoons and then shouted, "All privates, drop and give me twenty!"

Chaos erupted when the privates scrambled for an area to perform the ordered pushups, shouting the count as they did so.

"Recover! All NCO's drop and give me twenty! First Sergeant Atkinson, give me twenty."

Many of the company privates were laughing as the non-commissioned officers performed the required pushups.

"Recover! The battalion commander woke us early for an EDRE. For the new people, that means Emergency Deployment and Readiness Exercise," Captain Ibanez said.

"Sir! On behalf of the company, I request that all officers drop and give us twenty!" First Sergeant Atkinson's deep booming voice and tall, muscular stature automatically commanded attention and respect.

Stunned silence caught everyone when the captain looked at the first sergeant until he said, "Officers, drop and give the company twenty!"

The officers performed the required pushups, including Captain Ibanez, who was laughing rather than counting.

"Officers, recover! At Ease! Platoon sergeants, up here," Captain Ibanez said, gesturing us toward him. "Staff Sergeant Webber, who're you missing?"

"Sir, Sergeant First Class McFadden, Sergeant Wright, Corporal Breckenridge, Private Sanchez, and Private Hernández."

"Sergeant McFadden's wife went into labor early this morning. We'll take up a collection for his new family addition after the EDRE. Sergeant Wright and Corporal Breckenridge are accounted for in the arms room. Now, on a very serious matter, the Staff Judge Advocate has recognized an increasing trend of racist complaints from this company, generally directed at non-commissioned officers for the apparent purpose of discrediting them. I've said it many times, racism will not be tolerated. Those involved will be dealt with swiftly and severely. Put the word out among the men again. Staff Sergeant Webber, you're an Alamo enthusiast, and I know—"

"Sir, please don't get him started," First Sergeant Atkinson said.

"Did you know today in 1836, the siege of the Alamo began? Did you also know the Alamo was named for the Spanish word for cottonwood?" I said.

"Not now, Staff Sergeant," Atkinson grumbled, bored with my talks about Alamo history.

"I know you said nothing that could be considered racist or prejudicial in your discussions about the Alamo, despite the accusations made against you," Captain Ibanez said.

"Sir, I've been accused five times in the past three months. I'd like to know who made the complaints, as if I don't already know." I had good reason to be bitter when I turned to see if our two missing soldiers had arrived yet.

"Anyone can use Mexico and Mexican in the same sentence without being a racist," Ibanez said, sidestepping my question. "Battalion legal has completed its investigations and dropped charges against all NCOs in this company." There was a quiet sigh of relief from the gathered platoon sergeants, and not entirely for the accused men in their platoons.

"Sir, Hernández and Sanchez have decided to join us," Atkinson said quietly, nodding his head toward second platoon, where Hernández and Sanchez were easing themselves into the end of First Squad. As assistant squad leader, Sergeant Sutter moved toward them just as the first sergeant left the impromptu meeting and walked toward fourth platoon. Sutter got into Hernández's face, and began an earnest conversation with him.

"Sergeant Sutter's going to declare war on them," I commented, while the platoon sergeants covertly watched the confrontation.

With an exchange of comments we couldn't hear, Sutter pointed to the rear of the formation where Hernández and Sanchez should have remained when arriving late to any formation. Hernández said something and flipped him the finger. When I saw Sutter ball his fists I started to shout and wave him off, but the captain put his hand on my shoulder, and said, "At ease, Staff Sergeant."

The first sergeant swept in from behind the platoon and grabbed Hernández and Sanchez by the collars of their body armor and dragged them stumbling behind the platoon. Sergeant Sutter looked at me with a surprised expression, and then returned to his position at the head of the squad.

"Gentlemen," Captain Ibanez regained our attention. "Since our first sergeant is occupied, I'll give the briefing. We have a change to our training schedule. We'll use the EDRE to begin an overnight exercise. When everyone has drawn their M16s, we'll move to the range for a familiarization fire of the M203 Grenade Launcher. When it's completed, we'll force march to range fifteen alpha to zero and qualify with our M16s. Then we'll wait until dark to night qualify. At 2300 hours we'll begin an escape and evasion exercise. The company will be broken into squads and given a thirty-minute head start. We'll be pursued by elements of the 18th Military Police Battalion, who are also on a training exercise. Everyone will be carrying all their equipment, and they will try to get to a position ten klicks north of the start point without being captured. If you're caught, you will be returned to the start point to escape again. You will not ambush or take prisoners during this exercise." Ibanez looked directly at me.

"Sir, there were no instructions about ambush or prisoners, other than that there were ambushes waiting for us," I said, quick to defend the squad.

"During our last exercise, a lieutenant, three NCO's, and several of their squad members were tied up and left out all night before they were found. They were not happy about it."

"Sir, that was three months ago. Why am I just hearing about it now?"

"Since no one could be conclusively identified in the dark, it's the primary reason why no disciplinary actions could be taken against First Squad, or you. Keep that in mind during this exercise."

"Yes, sir."

"And, there's the unresolved matter of a stolen vehicle."

Knowing I could be in deep trouble over this, I had to choose my words carefully. "Sir, as I understand the situation, a truck was found unlocked and was…borrowed. From what I heard it was returned and secured in accordance with post regulations, like it should've been before it was found."

"Because you adapted to the situation, most of the company reached the rally point in record time. Don't do it again."

"Yes, sir." I was relieved that no one would be punished for our adaptability. In fact, it was our adaptability that had saved us from punishment.

"Platoon sergeants, make sure you and your squad leaders have compasses. Squad leaders will be responsible for the location of their men at all times. Don't let anyone get lost this time. Staff Sergeant Webber, First Squad has ammo duty. Take your squad to the arms room and draw your weapons. The armorer has already fitted your M16s with the grenade launcher. The company will use your weapons for the M203 familiarization fire. Fall out," Captain Ibanez said.

"Yes, sir," we said in unison, and returned to our platoons.

"Company!" Captain Ibanez shouted.

"Platoon!" the platoon sergeants responded.

"Ah…Ten…Shun!"

"Lock and load!"

"Platoon sergeants, take charge." The captain saluted before returning to the orderly room.

Turning to the platoon, I said, "Sergeant Davis, front and center." The Second Squad leader came to attention in front of me. "First Squad has ammo duty, so you're acting platoon sergeant. We're going on an overnight exercise, so make sure you and your squad leaders have their lensatic compasses. When you get your helmet radios and night vision goggles, double check their operation, and turn them off to conserve batteries. If you have time, get spare batteries from the supply room. The company will get detailed instructions from the range safety officer when we get there. First Squad, fall out, pick up your gear, and fall in at the arms room. Sergeant Davis, take charge. Sergeant Sutter, what did Hernández say that has the First Sergeant in an uproar?" I asked as I picked up my duffle bag.

"*Pegue esto en el culo,*" Sutter said in Spanish.

"What?"

"I'm supposed to stick this up my ass." He showed me his middle finger. "I was going to deck him, but the first sergeant pulled him out of range."

"If it'd been me, I would've had to take the abuse and disrespect again, and let McFadden handle it. I'm getting tired of dealing with those two."

"Yeah, me too. What're we doing today?"

"We've been selected for ammo duty. When we're done with that, we'll familiarize with the M203 grenade launcher; then we'll zero and qualify with our M16s. Our rifles have been outfitted with the M203, and the entire company will use them to fire with. Tonight we'll night qualify, followed by an escape and evasion exercise. The company will be pursued by the military police again."

"Can we take prisoners?" Sutter asked hopefully.

"Unfortunately, no. I think the captain got his ass reamed for what we did last time."

"I'll bet we have to wear our heavy bags and carry our weapons again."

"It's good training. First Squad, put your duffle bags in the truck, and fall in along the wall," I said when we arrived at the arms room.

"Staff Sergeant Webber!" First Sergeant Atkinson's voice boomed as he walked toward me with Hernández and Sanchez in front of him. They were holding their duffle bags in their arms instead of wearing them on their backs. "Take charge of these two."

"Yes, First Sergeant. Hernández, Sanchez, fall in at the end of the squad. Sergeant Sutter!" I pointed at our wayward squad members, and he made sure they arrived and stayed at the end of the squad, still carrying their bags in their arms instead of dropping them in the truck.

"Webber, walk with me. Immediately after we get back from the escape and evasion exercise, take Hernández to the company commander."

"First Sergeant; non-judicial punishment, extra duty, all the disciplinary actions given to him does nothing to change his attitude. In fact, it makes it worse."

"After seeing his actions for himself this morning, the captain is going to recommend to battalion that Hernández be discharged."

"Does he know?"

"Not yet, but the captain has had enough of him, even before this morning."

"Does Sergeant McFadden know?"

"He'll be notified of the captain's decision when he returns."

"First Sergeant, I'm concerned about having Hernández on a live-fire exercise. I request he be relieved and stay behind."

"Request denied. You and Sergeant Sutter will keep him out of trouble until we get back."

"What about Sanchez?"

"The captain thinks there's a chance to turn him into a soldier once he's away from Hernández's influence. Report to Sergeant

Wright in the arms room," Atkinson ordered, unwilling to listen to me argue over what he already knew.

"Yes, First Sergeant." I turned and trotted to the arms room.

"Staff Sergeant Webber, I heard you have the duty," the armorer, Sergeant Wright, observed.

"You can tell I'm overjoyed. I see we have the five-ton excuse for a truck again. Are we the only unit on post with that antique?"

"It may be old, but it beats walking."

"We're infantry! The Queen of Battle! We love to walk!" Laughter at my enthusiasm followed from outside the door.

"Is insanity necessary for promotion?" Wright said, scowling at me.

"Probably not."

"If it were, you'd be a general by now. Have your squad sign for their M16s and night vision goggles."

"No helmet radios?"

"Patience, Staff Sergeant. They'll be issued, but I'll give you a short block of instructions on this new model. It's basically the same, but in addition to the push-to-talk button, there's a switch where you can activate the VOX."

"Voice Operated Switch. I heard it was going to be put on the radios."

I was intrigued by this addition to the radio. To be able to talk during a firefight, without letting go of the rifle to push a button, put a new level of communication and control in the hands of the soldier. The ability to listen to the men's comments, hear what they were experiencing first hand, and being able to respond to their needs immediately was immeasurable.

"Here's the switch." Sergeant Wright pointed to the setting. "Push this way for the voice-operated-switch, and this way for push-to-talk."

"Sergeant Wright, this is way too confusing for me. I don't think I can figure it out."

"Adapt, Staff Sergeant," Captain Ibanez said from the door behind me.

"Yes, sir; I was being sarcastic."

The captain gave me an amused snort before turning to leave.

"If you think you can handle the radio, put the M16s in the weapons rack on the truck," Sergeant Wright said.

"We always carry our weapons," I stated, reacting to the unusual instruction.

"Not on ammo duty. You'll need to keep your hands free to load the truck and help set up at the range. When we're ready, we'll go the ammo bunkers and draw our ammo."

"Do you and your driver need to qualify?" I asked.

"Our M16s with M203 modules are already in the weapons rack."

"Okay. What about the truck radio?"

"Mounted and checked."

"Have the call signs been assigned?"

"The company call sign is Veto Bravo, and the ammo detail is Veto Bravo Three Seven."

"Sounds familiar. Who's the medic?"

"Corporal Taylor's in the supply room, checking the trauma backpack and the Unit One med kit. We've done this before, Staff Sergeant."

"Yeah, about three months ago. Weapons signature sheet?"

"Get your equipment from Corporal Barnes, and sign here."

I went to Barnes's location. "Corporal Barnes, my weapon's butt stock number is Bravo Four Six."

When I received my rifle, helmet radio, and night vision goggles, I checked the serial numbers, confirming them with the sheets. With a quick signature, I was armed long enough to put my M16 in the weapons rack. While I attached the radio and goggles to my helmet, I made certain the squad understood the operation of the new radio setup and had everyone load on the truck. Despite the generous size of the truck bed, it was already crowded with boxes of MREs, duffle bags, and armorers' equipment. It was going to get even more crowded, because we still had several boxes of ammunition to load. I silently sympathized with everyone who'd be riding there because, as the senior non-commissioned officer in charge of the detail, I'd be riding shotgun with the driver.

When the squad had been seated on the wooden slats in the truck bed, I climbed on a rear bumper and said, "Equipment check, night vision goggles first. Give me a thumbs up if you can see. Hernández, that's not your thumb! Turn off and stow the goggles. Verify your radios are set to VOX. Radio check; by the numbers, sound off." I listened as an individual count was given. "Good. Turn off the radios. As soon as Sergeant Wright, Corporal Barnes, and Corporal Taylor are aboard, we'll head out."

***

Live ammunition was tightly controlled on the main post, so we drove to the ammo bunkers, which were a safe distance from everything should an explosive mishap occur. Sergeant Wright inventoried the issues of the 5.56-millimeter rifle rounds and 40-millimeter grenades. When he was satisfied with the count, we loaded the ammo boxes onto the truck.

"Staff Sergeant Webber, what about breakfast?" Corporal Taylor said.

"Sergeant Wright, when do we have to be at the range?"

"As soon as possible. We still have to set up and load clips before the company arrives."

"You heard the instruction. We'll have an MRE breakfast when we get to the range. MRE, what does it stand for?"

"Meal, Ready to Eat."

"Wrong! Meal, Rejected by the Enemy." When the squad seated themselves in the truck bed, I said, "Corporal Barnes, let's get rolling."

***

We'd been on West Range Road for about twenty minutes when I said, "Corporal Barnes, it looks like fog ahead. Slow down before we get to it." When we started slowing, I looked at the rear-view mirror. "Watch out for the speeder behind us. Damn, he's coming up fast. Give that maniac all the room he wants."

"Yes, Staff Sergeant."

As we slowed, the fog seemed to lunge at us, engulfing us completely. As it got thicker, electrostatic arcs began leaping from every surface. Complaints from the squad in the truck bed were getting louder when everyone was repeatedly shocked.

"Pull over and stop," I told Corporal Barnes when I saw him repeatedly release the steering whenever he was shocked.

Barnes complied, applied the parking brake, and turned on the safety flashers.

"Damn! What in the hell's happening?" I exclaimed when I was shocked through my leather glove by a vicious electric arc.

Fog invaded the truck cab through every vent, crack, and crevice. The rapid staccato of static arcing became louder, deafeningly loud. The last thing I remember was everyone shouting and cursing about the increasingly violent shocks before I slumped against the truck door.

CHAPTER 2

DAY ONE - TUESDAY, FEBRUARY 23, 1836

The next thing I remember was leaning against the passenger window of the truck. When I pushed against the door to straighten myself up, I jerked my hand back. Tentatively I tapped my gloved fingers on various surfaces, fully expecting to be shocked. Whatever had electrified the truck had passed. Corporal Barnes was slumped against the steering wheel when I gave him a push on his arm. He let out a groan and slowly sat upright. I opened the pass-through window behind me and checked the squad in the truck bed.

"Is everyone all right?" I asked and was glad to hear the typical grouching and grumbling. "Sergeant Sutter, make sure everyone's okay. Sergeant Wright, contact the company and tell them about our delay."

"I'm on it." The radio cooling fan whined when he keyed the mike. "Veto Bravo Two One, this is Veto Bravo Three Seven, over. Veto Bravo Two One, this is Veto Bravo Three Seven, over."

"Check the frequency setting," I said, not hearing a response from the radio.

"It's set correctly. Veto Bravo Two One, this is Veto Bravo Three Seven, over. There's no answer. The static might've knocked out the radio."

"Gimme me the mike. Any monitoring station, this is Veto Bravo Three Seven, radio check, over. Damn, I hate doing this. Any monitoring station, this is Veto Bravo Three Seven, transmitting in the blind, radio check, over. This is Veto Bravo Three Seven, negative contact, out."

"Transmitting in the blind? I've never read that call in the radio field manual," Wright said.

"It's there, normally used with authentication."

"Any monitoring station sounds like a citizen band radio call."

"Sometimes, a nonstandard procedure gets results; especially from officers and NCOs who're anxious to make on the spot corrections. Run the dial and check all the known Fort Hood frequencies. Also, check the civilian FM radio stations and see if we can receive anything. Who has a cell phone?"

"Staff Sergeant Webber, we're not allowed to have phones on a field training exercise. You know that." Hernández had an irritating, sarcastic way of speaking to his superiors. I bit my tongue to keep a caustic remark from getting me in trouble again.

"I know most of you ignore the commander's directive, especially you Hernández; always jaw-jacking with the girlfriend you live with."

"Girlfriends." He smiled, and bumped Sanchez with his elbow.

"Who has a cell phone?"

After a few seconds of the men guiltily looking at each other, Carpenter produced a phone from his pocket.

"Turn it on and see if you can call your wife."

"It's on, but I don't have any bars." He tried to get a response by tapping the phone on the palm of his hand.

"Maybe the cell towers are down." I looked outside for any towers, but there were none to be seen. "Do you have a GPS locator on your phone?"

"Yes, Staff Sergeant. It's searching for a signal. Still searching… it says no signal."

"Keep checking. If you get anything, let me know."

Surrounding us in the early light of dawn was a typical Texas winter field with tall, dry, sage grass, clumps of brush, and widely spaced cedar trees. There were no roads, fences, or houses as far as I could see.

"I hope we're not in the impact area," I said, looking at Corporal Barnes.

"I stopped when you told me, Staff Sergeant," Barnes said defensively.

"We were still on the shoulder of the road when you did, but we might have coasted into the impact area."

"We couldn't coast anywhere. The transmission's in park and the parking brake is still on."

I unfolded and studied a laminated training map of the Fort Hood area. "We were driving north on West Range Road, and we just crossed Cowhouse Creek, so that puts us about here. Turn around and drive south."

"Which way's south?" he said.

I pulled the lensatic compass out of the case clipped to my equipment strap.

Barnes was looking at me when I asked, "You're going to make me get out, aren't you?"

"A compass can be affected by the truck's magnetic field, Staff Sergeant."

"How can a truck get magnetized?"

"From the electrical system and metallic mass."

"Well done." I smiled because he was right. "It looks like I have to get out."

When I looked at the compass it steadily pointed north over the truck hood, then I got out and carefully walked away from the truck, checking every step before I made it. I swept the compass around, but it still pointed north, apparently unaffected by the truck. When I got back in, I said, "Turn completely around and drive slowly. There may be unexploded ordinance, so watch for craters, rockets, and artillery rounds lying around."

"How far?" Barnes asked.

"About ten klicks, or until we find a road. Watch the odometer and tell me when we've driven six miles. Sergeant Wright, how many MREs do we have?" I said through the truck bed window.

"We loaded thirty-six boxes for the company. That's four hundred thirty-two meals."

"While we figure out where we are, break open a box and let's have breakfast."

***

We crawled along until six miles came and went without seeing a road or any other vehicles. Believing we had cleared the impact area, I told Barnes to increase speed until we had to stop at clear, wide stream.

"Staff Sergeant, this could be Cowhouse Creek," Barnes suggested.

"No, the creek was dry when we crossed the bridge."

"Sergeant Webber, are we lost?" Wright asked through the window, annoying me with his suggestion.

"Get on the radio and try calling the first sergeant."

"Veto Bravo Two-One, this is Veto Bravo Three Seven, over....

Veto Bravo Two-One, this is Veto Bravo Three Seven, over.... No contact, Staff Sergeant."

"Carpenter, do you have any bars on your phone yet?"

"Negative, Staff Sergeant."

"Check the GPS again."

"Checking...there's still no signal."

"Sergeant Wright, Sergeant Sutter, Corporal Barnes, meet me in front of the truck." While I waited until the four of us had gathered in the truck headlights, I checked the map and looked around. "This whole area is basically flat without any decent hills or mountains we can get a contour from. Without GPS coordinates we can apply to the map, we'll have to guess where we are. The only things we can use reliably are rivers and streams."

"This could be the Lampasas River," Sutter suggested, pointing at the map.

"We couldn't have driven that far without seeing Killeen, or crossing Highway 190," Wright said.

"We'll ford the stream and keep going. We've got to see something sooner or later. Load up."

We easily crossed the three-foot-deep stream without incident.

***

We'd been bumping along for about an hour when we topped a rise and spotted a town. After quickly eyeballing the area, I shouted, "Stop the truck! Back up, back up!"

Barnes slammed the truck to a stop, and then quickly backed down the rise. When I jumped out of the truck cab and climbed on one of the rear bumpers, I was assailed by complaints about the rough ride.

"Knock it off! Where's my bag?"

When it was located and rolled to me across legs and boxes,

I pulled out a small pair of camouflaged binoculars I had bought at an army surplus store.

"Everyone out of the truck. Stretch your legs, take a leak, but don't wander off."

I walked to the top of the rise, being careful not to silhouette myself to eyes beyond, and scanned the panorama.

Groups of people were leaving a town to my right, crossing a bridge, some walking, others riding horses and wagons toward an enclosed compound.

"What is it?" Sergeant Sutter asked when he joined me.

"Over there, about four klicks out." I pointed and handed him the binoculars.

"Okay, what am I looking at? No, no, that can't be right."

"Talk to me; what do you see?" I said, wanting confirmation of what I thought I'd seen.

"What's happening?" Sergeant Wright asked when he joined us.

"Something I don't want to believe. Sergeant Sutter, let Sergeant Wright have a look."

"Yeah, yeah." He released the binoculars to Sergeant Wright, but continued to stare at the area.

"It's an old town, so what?"

"That's San Antonio," I stated.

"I've been to San Antonio, and that's not it."

"Look to the left of the river. What do you see?"

"It's an enclosed compound with what looks like the remains an old church."

"Take a closer look. What do you see on the walls?"

"Cannons? Muzzle loading cannons?" Wright's jaw dropped in disbelief.

"Get back to the truck. Sergeant Wright, let's go." I took the binoculars from his reluctant hands, and we trotted down the rise.

"What's going on, Staff Sergeant?" Corporal Thompson asked when we joined the squad at the back of the truck.

"We're outside San Antonio, but— "

"We couldn't have gone over a hundred and fifty miles that fast," Thompson said.

"Go take a look, and be sure to check the buildings to the left of the river," I said as I handed him the binoculars. "We'll wait until he gets back with his observations. PFC Carpenter, are there any bars on your phone yet?"

"Not yet, Staff Sergeant."

"You may as well turn it off because you're not going to get any. I think we're outside San Antonio, and today is February 23, 1836."

"Have you lost your mind?" Private Hernández said.

He knew I hated that phrase above all others, but instead of losing my temper, I said, "'Have you lost your mind, Staff Sergeant?' Don't say another word!" I pointed my finger in his face to keep him quiet.

When Thompson returned, he handed me the binoculars, deliberately dusted his hands in front of me, and stated, "I'm done. I'm not playing anymore."

"Thompson, what'd you see?" Hernández asked.

"I'm not playing anymore!" He stated as he climbed into the back of the truck.

"Load up. We're going to drive to what I think is the Alamo to confirm where, and when, we are."

"The Alamo?" Someone exclaimed.

"Is this some kind of training exercise?" Sutter asked.

"If it is, it's got my attention. Load up."

When we got under way again, Sutter put his head in the pass-through window behind me. "Could that be the Alamo movie set? You know, the one John Wayne starred in."

"You mean the Alamo Village north of Brackettville? Definitely not. I was there on a tour last year, and they put the San Antonio filming area north of the Alamo compound, which was historically wrong. This one's west, where it should be," I said, pointing at the town across the river. "They also got the movie set orientation wrong. It was turned completely around. This one's correct."

"Going on the assumption that's the real Alamo, and this is 1836, we're riding in something they've never seen before."

"Yeah, and they've got cannons. Corporal Barnes, stop the truck. Do you have any white rags?"

"We have some for weapons cleaning in the armorers' box."

"Sergeant Wright, get two of the largest white rags you have. Tie one to the radio antenna and give me the other one. Sergeant Sutter, get everyone out and take cover behind the truck, and have everyone turn on their helmet radios. PFC Snyder, let's go for a walk."

When a stained white T-shirt had been tied on the radio antenna, and with a white towel in my hand, Snyder and I left the truck. Ironically, we'd stopped near the place where the Mexicans would set up their northern cannon battery. Waving the stained white towel over my head, we had walked to about fifty meters of the wall when a puff of smoke appeared, heralding the sharp bang of a musket gunshot that hit Snyder. He grunted, doubling over as he staggered backward, and went down. I dropped to the ground and yelled "Medic!" into my radio, just as a cannon fired with an ear-ringing report. I lifted my head and saw the cannonball strike the ground, bounce up, and impact the truck bumper with a deafening metallic bang. Like swarming ants, everyone left the area behind the truck and concealed themselves as best they could in the sparse vegetation.

I jumped up, frantically waving my arms and the white rag over my head, shouting, "Hold your fire! Hold your fire!"

"Hold fire!" Someone shouted from the Alamo wall.

Hoping no one else would shoot at us again, I went to Snyder. "The medic's on his way. Where are you hit?"

"Stomach." Snyder was breathlessly clutching his midsection.

I checked his back for an exit wound before rolling him onto his back.

"Move your hands. I need to see what I'm doing," I said, opening his bandage kit, preparing to render first aid.

While I was ripping the Velcro straps from his body armor, Corporal Taylor arrived at a run. "I have him. Where's he hit?"

"Stomach. There's no exit wound. What can I do to help?"

"I'll let you know," Taylor said, unstrapping another section of armor, and slipped his hand under. When he pulled it out, we looked at it. "As I expected, there's no blood. You're lucky you only got the wind knocked out of you."

"Lucky? I've been shot!" Snyder painfully exclaimed.

"It's going to leave a bruise for sure. Stay still a minute." Taylor pulled out a pocket knife.

"What're you doing?" I asked.

"Souvenir."

"Doc, we ain't got time for souvenirs." I turned and looked at the Alamo wall with their muskets and cannons all pointing at us.

"Patience. We're under a flag of truce and I'm treating wounded."

"It didn't work for me," Snyder said, painfully straining to speak.

After some gentle digging, Taylor pried out a partially flattened mass of a lead ball from a section of the body armor. "Looks to be about a fifty caliber. To my knowledge, no one has been hit by a round this large and lived to tell about it." Taylor put the ball in Snyder's hand.

"Doc, can I get up?" Snyder asked.

"You have to take it easy. There may be some blunt force trauma to your internal organs."

"Do you think I'll get a Purple Heart?" Snyder asked as Taylor and I helped him to his feet.

"I'll recommend it, but the chain of command must approve it. You two wait here." Snyder staggered and then tentatively walked a few steps, noticeably bowed over at the waist while Taylor carefully watched his movements.

When I walked toward the north wall with my hands in the air, there were several muskets trained on me while the cannon was being rolled forward after being reloaded.

"I request permission to speak to your commander."

"I'm in charge of this garrison."

I recognized Lieutenant Colonel William Barrett Travis from a sketch I'd seen during one of my several visits to the San Antonio Alamo Shrine, but he looked thinner than in the sketch.

"Sir, Staff Sergeant Webber reports." I put down my arms and gave a salute.

"What is that thing out there?" Travis asked when he looked at the truck through a handheld telescope.

"Sir, we're under a flag of truce. Why did you shoot at us?"

"I'll ask you again, what is that thing out there?" he said sternly.

"Sir, it's…um…a horseless wagon. You already know Santa

Anna's approaching from the south. Can I bring my men inside?"

"Just you. No one else," Travis said.

"Thank you, sir. First Squad, stand fast," I said as I walked around the northwest corner toward the south gate. I had to be careful of what I said to Colonel Travis. His suspicion had already gotten one man shot.

Despite the many muskets trained on my every move, I was experiencing a growing excitement. As I approached the southwest corner, a fit of coughing got my attention. Among the faces gazing down at me I recognized Lieutenant Colonel James Bowie from a print in a book I'd once read. I looked at the famous eighteen-pounder cannon barrel pointing over the wall toward San Antonio de Bexar, as it was called in this time.

When I turned the corner, I was facing men with muskets pointed directly at me from behind a dirt breastwork. When I stumbled through the defensive ditch and climbed over the breastworks, I raised my hands again as I walked through the gate. Inside there were two cannons pointed at me from behind another dirt breastwork, as well as more men with muskets.

"What is your name again?" Colonel Travis asked when he walked toward me.

"Sir, I'm Staff Sergeant Elliot Webber, Bravo Company, 1st Battalion," I said, deliberately not giving him any more information than he would understand.

"Where are you from?"

"Sir, we're not necessarily from where, but when."

"I'm not accustomed to repeating myself!" Travis stated loudly.

"Sir, we're from the future, and we're here to help you."

Colonel Travis regarded me with a steely gaze for an uncomfortably long time, and I fully expected to be shot by his order at any moment.

"You say you're from the future," he said skeptically.

"Yes, sir."

"Are you drunk?"

"No, sir. Not when I'm on duty."

"That contraption you were in; you say it's a horseless wagon?"

"Yes, sir."

"You have the bearing of a trained soldier, and your uniform tells me you're not from Santa Anna's army, or any army I'm familiar with. Put your hands down. Does your wounded man need our surgeon's help?"

"No, sir. He was protected by the body armor he's wearing," I stated, suddenly wishing I hadn't mentioned the armor because he might want to test it, on me this time.

"Armor? Like...knights used to wear?"

"It's something similar, yes, sir," I said, thumping my armor with my fist.

"I want to see this horseless wagon of yours. Go tell it to come here."

"Sir, I can do it from here." I unnecessarily put my hand up to the microphone. "Corporal Barnes, what's the damage to the truck?"

"It's drivable. The bumper's got a big dent that almost pushed into the radiator."

"First Squad, load up. Sergeant Sutter, make sure everyone's loaded, and bring the truck to the gate on the other side of the compound. Corporal Taylor, PFC Snyder, load on the truck when it gets to your position."

"Colonel Travis, that thing is moving again!" shouted voices relayed across the compound.

"Hold fire! Let it approach! How did you do that?"

"Sir, we need to meet with your staff and I'll try to explain."

"You'll do much more than try."

"Yes, sir."

Muskets were trained on the truck as it grumbled toward the gate. Admittedly, it would be frightening to anyone who'd never seen one before. When Travis and I walked out the gate, I escorted him as he regarded the truck with obvious suspicion.

"Colonel Travis, can your men stand down? I don't want any more accidental shootings."

"Sergeant Major Williamson!" He shouted, waving his hand at the wall. Someone shouted an order, and those in uniform pointed their muskets elsewhere. A few of the non-uniformed men, those I recognized as volunteers, where not as compliant.

"Sir, this is made of metal, like your cannons and muskets." I slapped the fender to show him it was real, and that he could touch it as well.

"Crockett, come out here!" Travis shouted.

I immediately recognized the man walking through the gate as David Stern Crockett from his buckskin clothes and musket he cradled in his left arm. He was taller than I expected, and I tried not to smile at the coonskin cap he wore; unsuccessfully, I might add.

"Congressman Crockett, I'm Staff Sergeant Elliot Webber. It's an exceptional honor to meet you, sir," I said, as I saluted him.

"Staff Sergeant Elliot Webber, I'm not a congressman any longer, nor am I a military officer."

"Sir, I'm aware of your request to be regarded as a high private. Because you were a congressman, you'll always have the title, and the respect of that position."

"Much obliged," he said, regarding me with a puzzled

expression.

I followed Travis as he slowly walked around the truck, looking it over. When he got to the back, he said, "How many men do you have?"

"Sir, there are eleven men in there, and the wagon driver is in the front," I said, pointing to each position.

"All of you, get out of the wagon!" Travis ordered.

"First Squad, fall in by rank behind the truck," I shouted, banging my fist on the tailgate. "Sergeant Sutter, anchor the squad. Sergeant Wright, Corporal Barnes, fall in on Sergeant Sutter."

When everyone had jumped out and lined up, I said "Squad, Ah…Ten…Shun!"

"Lock and load!" the squad shouted, causing muskets to be trained on us again as Travis took a step back in surprise.

"Sir, the squad is prepared for your inspection," I stated after I turned and saluted Travis.

Colonel Travis went to inspect the squad. He looked at each man and his equipment as we walked slowly down the line. After he finished inspecting the squad, he said, "Who is the man that was shot?"

"I am, sir. Private First Class Snyder."

"How badly are you injured?" Travis said, and went to face him.

"Sir, I'm a bit sore, but I'll be all right. This is the bullet that hit me." He showed Travis the lead ball.

"Your…armor stopped it?"

"Yes, sir."

"Sergeant Webber, it appears that you and your men are well disciplined. I notice you and your men have US Army on your shirts."

"Yes, sir. We're professional, all volunteer soldiers from the United States Army of the future," I said, but worried about Hernández, Sanchez, and Thompson who, for the moment at least, were playing the part.

"So you say," Travis said, looking at the squad still standing at attention. "If you're professional soldiers, where are your muskets?"

"Sir, they are secured in the wagon. I don't want our wagon to fall into Santa Anna's hands. With your permission, I'd like to move it inside the compound."

"Do you think it will fit through the gate?" Travis looked first at the truck, then at the wooden gates.

"Yes, sir, but the cannon will have to be moved. Considering how close Santa Anna's army is to Bexar, I'd like to begin immediately."

"I'll order the cannon to be moved inside."

"Thank you, sir." With a salute for Travis, I turned to the squad and said, "We're going to take the truck inside the walls. Barnes, Ruiz, remove the cab cover, fold the windshield on the hood, and pull in the mirrors. Taylor, Carpenter, Hernández, Sanchez, take the canvas off and unseat the bows. Everyone else, help move the cannon inside, and then get shovels from the truck and the compound. Prepare to help fix any damage done to the breastworks. Fall out."

It took about fifteen minutes before we were ready, and just in time because a bugle sounded from Bexar announcing the arrival of Santa Anna's cavalry vanguard. I had Barnes drive the truck in a wide arc and lined him up with the gate. Then I jumped up on the running board, and said, "It looks like a tight fit, but you should be able to get through."

"It won't fit between the wooden gates, Staff Sergeant."

"They'll have to fix the damage once we're in. Put it in all wheel drive and make a tight left turn to avoid the cannons inside. Watch your head," I said, and ran to the front of the truck to guide him in.

The roaring engine, black cloud of diesel exhaust, and dirt kicked up by churning tires as it climbed over the breastworks had everyone, except the squad, nervously staying well away from the activity. As Barnes began his turn to avoid the breastworks inside, the corner of the truck bed shattered one of the gates. After Barnes pulled into the compound, we surveyed the damage to the truck.

"Captain Ibanez won't be happy about the bumper," Barnes said, trying to pull on the massive dent as if he could fix it with his hands.

"I'll tell him we had to adapt to a situation. He's fond of hearing that. Barnes, Ruiz, set up the cab cover. Taylor, Carpenter, Hernández, Sanchez, set up the bows and canvas. Everyone else, grab shovels, repair the breastwork out there, and help move the cannon outside the gate," I said over my radio.

I looked around at the courtyard in fascinated disbelief. Everything was as I had read it would be. Ramps that allowed the cannons to be pushed up to their firing positions were in place, extending much farther into the compound than what I'd seen in the Alamo Village movie set, which was noticeably smaller. The second floor above the barracks was as tall as the Alamo church, which lacked the iconic curvilinear parapet that had been rebuilt over the modern-day shrine. Missing from several drawings and some Alamo movies was a wooden watchtower, constructed over the right side of the church and supporting a flagpole. I recognized the Flag of the State of Coahuila y Tejas with two yellow stars as it gently folded and unfolded itself in the breeze.

Music began playing from the town.

"Santa Anna brought a band with his army," Travis said.

"They're playing music for his arrival," I said.

I followed Travis when he walked up the ramp toward the eighteen-pounder cannon. When we reached the top of the ramp, Colonel Bowie was slumped against the wall next to the cannon, having obvious difficulty breathing.

"Colonel Bowie, it's an honor to meet you, sir." I saluted, and then extended my hand. He nodded at me and shook my hand. Despite his weakened condition, his grip was strong.

The band stopped playing, and a bugle sounded from the town. With some dread, I said, "Colonel Travis, Santa Anna is going to raise a red flag over the San Fernando De Bexar Cathedral. He will make the cathedral his headquarters."

"How do you know?"

"Sir, the bugle call you hear is *El Degüello,* also called slit throat, or throat cutting. It's used by Spanish armies to signal no quarter to their opponent," I told Travis, while others nearby listened and stared at me.

"Colonel Travis, a red flag is being raised in Bexar!" a uniformed soldier shouted and pointed.

"Sir, Santa Anna wants to talk terms of your surrender," I stated.

With the briefest glance at me, Travis grabbed a long rod called a linstock, with a specially prepared piece of smoldering rope, and put it on the touch hole of the cannon. With a sudden whoosh of smoke from the touch hole, and a deep boom, the cannon fired. The recoil rolled the cannon back a couple of feet, prompting the cannon crew to set about reloading it. That was the first time I'd been so close to any artillery cannon being fired, and unbelievably, I enjoyed the chest thumping, ear ringing marvel of it.

"Sir, Santa Anna has light cannons following close behind his army. He also has heavy cannons coming in about two weeks."

When I looked at Bowie having a fit of coughing, I said, "Colonel Travis, can I have a private word with you? Colonel Bowie would like to send Major Jameson to talk with Santa Anna."

Travis scowled at me as he turned and said, "Bowie, are you planning to parley with Santa Anna without telling me?"

"I do not need to…tell you anything. I'm in command…of my men…not you," he said, coughing and wheezing as he spoke as he put his hand on the hilt of his knife. I had to get a closer look at that famous blade.

"Santa Anna wants a formal parley," I offered.

"How do you know?" Travis said, whirling around and glaring at me.

"Sir, you're going to find that I know a lot about what's going to happen. For example, if you'd followed General Houston's orders, this fort would have been burned to the ground, and you'd be on your way to join him. Instead you'll be facing Santa Anna, who will have over 2400 soldiers and several cannons." My revelation stopped everyone within earshot.

"You said he wants a parley. Who will he send?" Travis asked, regarding me suspiciously.

"Sir, history records two of Santa Anna's officers are on their way to the bridge as we speak," I said, took a step back, and pulled out my notepad. "I'm going to write down who they are, who you will send, and what will happen afterwards. I'll keep it here in my top pocket and give it to you when it's done."

"Colonel Travis, someone's crossing the bridge with a white flag."

"Just because you guessed what was expected does not convince me."

"Yes, sir." I finished scribbling the note and put it in my pocket.

"Captain Martin! Go and…." Travis stopped and looked at me as I pointed to my pocket. Then he walked down the ramp and spoke privately with Captain Martin. After several glances at me, Martin shouted for horses and two were brought. He and a Tejano mounted the horses and trotted toward the bridge carrying a white flag on a stick.

"Sergeant Webber, what were my orders to Captain Martin?"

"You asked for an honorable surrender."

The stunned expression on his face was enough to tell me history was right. While we watched, there was a brief negotiation at the bridge and they returned at a gallop.

"What does he want?" Travis shouted when they reached the wall.

"We are to immediately place ourselves at the disposal of the Supreme Government of Mexico, from whom we may expect clemency after some considerations. They are waiting for an answer."

"Sir, Santa Anna wants you to surrender at discretion, or you and your men will be put to the sword. From what future history knows about Santa Anna, surrender at discretion means you'll be killed, whether you fight or surrender. He's already killed all the pirates he can find between here and the Rio Grande."

"Pirates?" Travis exclaimed.

"Yes, sir. The Government of Mexico considers all foreigners to be pirates, not deserving of a trial or mercy. That's the reason for the red flag and the demand for surrender."

"He wants us…to surrender? Travis…you better…answer

him," Bowie wheezed loudly, weakly waving his hand at the cannon.

"Captain Martin, get clear!" Travis shouted, prompting them to ride for the gate.

Travis put the linstock to the touch-hole of the reloaded cannon. This time I plugged my ears with my fingers just before the cannon fired with another chest thumping boom, bringing cheers and shouts of defiance from soldiers and volunteers on the walls.

"Sir, in case you're interested, that last shot hit Santa Anna's headquarters, but he wasn't in it yet."

"Give me the paper." I handed Travis the note from my pocket. "Captain Martin, who did you talk to out there?"

"Colonel Almonte and one other."

"Colonel Juan Almonte is one of Santa Anna's staff officers, and Colonel José Bartres is an aide to Santa Anna." Travis looked at me and the note again. "It seems that you're good at guessing what is going to happen."

"Sir, I'm not guessing. Some of Santa Anna's soldiers will be attacking from the bridge. We should watch Congressman Crockett and see what he does."

"Yes, you wrote that down." He looked at the note again.

We turned just as Crockett was drawing a bead on the bridge, steadying his musket on a cannon wheel. A uniformed officer quickly put his gloved hand over the loaded cannon's touch hole to prevent a spark from the musket's flash pan from accidentally firing the cannon.

"The bridge is out of range," Travis stated.

"Yup…it is." Crockett gently squeezed the trigger. The hammer dropped with a click, and smoke jetted up from the flash pan, immediately followed by the musket's report. The lead man on the bridge staggered backward into those behind him, and then fell into the river. The remaining soldiers beat a disorganized retreat.

"Great shot, Congressman! That was over three hundred meters," I said.

"What are meters?" He said with a confused look.

"It's about three hundred yards."

"It was more near three fifty," he said as he reloaded his musket.

"Colonel Travis, when can we have a meeting with your staff?"

"We'll do it now. Private King, officers' call in my headquarters."

"Yes, sir," King said, and ran down the ramp, shouting Travis's order.

"Sir, can we have Congressman Crockett join us?"

"Call me David."

"He'll be there," Travis said.

When we walked down the ramp, I couldn't help looking around again. I'd studied several historical battles, but I'd always had a special, perhaps even a strange affinity for the Battle of the Alamo. Texans, or Texians as they were called at the time, fought a hopeless battle against overwhelming odds in this place. History recorded that most of them would die, but I—we—had to change that outcome. I was responsible for the men with me, and we were not leaving, mostly because we'd nowhere to go.

When we walked toward Travis's headquarters, I looked around and wondered why Santa Anna had chosen to attack the north wall on the last day of the siege. He sent soldiers toward all the walls as a diversion, but his focus was the north wall, where he needed ladders to enter the compound. It would have been less costly in manpower to take the lower and weaker south palisade, where he wouldn't need ladders. Foreknowledge of events would be our greatest tactical advantage.

When we walked into Travis's headquarters, I said, "Sir, you're going to send a rider to Gonzales and warn them the Mexican army is here."

He stopped short and turned to look at me. "How do you know what I was thinking?"

"Sir, I'll be happy to explain when your staff arrives."

Travis took off his hat and sat at a table next to an unshuttered window, and dipped a metal tipped quill into an ink well. When he started writing, two uniformed men entered.

"This is Captain Dickinson and Major Jameson—"

"Captain Almaron Dickinson, Artillery Officer. Sir, I thought it might be you on the eighteen-pounder. And Major Green Jameson, Staff Officer," I said, saluting the officers.

Another uniformed man entered. "This is Sergeant Major Williamson."

"Sergeant Major Hiram Williamson, sergeant major of the garrison, and in charge of the uniformed infantry, what you might call the regulars." I shook his hand as another uniformed officer entered.

"Do I need to introduce him?" Travis asked.

"Just his last name, sir."

"Baugh."

"Captain John Baugh, the garrison adjutant." When I saluted him, Crockett entered.

"Congressman Crockett, when you were voted out of office, you told your constituents to go to hell, and you were going to Texas," I said, extending my hand.

"Not many people know 'bout that, 'cause I told that story

for the first time when I got here." He almost crushed my hand when he shook it.

"Congressman, you arrived in Bexar on February eighth with twelve volunteers."

"Call me David."

"Yes, sir." A fit of coughing outside the door caught my attention. "I believe Lieutenant Colonel James Bowie has arrived."

"Travis, I hate your meetings. Why am I here?" Bowie was worn out from the effort of walking from the eighteen-pounder cannon when he seated himself on a box, wheezing and coughing even more than before.

"We're going to find out what this man's story is. Explain yourself, Sergeant Webber."

"Gentlemen, everything I'm about to say will be hard to believe, so I'll start by saying that my men and I are from the future; specifically, the year 2010."

My statement started mutterings of disbelief, quickly turning into a battering of overlapping questions I couldn't answer quickly or completely enough, while Travis and Bowie listened.

"Gentlemen, Santa Anna left Mexico with his army on—"

"We've known Santa Anna's been on his way here for many weeks. We didn't know he'd be here this quickly," Travis interrupted.

"He would've been here sooner, but he had to split his army into sections to allow for wells found on the way here to refill. He also stopped several times to capture and execute anyone suspected of being a pirate."

"Pirate?" Bowie exclaimed.

"Yes, sir. Last December, Santa Anna coerced Mexico's Minister of War, José Maria Tornel y Mendívil, to write what we call the Tornel Decree. The decree says all foreigners bearing arms against the Government of Mexico will be treated as pirates and killed immediately without trial. Santa Anna is exceeding the decree by executing anyone seen carrying a musket or pistol, even his own countrymen."

"How do you know this?" Travis asked.

"Sir, as I stated, we're from the future. I've personally studied what will be called the Battle of the Alamo, and I can give you daily events before they happen."

I was hammered again with more questions, but when they took a disagreeable turn with an accusation of witchcraft, I had to take charge of the conversation.

"Gentlemen! Gentlemen! There's no witchcraft here!" I shouted over the bedlam. "There's no such thing as witchcraft; only superstition and ignorance."

"Are you saying we're ignorant?" Captain Dickinson asked.

With my head full of Alamo lore anxiously waiting to get out, I wanted to say yes. Instead, I said "Sir, I'll answer your question this way. Has anyone ever heard about steamboats?"

"I have," Sergeant Major Williamson said. "I saw one on the Mississippi River last year, but I would not get on one of those things. I used a raft to cross with my horse. Is your wagon a steamboat on land?"

"It's similar. What you call a wagon, we call a truck. The truck, our equipment, all we brought with us, are just tools; things not known in this time. What can I do that'll convince you we're soldiers from the future?" I looked around but didn't get a response. "Colonel Travis, would you like a demonstration of our rifles?"

"Yes, I think we all would."

"Not me," Bowie said, pulling a flask from his pocket, continuing to wheeze and cough between drinks.

"Yes, sir." I put my hand up to the radio microphone again. "Sergeant Wright, unlock the weapons rack and give Corporal Breckenridge his rifle. Break out a bandoleer, and load two clips with twenty rounds each. Meet me at the palisade."

"Where's the palisade?"

"It's the dirt and wood fence on the right of the church."

"Wilco, Staff Sergeant."

"We'll be ready for the demonstration in a few minutes."

"How do you do that?" Travis asked.

"Sir, this device on my helmet is called a radio. We use it send messages across short distances where we can't see or hear each other."

"I want to hear this radio of yours," Travis stated.

"Staff Sergeant Webber, we're ready," Wright said.

"Sir, I've just been told we're ready for the demonstration." I extended my hand to the door and preceded everyone when I walked out, not looking back to see if I was followed.

Breckenridge hopped off the truck bed and walked toward the palisade with his rifle, tucking the loaded magazines into an ammo pouch on his pistol belt. Wright stayed with the truck and the open ammo box.

When Travis and several others had arranged themselves around us, I said, "Sir, I'll have Corporal Breckenridge demonstrate the operation of the rifle. Corporal Breckenridge, load and prepare to fire." As I stepped back, I quietly said over the radio, "Fire the first ten rounds at one second intervals, then switch to auto and fire the rest in a burst. Control the muzzle rise."

"Yes, Staff Sergeant."

"Fire when ready," I said, loud enough to be heard by everyone.

With every single round fired, the skeptics became fascinated by the operation. When Breckenridge selected automatic and fired one long burst, a few observers took a cautious step back.

"Cease fire. Gentlemen, that was twenty rounds in about fifteen seconds, and that's not as fast as the rifle can fire. Will you agree this is not witchcraft?"

While everyone was looking at each other and speaking in hushed tones, Travis went to Breckenridge. "How can you fire without ramming a ball down the barrel? How is it done?"

"Sir, we use a self-contained cartridge." He reached into his ammo pouch, lifted a cartridge out of the magazine, and handed it to Travis. "This is a 5.56 millimeter standard NATO round. The cartridge automatically feeds into the chamber when the bolt closes on it. When I pull the trigger, the round fires, and the brass ejects from this port." He stooped to retrieve an empty brass cartridge from the ground for comparison. "Then the bolt moves forward, stripping another cartridge from the magazine, and it's ready to fire again."

I almost smiled at the confused look on Travis's face.

"Give me the musket." Travis held his hand out.

"Sir, before a rifle is given to an inspecting officer, it will be cleared and made safe." I nodded at Breckenridge.

Breckenridge verified the firing selector was on safe, ejected the empty magazine, and visually observed the bolt was locked to the rear. Then he held the rifle up and looked into the ejection port to see if there was any brass in the chamber. Having made the weapon safe, he offered it to Travis.

When Travis took the rifle, he said, "It's light, and too short to be accurate."

"Sir, this is the M16 rifle. The maximum range is 3,500 meters… yards. This rifle was made by the Colt Manufacturing Company."

I pointed at the rearing horse stamped on the magazine well.

I was going to explain the rifle's firing capabilities such as muzzle velocity and other rates of fire, but after seeing Travis's confused reaction to Breckenridge's explanation, it was unimportant in light of the demonstration.

"What is this large barrel for?" Travis asked.

"Sir, that's the M203 Grenade Launcher," Breckenridge said.

"It throws grenades? How far?"

"Sir, I'd like to demonstrate the grenade launcher two days from now when Santa Anna will attack from the south," I said.

"How do you know that?"

"Sir, for the time being, you'll have to trust me. I don't want to give away our tactical advantages to Santa Anna, yet."

"You still claim to be from the future?"

"Sir, I've already proven part of what will happen with the note I gave you. Santa Anna will set up three cannon batteries. One to the north, and two to the southwest in Bexar."

As if on cue a uniformed soldier ran to us, and breathlessly said, "Colonel Travis, cannons are being moved to the north."

"Return to your post," Travis said, and then examined the rifle again.

"Sir, would you like to fire the rifle?"

"Yes, I would."

"Corporal Breckenridge, prepare your rifle for the colonel, and brief him on its operation."

Breckenridge respectfully asked for the rifle, loaded the second magazine, released the spring-loaded bolt, and handed it back.

"Sir, you sight the weapon through the hole in this rear sight and center this front post on your target." Breckenridge pointed at the two sight components.

Travis put the rifle up to his shoulder and sighted over the wall. When he tried to fire, the trigger wouldn't move.

"Sir, the firing selector is on safe." Breckenridge switched it to semi. "Fire when ready."

Travis fired one round, lowered it from his shoulder, and said, "There's not much kick. How do I reload?"

"Sir, it's already reloaded. Fire again," Breckenridge said.

After he fired several more rounds, he said, "How does it fire faster?"

"Sir, allow me." Breckenridge switched the firing selector to auto. "Aim, squeeze, and hold the trigger. Be careful, sir. On automatic fire, the weapon will rise up and to the right."

Unlike some soldiers I'd seen, he controlled the automatic recoil surprisingly well. When he fired the last of the magazine, I could see he was impressed. Despite the forty rounds fired so quickly, I wasn't concerned by the wisps of smoke rising through the cooling slots over the hot barrel.

"Sir, can I have my rifle?" Breckenridge recovered the weapon and made it safe again.

"Sir, I think you and your staff have something to think about. In the meantime, I'd like to bunk my squad before it gets dark. Where can we stay?" I asked, as if I didn't already know.

"Lieutenant Melton! Lieutenant Melton!" Travis shouted, looking around for him as other voices relayed around the Alamo.

"Lieutenant Eliel Melton, the garrison quartermaster."

"Do I need to introduce anyone to you?"

"Sir, I'm familiar with almost every officer and senior non-commissioned officer by name and position."

When Lieutenant Melton arrived, Travis said, "Make room in the barracks for Sergeant Webber and his men."

"Lieutenant Melton, I'd like to keep my men together in the

same area, preferably on the south side of the barracks. We won't need bunks."

"How many men do you have?"

"Thirteen, sir," I said, hoping the number wouldn't add to the superstitious accusation of witchcraft. That, and the fact the siege would last thirteen days. Somehow, this didn't bode well, even to my non-superstitious mind.

"There are enough bunks for everyone. I'll make room for you and your men," Melton said, and walked toward the barracks.

"Colonel Travis, with your permission, I'd like to move the truck and unload our equipment into the barracks." When he nodded agreement, I said into the radio, "Corporal Barnes, back the truck up to the walkway to the right of the barracks. Sergeant Sutter, eyes on me. Lieutenant Melton is the uniformed officer walking toward the barracks." I pointed to him. "Get with him about our accommodations and give him whatever help he needs."

"Yes, Staff Sergeant," I heard as he jogged to catch up with the lieutenant.

"Sergeant Wright, when space has been made for us, have everyone unload our gear."

"Yes, Staff Sergeant."

"Sergeant Webber, I want to use your radio," Travis said.

"First Squad, Colonel Travis wants a demonstration of the radio. Webber is offline." I took off my helmet and gently put it on Travis's head, after he removed his wide brimmed hat.

"Sergeant Wright, talk to Colonel Travis," I said close to the microphone.

"Sir, this is Sergeant Wright."

"Where are you?" Travis said, looking around.

"Here sir, in the back of the truck," Wright said, leaning out from

under the canvas, waving to get his attention. Travis tentatively waved back.

"We can hear each other, without shouting," Travis said incredulously. "How far can you talk with this?"

"Using line of sight, about a mile."

"I can hear people talking to each other."

"Yes, sir. Can I have the helmet back?"

He listened to conversations for a while longer before reluctantly removing the helmet. He examined it for a few moments before handing it to me.

When I put it on and snapped the chin strap, I said, "Webber's back on line."

"Webber's back on line. Big fucking deal."

"Knock it off, Hernández!" Sutter shouted.

"Sir, you've seen some of our equipment in operation. Would you agree we are who we say we are?"

"I still have no evidence you're from the future."

"Sir, I don't think there's any indisputable evidence I can give you, other than what I've shown you so far."

"I believe what I've seen and touched, but despite what you say, I say it's impossible that you're from the future."

"Sir, if all things were equal, I'd agree with you; but things are not equal, and…here we are," I said as I shrugged my shoulders.

"The things you've shown me could have been ordered by the president and made in the East."

"Sir, you met with President Jackson prior to coming here. Did he mention anything about new weapons like we have?"

"You come up with answers too easily, and too quickly. You could be a spy."

"Sir, what can I say or do that'll convince you of who we are?" I said with a sigh.

"You can say anything you want, but is any of it true? I do not know. My officers and I will be watching you."

"Sir, I welcome the opportunity for you and your officers to question any of us at any time. I'm sure your men are afraid of us; but curiosity will replace fear, and trust will follow."

"Since you know so much about the future, tell me something that is not known beyond these walls," Travis stated.

"You and Colonel Bowie had…differences of opinion over command here. You settled your differences by arranging a joint but separate command. You have command of the regulars, and Colonel Bowie's in command of the volunteers. With your permission, I'd like to have a similar arrangement."

"You do not trust my leadership?"

"Sir, it's not a lack of trust. No one here knows how we've been trained, or how to operate our equipment, except us. I'll report directly to you and follow your orders."

Loud, ragged coughing from across the compound caught our attention. We saw Bowie lean against a wall and then collapse to his knees. Several volunteers ran to him and helped him to his headquarters.

"Sir, tomorrow morning, Colonel Bowie will give his command to you."

"He'd rather die than give me his command. Even if he does, his men will not follow me."

"He's too sick to carry on, and he'll encourage his men to follow you. If you take advantage of Congressman Crockett's popularity among the volunteers, you will gain their cooperation. It's getting dark, and I'd like to brief my men before turning in. Knowing what will happen starting tomorrow, you should turn in early as well."

"What will happen tomorrow?"

"Before dawn, Santa Anna will begin a cannon bombardment that will continue for the next eleven days."

"I'll believe that when I see it."

"By your leave, sir." I saluted him and walked toward the barracks.

I understood his skepticism, but how long would it take before he'd accept who we are? I needed his trust.

The squad had almost finished unloading the truck when I arrived in the barracks.

"First Squad, listen up. Turn off the radios for tonight. Tomorrow, we'll join the garrison under Colonel Travis's command."

"We're not leaving?" Hernández asked.

"We've nowhere to go."

"We can go anywhere we want," Hernández argued.

"There's a lot of bad things beyond those walls; bandits, criminals of every sort who'd shoot you for your boots. We're in Comanche territory, and they'd be happy to scalp you while you slept. And let's not forget the Mexican army has arrived. If you want to take your shelter half and camp outside the walls, be my guest."

"*Mierda*." Hernández mumbled his usual explicative when someone goes against what he wanted to do but didn't have an easy alternative.

"Finish unloading the truck and then set up your sleeping areas. Turn in early and get as much sleep as you can. Santa Anna will start his bombardment tomorrow morning, and you won't get much sleep from then on." I took my duffle bag into the barracks to claim an area near the door.

The bunks we were given were simple wood frames with ropes strung between the rails. Short legs raised it above the floor for comfort against the cold, and to keep vermin from biting.

While we were unpacking, I felt a cold breeze on the back of my neck. Turning around, I snapped to attention with a salute and said, "Sir, I apologize. I didn't know you were there. First Squad, this is Lieutenant Melton. He's the garrison quartermaster."

"Settle down, men," he said when the squad came to attention, and he handed me a well used ceramic jug.

"What's this, sir?" I asked.

"Whiskey, compliments of Colonel Travis."

"Thank you, sir." I handed the jug to Corporal Barnes.

"You're not having a drink?" Melton asked.

"No, sir. I'm still on duty." I had the suspicion I was somehow being tested.

Barnes eagerly popped the cork, and confidently slung it on his elbow with practiced ease.

"Is that how they do it in Tennessee?" I said.

"Yup."

"Get drunk on that stuff and you'll pay for it tomorrow."

"I don't have to drive, so I'll take a chance." Barnes lifted his elbow and took a drink.

"How many have drunk from that jug?" I asked.

"Whew!" Barnes said, screwing up his face. "Wow! It doesn't matter. This is really good stuff. It'll sterilize anything."

"Including you, if you're not careful. Sir, please thank the colonel for us." I saluted Lieutenant Melton before he left. "Barnes, cork the jug until we get settled."

"Staff Sergeant Webber, have you thought of a way to get home?" Carpenter said, opening his phone again.

"No, but if an opportunity presents itself, we'll take it no matter when it occurs. It's my guess it'll come with the electric fog we ran into this morning, so keep your eyes and ears open, and shout if you see it so we can all get in."

"If we can't get back before the shooting starts, how can we hope to defend this place with the Mexican army out there?" Ruiz said.

"This is a good, defendable position. The walls are thick, and there are parapets we can take cover behind," I stated, appreciating his concern.

"They're setting up artillery all around us, and they're going to use it to kill us all," Hernández said.

"Cannons will be set up to the north and southwest, not all around us. The walls are made of three-foot-thick adobe, and round cannonballs will not be able to break through them. Despite the bombardment, the walls will stand. Some rounds will arc over the walls and hit the buildings, so stay under cover as much as possible. History is unclear if Santa Anna used explosive cannonballs, but from what I've read, none were used. There were a few injuries, but no fatalities due to cannon fire."

"Staff Sergeant, how can you be so calm about this?" Private Wallace asked.

"I've been through it in Afghanistan, twice."

"We've been through it," Sutter corrected me.

"Santa Anna doesn't know it yet, but he has a lot more to worry about than we do. When he sends his troops, we'll bring our force multiplier to bear."

"What's a force multiplier?" Wallace asked.

"The grenade launcher," Sutter stated.

"Right. The grenade launcher will help decimate and demoralize Santa Anna's army before they can reach the walls."

"Staff Sergeant, I've never fired the grenade launcher. We were supposed to fire it this morning," Barnes said.

"Show of hands—how many have never fired the grenade

launcher? Okay, that's just about everyone. Tomorrow after breakfast, I'll give a block of instructions on its operation."

"What can we expect from the Mexicans?" Ruiz said, prompting Hernández to give him a look that he ignored.

"Santa Anna is a self-proclaimed dictator, calling himself the Napoleon of the West, and he's trained his infantry in the Napoleonic style of fighting."

"What's the Napoleonic style?" Ruiz asked.

"Soldiers line up shoulder-to-shoulder, usually two ranks deep, where they volley fire, and reload standing up. This style of fighting will be used through the Civil War. After that, generals have to rethink their tactics when lever action cartridge firing rifles and the Gatling gun become common."

"I've never shot anyone," Snyder stated.

"In our platoon, only McFadden, Sutter, and I have. Sergeant Sutter, care to weigh in here?"

"Think of it like field firing on the range. Pick your target, take the shot, and move on to the next."

"Yeah, but—"

"Don't think about it, just do it. When you're being shot at, it's kill or be killed."

"Staff Sergeant, you said there were about one hundred eighty in the Alamo, against two thousand Mexicans," Snyder said.

"During the final attack on March sixth, yes. When Santa Anna's at full strength, he'll have about twenty-four hundred soldiers, if you count the cavalry, but they're not going to dismount and fight with the infantry. They'll patrol around us to prevent desertions by both sides."

"Sarge, can we—?" Sutter elbowed Carpenter into silence.

"It's okay, Sergeant Sutter. We can afford to relax a bit, but

I want everyone to remember who and where you are. Do you understand?"

"Yes, Staff Sergeant," almost everyone said in unison.

"Sergeant Wright, open the weapons rack and give everyone their weapons. Keep your weapon with you at all times, and when you're out of the barracks, wear your helmet and armor. You can take the armor off when sleeping but cover yourself with it. Tomorrow will be a loud and busy day, so go easy on the whiskey. Finish setting up your bunks and get as much rest as you can."

When I finished setting up my bunk, I set my watch to wake me at 0500 hours, then tucked myself and my rifle in the sleeping bag. While I was struggling with the zipper on the overcrowded bag, Sutter sat on his bunk next to mine.

"Hernández and Sanchez are going to be a problem," he stated bluntly.

"I know, and it's going to get worse."

"How do you know?"

"Back in the company area our usual duties would separate us, leaving less chance for confrontation. Now we're jammed together in each other's faces for the duration."

"The first sergeant seems to be the only person they had any respect for."

"And he's not here. You and I have combat experience, the others don't. If they're scared and confused, they'll freeze under fire. I'll relax discipline a bit and offer certain opportunities for them to concentrate on."

"I hope you're not thinking of becoming their friend."

"Hell no. Followers want to be liked. Leaders don't give a damn about being popular. I know if I relax discipline too much, I lose respect. If I tighten too much, there could be a breakdown in discipline, maybe even a mutiny."

"Yes, sir, Captain Bligh, sir," Sutter joked with a mock salute.

"Thanks," I agreed with a derisive snort.

"What'd you say to the first sergeant about Hernández and Sanchez this morning?" Sutter asked.

"I wanted them to stay behind, but he said we, meaning you and I, have to keep them out of trouble. I'll keep them separated as much as possible so they're easier to manage, and I'll brief Sergeant Wright about them tomorrow."

"Roger that. Goodnight...Sarge." Sutter smiled when he stood.

"After so much training and conditioning, it sounds strange, doesn't it? Goodnight, Sarge."

I finally got my sleeping bag zipped up, and before things got too rowdy around the whiskey jug, I went to sleep.

CHAPTER 3

DAY TWO – WEDNESDAY FEBRUARY 24, 1836

Boom! Boom! Boom!

"What's happening?" Someone's panicked shout came from the darkness.

"The bombardment has started," I said calmly, unzipping my sleeping bag.

"Everybody gear up! Move it!" Sutter shouted.

"What time is it?"

"Zero dark thirty," a tired voice in the darkness said.

"It's 0410 hours," I said, looking at my watch.

"Will this go on all day? The cannons, I mean," Carpenter asked.

"All day today and into tonight. After that, it'll lighten up during the day, and be heavier at night. Like I said, you won't get much sleep."

An Alamo soldier, partially dressed in what looked like long-johns, was walking around, lighting candle lanterns hanging on the walls and giving us some limited, but much needed light.

BOOM!

"That was the eighteen-pounder on the southwest corner, responding to the Mexican cannons in Bexar," I said while speed lacing my boots. "Until something changes, there'll be skirmishes almost every day, cavalry charges and such, and we'll be defending the walls. Remember, always wear your armor and helmet, and take your rifle wherever you go. Sergeant Wright, what's for breakfast?"

Boom! Boom! Boom! Boom! Boom! Boom!

"Hold on a minute." He read a package with his flashlight. "How about meatloaf with gravy?"

Boom!

"The breakfast of champions. Toss it."

I lost track of the airborne package in the poor light, and it bounced off my helmet.

"Thanks. Everyone, listen up. I'm going to form four fireteams. I'll take team one with Corporal Thompson and Private Hernández. Sergeant Wright, take team two with Corporal Barnes and Private Sanchez."

"Hey, you can't separate us," Hernández objected.

"No, it's done! Corporal Breckenridge, you have team three with PFC Carpenter and PFC Ruiz. Sergeant Sutter, take team four with PFC Snyder and Private Wallace. Corporal Taylor, you're the odd man out. Since you don't have a weapon, you'll float in addition to your medical duties."

When I saw Hernández rolling his eyes, I asked, "What's your problem?"

"Where's the bullshit you always come up with?"

"What are you talking about?"

"The bullshit. Every time you say something, bullshit follows."

"I think he means an unnecessary explanation of the orders

you give. You do, you know," Sutter said when I looked at him.

"What you call bullshit is called training, reinforcement, and keeping you informed. I've distributed everyone's skills to make the fireteams more effective. And, speaking of bullshit, what did you qualify as the last time you were on the range?"

"Marksman."

"That's it? You've nothing else to add?"

"What's to add?" Hernández asked.

Boom! Boom! Boom!

"You don't want to add the fact that couldn't zero your weapon with our company, and you had to be sent out with Alpha Company a month later, where you took all day to zero and qualify?"

"I qualified, that's all you need to know. And the trip with Alpha Company got me away from you for a whole day."

"Ah-ha, his secret's out," Sutter observed sarcastically.

"I've always qualified expert because I understand my life depends on it. Sergeant Wright is an expert, as is Corporal Barnes; Sanchez is a marksman. Corporal Breckenridge and PFC Ruiz are experts. PFC Carpenter is a sharpshooter. Sergeant Sutter is an expert. Private Wallace is a sharpshooter, as is Corporal Thompson."

"I missed expert by one target," Wallace said, miffed by his rating.

"And you, Private Hernández, are a marksman. I didn't see you qualify, so you're questionable at best."

"After all that bullshit, what you really mean is you've put the most trusted with the least trusted and keeping the beaners separated."

"I won't dignify that ignorance with a comment."

"Are you saying I'm ignorant?"

"Not in the least. With a slight attitude adjustment, you could become a decent soldier."

"A major attitude adjustment," Sutter corrected me.

"Do you mind?" I said to Sutter.

"How do you know all our qualifications?" Hernández said.

"The hallmarks of an NCO: service, professionalism, leadership. I personally add training, attention to detail, and a good memory to that hallmarks list. For your information—"

"And here comes the bullshit," Hernández interrupted.

"Yeah, here comes the bullshit, because you asked. During the dress greens inspection last month, McFadden had an appointment and I had to make sure everyone had their uniforms squared away, which included verifying weapons qualifications."

"I've seen your uniform. You're a real post exchange hero with all the ribbons you wear. And we're all impressed by your expert infantryman badge." Hernández pointed at the musket patch sewn above my left breast pocket. "I know that all you did was take a test to get it."

"It was a lot more involved than just taking a test," I stated, tightly holding on to my temper.

"In case you haven't noticed, he's also earned the parachutist badge, and we earned our Purple Hearts in Afghanistan." Sutter jumped headlong into the conversation.

"I've earned everything I wear. Maybe someday you'll wear something other than just a national defense ribbon. Is my bullshit clear enough, or was it too much for you to understand?" I shook my head at Sutter's advocacy.

"Are you saying I'm stupid?" Hernández asked, deliberately twisting what I'd said.

"At ease!" My patience finally snapped as I shouted in his face, bumping helmets with him.

Boom! Boom! Boom! Boom!

"I'd like to see you try and knock me down," Hernández said defiantly.

"If I did, you wouldn't get back up," I said, nose to nose with him.

"Get out of my face! I'm not your ass fucking buddy, like Sutter is." Despite our proximity to each other, Hernández didn't dare touch me because he knew I'd break his face and take a chance with a court martial.

"What about you and Sanchez? Yeah, you'd better have your shit together before you come at me with something like that." I turned to see Sutter advancing on Hernández. I shook my head, and he reluctantly stopped when he bumped into my outstretched hand.

"Your assignments are team one, south wall. Team two, west wall. Team three, north wall. Team four, east wall." I pointed to the general directions of each area. "Team four, take up your positions in the back of the church with the cannons. It's elevated, so you'll have an excellent observation and firing position. When you get to your positions, coordinate with your team leaders and interlock your lines of fire wherever possible. Sergeant Wright, does everyone have their weapons?"

"Yes, Staff Sergeant. Should I issue the basic load of ammo?"

"What does our inventory look like?"

"Six thousand six hundred rounds of M16 ammo, minus forty from yesterday. One hundred eighty rounds of high explosive grenades for the M203, and eighteen parachute flares."

"Why do we have flares?"

"The officers were going to fire flares during the night escape and evasion exercise."

"Since our training is always ongoing, what's a basic load?

Anyone but Sergeant Wright and Sergeant Sutter answer the question," I said.

"Two hundred ten rounds in seven, thirty round magazines," Ruiz answered confidently.

"Correct. Sergeant Wright, do we have any thirty round magazines?"

"Negative. We left the banana clips behind when we found out we were going to the range again."

"For now, issue everyone four full clips."

"Will eighty rounds be enough? We'll be facing a lot of Mexican soldiers," Sutter noted.

"Santa Anna will not attack in force for another ten days. Without resupply, we've got to carefully manage our ammo."

Being a practical man, Corporal Taylor said, "Speaking of supplies, eventually we're going to run out of MREs. When it happens, where do we eat?"

"There's a kitchen in the building in front of the church, but I don't recommend eating there."

"You want a five-star restaurant?" Hernández asked.

Boom! Boom! Boom!

Everyone ducked when a cannonball struck the hospital wall above us.

"There's no telling how well the food is prepared, or even what it is. Most likely it's a stew made of beans, corn, pork, or salted beef. I'll eat MREs because I know where they came from. To make them last, we'll each get two MREs per day. Keeping warm is going to be a problem because wood for fires is already scarce. Save your boxes and put the wrappers in them. We'll burn them when we need to. Sergeant Wright, you'll be responsible for distributing ammo and MREs. Corporal Taylor, you'll guard the ammo and our equipment during the attack against the south wall tomorrow."

"He gets to stay under cover while we're getting shot at?" Hernández said.

"If you don't like the arrangements, we can report to Colonel Travis and you can give him your opinion. Travis doesn't strike me as the type of officer who takes any backtalk, and you won't be able to sweet-talk him, like you do Captain Ibanez. Disrespect Travis and he could have you shot."

"Not without a court martial," Hernández said confidently.

"Commanding officers in this time have the final authority over their men, and they vigorously exercise it to maintain discipline. If you show him some respect, he might throw you in jail instead of having you shot."

"Manny, can he really shoot us?" Sanchez wailed.

"Shut up, Juan. He's trying to scare us."

"Am I? Go ahead and test Travis's patience, if you've got the balls. Wait, what's the Mexican word? *Cajones*, isn't it?"

"*Bolas*, if you've got two balls. *Pelota*, if you have only one ball. *No bolas* if you have no balls." Sutter grinned at Hernández.

Boom! Boom!

"First Squad, are we ready?" Mixed answers and light from red lens flashlights dancing around told me, not yet. "It's going to rain later today, so keep your rain gear handy. Wear the poncho or the rain suit and boots, your choice."

"How does he know it's gonna rain?" a voice asked from the semi-darkness.

"Do you really need to ask?" Sutter replied.

"Sergeant Sutter, Sergeant Wright, get 'em motivated." I stuffed my MRE into my thigh pocket and walked outside.

I was making my way toward Travis's headquarters when I was challenged.

"Stop! Who goes there?"

"Staff Sergeant Webber."

"What is your business?"

"I've been called to meet with Colonel Travis to…receive my orders of the day," I responded in the jargon of the time.

"Go inside. The colonel is expecting you."

When I opened the door, Colonel Travis was talking with several of his officers until he pointed at me and said, "You said this would happen."

"Sir?"

"The bombardment—you said it would happen this morning."

"Yes, sir. Santa Anna wants to keep us from getting any sleep."

"What happened last night?"

"Last night, sir?" I asked, confused.

"After you turned in, what happened?"

"Umm…as I recall from history, you sent out a patrol. When they returned, they brought back pack mules with some supplies, and a prisoner."

"He's beginning to convince me of who he is," Travis said to the gathered officers.

"We can't afford to keep prisoners," Lieutenant Melton said. "Our supplies are low, and we'll have more men to feed when help arrives."

Boom! Boom! Boom! Boom! Boom!

"Sir, why don't you use the prisoner to identify Santa Anna's bugle calls? Then he can earn his keep," I said, recalling something I'd once read.

"Sergeant Webber, what will happen today?" Travis said.

"Today's barrage will be the most intense, but it will ease off in the mornings, and become heavy again at night."

"Do you know why?" Captain Dickinson said, eyeing me carefully.

"Like us, Santa Anna doesn't have unlimited power and shot. It will ease off during the day because he knows it's harder to sleep during the day."

"It's what I would do," Dickinson said to Travis.

"Captain Dickinson, the Mexican artillery will hit two cannons today, but you'll quickly bring them back in service. Colonel Travis, you will send an important letter today."

"Who will I send with the dispatch?" Travis said. I was reaching for my notepad when he said, "Tell me who it is."

"You'll send Captain Albert Martin to Gonzales."

"I've already informed Captain Martin that he's the next courier I'll send, but I didn't tell him where he would go," Travis said to his officers.

"Sir, when Captain Martin arrives in Gonzales, your letter will be taken to San Felipe, where it will be read by Governor Smith. He'll tell the colonists in San Felipe to 'come to the aid of their besieged countrymen and to rally without one moment's delay.'"

"Will I get reinforcements?"

"Yes, sir, but not right away, and not in the numbers you need. Before dark this evening, Mexican Colonel Juan Bringas will lead scouts across a footbridge being built over the river—"

It seemed like every Mexican cannon fired at once, pounding various points along the walls. Everyone in the room crouched when one round solidly struck the outside wall of Travis's headquarters, chipping adobe from the inside wall and drifting dust on us from the rafters.

"Sir, they hope to cross the footbridge and surprise you. Your men will kill one soldier and force the rest to retreat. Congressman, you'll shoot a second soldier before they can reach cover."

The door burst open and a uniformed private shouted, "Captain Dickinson, the eighteen-pounder is out of action. Two men are hurt." Dickinson looked at me before rushing out of the room, taking the private with him.

"Corporal Taylor, injuries reported on the southwest corner near the big cannon," I reported over my radio.

"I'm on my way."

"Colonel Travis, what are my orders of the day?"

"Are you certain the only skirmish today will be this afternoon, over the new footbridge?"

"Yes, sir. The first major action will come tomorrow morning."

"Put your men on the walls, and report to me after the skirmish this afternoon."

"Yes, sir." I saluted Travis before leaving the headquarters. I'd noticed salutes were not often returned, so I didn't wait for them anymore. *"Sergeant Webber, what are your instructions?"* Sutter asked over the radio.

"Keep everyone under cover and eat. After breakfast, we'll gather outside the barracks, and begin training on the M203."

"What about the colonel's orders?" Wright asked.

"Training first. We need to prepare for tomorrow's attack."

"Roger that."

Boom! Boom! Boom! Boom!

I went back to the barracks, got my binoculars, and passed Corporal Taylor as he helped a soldier with a bandaged leg to the hospital. When I walked up the ramp, men were using a long wooden lever to raise the cannon and set a replacement wheel on it. I selected an unoccupied spot on the wooden scaffolding, alternating between eating and scanning the Mexican positions with the binoculars, noting that the Mexican engineers were already building the footbridge. It must've been cold standing in the water.

"Sergeant Webber, are you the only one of your men on the walls?" Travis asked when he joined me.

"Sir, please keep your head down. Your hat is an attractive target."

He dropped to one knee, and said, "I want more of your men on these walls."

"Yes, sir. How long have you had your telescope?"

"I bought it a few years ago." He put his hand on a cylindrical case at his side.

"Try using this." I removed the strap from my neck and handed it to him.

"What is it?"

"They're called binoculars. It's actually two telescopes mounted side by side. Sir, you look through it with both eyes from this end." I reoriented it for him. "Look at the activity over the river to your right."

"Is that the footbridge you told us about?"

"Yes, sir. It's hard to see with the trees in the way. With these binoculars, we can see farther and clearer than you can with your telescope. I've already demonstrated that any one of my soldiers, using just one of our rifles, can fire faster than twenty of your best. And we can use the radio to call for reinforcements if we need to. We do more with less, which is why I'm the only one on the wall, for the moment. If you'd like, you can borrow the binoculars to observe the Mexican preparations."

"I want more of your men on the walls."

"Yes, sir. I have training planned for my men later this morning. We'll be in the courtyard near the corral, if you'd like to join us."

"I will." When he walked down the ramp, he admired his new toy, looking through the binoculars as he walked.

"Smooth, Staff Sergeant. Real smooth," Sutter chuckled at me over the radio.

"Do what you can, with what you have, where you are."

"Wait, I know this one. Grover Cleveland said it."

"Theodore Roosevelt. It's the basis of our adaptability. The men are quiet. Are they ready for training?"

"No, we're not!" Hernández shouted.

"Sergeant Wright, get one flare round to practice loading, and gather everyone in the barracks courtyard for M203 training."

"Why don't you use the dummy rounds?"

"Do we have any?"

"We were going to use them for training when we got to the range."

"Do we have the gun sight training board?"

"We have everything we need."

"Bring them out. Sergeant Sutter, get everyone outside." I crouched low along the scaffold before walking down the ramp.

"Fire!"

BOOM!

"Damn!" I exclaimed over the ringing in my ears when the repaired eighteen-pounder unexpectedly fired behind me.

While I waited for everything we needed to be brought outside, Colonel Travis joined me.

"Good morning, sir," I said without a salute, just to see his reaction.

"I want to see the training you mentioned." Travis apparently didn't miss the salute.

"Yes, sir. Would you like to participate?"

"Yes, I would."

"Sir, you can use my rifle." I ejected the clip before handing it to him. "First Squad, form a semi-circle around Sergeant Sutter. Quickly, people, quickly. Colonel Travis is here to participate in our training. Sergeant Wright, assist the colonel. I'm going to compress a one-hour block of instructions into about ten minutes, so pay attention. Eject the magazine from your weapons and put the M203 on safe by locating the curved lever in front of the trigger, and pull it rearward until it clicks." I walked around, checking the switches on both the M16 and M203 to verify they were on safe. "While we're here, we'll be using the M406 High-Explosive round. It has a maximum range of four hundred meters, but the sight on these weapons only goes to two hundred fifty meters. You'll get maximum range by angling the weapon about forty-five degrees. On impact, the grenade produces a kill radius of five meters, and a maximum casualty radius of one hundred thirty meters. What's a casualty radius?" I asked.

"It's the area in which a grenade causes injuries. It's most effective in an open area, like a field or desert," Taylor said.

"It's even more effective if you can manage an air burst, like bouncing it off someone's head," I stated.

"How can you say hitting someone's head is an air burst?" Carpenter asked.

"A head is about six feet off the ground, right? Don't drop a live round; it won't explode, but you could damage it. The barrel of the M203 is rifled and when fired, it spins the grenade, arming it within twenty-seven meters. In the unlikely event of a misfire, how long must you wait until you try to fix the problem?"

"Thirty seconds," Sutter said.

"Why wait that long? Someone other than Sergeant Sutter answer."

"It's like a misfire with the M16. It could go off when you

open the breech," Ruiz said.

"Exactly. Sergeant Sutter, use the training board to demonstrate setting the sight to one hundred meters."

"To sight the M203, lift your leaf sight by pulling it up from its housing and gently pivoting it toward you. Raise the barrel until the front sight is centered on your target, and on the number one of the leaf sight. Notice how the spread of the front sight is level between both pointers on the leaf sight. This is the sight picture for the one-hundred-meter range setting."

"Sergeant Wright, did you bring the training rounds?"

"Yes, Staff Sergeant." Wright produced four blue dummy rounds from his thigh pocket. I handed one to Sutter and another to Travis.

"Pass the others around for practice. Sergeant Sutter, demonstrate loading the grenade launcher."

"Loading is done by depressing the unlocking lever on the left side of the weapon and sliding the barrel all the way forward. Insert the round end of the grenade all the way into the barrel. Close the barrel by pulling it back until it clicks. Get your sight picture, take the weapon off safe by pushing the curved safe lever forward until it clicks, and fire. After firing, eject the empty cartridge by depressing the lever, and slide the barrel forward. The empty cartridge will be hooked by the cartridge extractor and fall out. If it doesn't fall out on its own, like mine just didn't, you can pull the cartridge out with your fingers." Sutter confidently demonstrated each step.

"Thank you, Sergeant Sutter. Sergeant Wright, check the extractor on Sergeant Sutter's grenade launcher. People, this is a real as it gets. Review and check yourselves and each other on what you've learned. If there are any questions, get with me or Sergeant Sutter. I would've liked to have everyone fire a practice grenade, but not today. You'll get your chance tomorrow."

"Staff Sergeant, can we get on the walls for some target practice?" Snyder asked.

With all eyes on me, I thought for a moment, and then said, "You'll get your chance tomorrow."

"Come on, Sarge. We got lots of ammo," Snyder argued.

"It's a good idea, especially for those who've never seen combat," Sutter said.

"We have to be careful with the inventory," Wright reminded me.

"Who wants some target practice?" Five hands went up. "You'll each get one clip with twenty rounds; no grenades."

"Sarge, why don't you give us grenades? We can practice on the cannons," Snyder said.

"Santa Anna doesn't know we're here, and he's expecting flintlocks and muzzle loading cannons. I want to keep what we have a surprise until tomorrow."

"What about yesterday's demonstration? They must've heard it," Wright said.

"They heard a new sound, but they don't know what it was. To maintain the surprise, when you're on the wall today, take one, slow, aimed shot at a time. Use Kentucky Windage to correct a round's strike over long distances. When firing your weapon, always wear your tactical shooting glasses. Sergeant Wright, supervise the shooters, and make sure they don't fire on automatic. Everyone listen up, because this is important; don't get comfortable with what you're doing. This isn't the rifle range, where you shoot at pop-up targets. When you shoot at a man and he goes down, that's a man you've killed. Those not shooting, get under cover. Fall out."

"Damn, Sarge. That was cold," Sergeant Wright said when

he walked past me.

"Truth often is. Corporal Taylor, walk with me." I led him through an archway into the Alamo compound; Colonel Travis was following with my rifle in hand. "Colonel Bowie didn't get to the staff meeting this morning because he's too sick to move. I want you to examine him in his headquarters. It's the last door on the northwest corner," I said, pointing in the general direction.

"Are you a doctor?" Travis said to Taylor.

"No, sir. I'm a combat medic."

"Combat Medic? What is a combat medic?"

"Sir, a medic is a person trained in the treatment of combat injuries," Taylor said.

"Doctor Pollard!" Travis shouted at the hospital on the second floor of the barracks. "Doctor Pollard, are you available?"

"The surgeon is with a patient," a man said when he walked out onto a balcony, wiping his hands on a bloody rag.

"Doctor Howell, have you met Corporal Taylor?"

"I have. He said our hospital is filthy, and Doctor Pollard said he's not to come up here."

"What?" I exclaimed at Taylor with total exasperation.

"Nothing's clean," Taylor explained, defensively pointing at the rag in Howell's hands. "They reuse bandages, and wipe their hands on unwashed smocks instead of washing them."

"Doctor Howell, I apologize for the rash words of my soldier. If you allow him to revisit your hospital, I assure you he will conduct himself professionally. He can show you medical techniques you may not know of."

"Doctor Howell, my compliments to Doctor Pollard, and ask him if he will speak with Corporal Taylor at his convenience," Travis said politely.

"I'll give him your message, Colonel."

A young man, far too young to be a soldier, ran to us and breathlessly said, "Colonel Travis, sir, Colonel Bowie is very sick, sir. He wants you to come see him, sir."

"Thank you. Return to Colonel Bowie and tell him I'll be there directly. Sergeant Webber, are you certain he'll give his command to me?"

"Yes, sir. Today's the day."

"I'd like to hear more about the future," Travis said as we walked toward Bowie, who was being carried outside on his cot by some of his volunteers.

"Sir, can we talk this evening? There's something I'd like to discuss with you, Captain Dickinson, and Davy Crockett."

"Call him David. He hates being called Davy," Travis warned.

"David; yes, sir. I'll remember to do so."

"I'll have them meet us after sundown," Travis said.

When we arrived at Bowie's headquarters, most of the volunteers had gathered outside. Bowie looked up at Travis, and then tried to get to his feet. When two men tried to help him up, he loudly wheezed, "No! I stand…on my own." Bowie struggled slowly to his feet, and in a barely audible voice said, "I give my command…to Travis." Mutterings of disagreement rippled through the gathering as Bowie's barely audible words were relayed through the crowd. "Follow him…obey his orders." Bowie nearly collapsed but was caught by two of his men.

"Thank you, Colonel Bowie." Despite the historically known differences between them, Travis was more gracious than I expected him to be.

"Travis…that's a…fancy musket…you have," Bowie said breathlessly.

Travis handed my rifle to me, and then said, "Take him inside. Corporal Taylor, would you like to examine him now?"

"Yes, sir."

"Sir, there's a crowd gathering around my men on the wall. I'll be up there," I said.

Travis nodded agreement, and then walked to his headquarters.

"Doc, before you go in, would you like to know what you'll be facing in there?"

"I need to examine him before I can make any kind of diagnosis."

"Historians say Bowie was bad tempered, drunk most of the time, and was suffering from a disease of a peculiar nature. No one can be certain of what he had, but it was thought to be tuberculosis, or typhoid pneumonia."

"That would explain his breathing problems. They're contagious infections of the lungs."

"I'm glad we've had our shots. What do you have for it?"

"I could give him a broad-spectrum antibiotic, but I can't give anything like that without a lab to confirm what he has, and a doctor's approval."

"If you give him the antibiotic, would it hurt him?"

"It could, if he has an allergy to it."

"You're the closest thing to a real doctor anywhere in this time, and I don't see a lab anywhere," I said, looking around. "Why don't you give it a try?"

"It's against regulations."

"He'll die for certain if you don't treat him. Is there some kind of medical loophole you can crawl through?"

"Well, medics are responsible for providing continuing medical care in the absence of a readily available physician," Taylor suggested.

"I'm no doctor, but I'll come in with you if you want."

"I'd rather you didn't. Besides, you have to watch those characters." Taylor jerked his thumb at our shooters before walking into Bowie's headquarters.

***

I was observing and critiquing the men shooting from the wall when I saw Taylor walking up the ramp toward me.

"How's Colonel Bowie?"

"I can't be certain of what he has, but it looks like the resolution stage of pneumonia. Like you said, he's difficult and uncooperative, using whiskey as a pain killer. And he's a big baby when it comes to needles. I had to sit on him to inject the antibiotic into his hip."

"I've never heard of a doctor sitting on a patient before."

"It's in my medical book from now on. I'll give him injections for a few days to see how he responds."

"Thanks, Doc. By the way, their hospital is typical for this time in history, and it is dirty by our standards, so let's not rub their noses in it, okay?"

"Sarge, you know I'm a medic, not a doctor."

"You're a combat medic."

"And I've been trained to treat combat injuries."

"I know where you're going with this. Take a look around; this is 1836. Santa Anna has raised the red flag of no quarter, and in case you don't know, it means kill everyone without mercy. If they get inside these walls, you'll have to go to the rifle. You'll have to do harm, to keep others from harm."

"I know what you want me to do, but I say *Primum Non Nocere*."

"What?"

"It's Latin, meaning, 'First, do no harm.' What you want me to do is a gross misinterpretation of the Hippocratic Oath."

"I didn't know medics had to swear the Hippocratic Oath."

"We don't—it's not part of our training, but I know it because I'm going to college, pre-med, to become a doctor."

"Pollard is the senior surgeon in charge of the hospital, so you'll have to kiss his ass. Go see what you can do to help, and make suggestions about techniques, cleanliness, and suggest the reasons way. While you're at it, get as much information as you can about…what are they called? —healing spices, I think?"

"Herbal medicine? You're kidding, right?"

"Our training is always ongoing, and you can help them in the process. It may put you in a better light because it appears you don't know as much as they do—if you get my meaning."

"Yeah, I get it." He left but met me several minutes later.

"Did you get kicked out already?" I asked when I saw him walking toward me.

"Not yet, but I heard the well's running dry, and there's talk about getting water from the river."

"I'd forgotten about that. Come with me. First Squad, gather at the well in the courtyard behind the barracks," I said over the radio as we walked toward the well.

"*What about my shooters?*" Wright asked.

"Stay where you are but listen in on the radio."

When everyone else had gathered, I said, "Listen up. This well is running dry, and they'll have to start getting water from the river until the new well is dug. Corporal Taylor, what are the dangers of drinking water from unapproved sources, including this well?"

"The most dangerous contaminates are single-celled protozoan parasites found in soil, food, or water that's been contaminated with the feces from infected people or animals. Some of the worst symptoms are severe nausea, cramps, diarrhea, and dysentery. Untreated dysentery can kill. The individual water purification kits won't last long under these conditions, so I'll try to get a pot to boil water and help the kits last longer."

"Thanks, Doc. I also have a Lifestraw in my pack. It's good for purifying a thousand liters of water."

"You have a Lifestraw?" Hernández scoffed. "You're a real Boy Scout."

"You never know where you're going to end up. Until we get a clean water supply, I'm suspending shaving until further notice. Corporal Taylor, what do you think?"

"It's a good idea. Without clean water, a small shaving cut can turn into a deadly infection."

"Another reason why we don't need to shave is because we don't need the gas masks. Take them off and store them in the truck." I set the example by unstrapping the mask from my waist.

"What if they get stolen?" Ruiz asked.

"Don't worry about it. They serve no purpose here."

"Are we supposed to pick them up if the fog returns?" Sutter asked.

"Are you going to try and recover everything you have before jumping in?"

"Webber loves this place. I vote he stays behind and guards our stuff," Hernández said.

"I'm sure you'd like that. I've often wondered what it'd be like to be here; but as they say, been there, done that. If the fog returns, I'll leave this place in an instant. I'll dive in naked if I have to."

"Let him go first. His dick will be a lightning rod and protect us from the static," Hernández said.

"Oh, my God. I'll never get that picture out of my head." Sutter rubbed his forehead with his fingers amid raucous laughter that erupted from everyone.

Hernández's ongoing disrespect continued to irritate me.

"Very funny, people. From now on, there won't be any formations. I'll take accountability every morning."

"Can you count that high?" Hernández asked.

"And it was going so well," Sutter mumbled.

Because of Sergeant McFadden's often repeated instructions, I had been tolerating Hernández's remarks, but this time, I almost went off on him. Instead, I said, "Uh-huh. Okay. Everyone listen up. Until further notice, we will Stand To. In case you missed it during training, Stand To means we get up before dawn and go to our firing positions, waiting for an enemy's sneak attack. This means everyone!" I said to Hernández.

"You can't do that. It's mass punishment."

"You're damn right it is. Next time, keep your pie hole shut!" I shouted.

"I've had enough of you. I'm going to the captain."

"Good! I want to see him too. What? He's not here?" I gestured at our surroundings. "Until he appears, you will Stand To with the rest of us. You will learn the names and ranks of all uniformed officers and senior enlisted men here, and you will treat them with the respect they are due. And, you will conduct yourself like a soldier. That goes for everyone! Fall out!"

When everyone started to disperse, Sutter loudly said, "Are we doing the right thing?"

It was unusual for Sutter to speak out like that, and everyone stopped to listen.

"What do you mean?" I asked.

"You said it. This place will be overrun, and everyone gets killed."

"It looks like we have to change history to save ourselves."

"Do we have the right to change history? Don't give me a history lesson. I want to know if we're right!" Sutter's voice rose, pressing his point home. It gave me a moment of pause—the moment needed to think.

"Everyone, gather around," I finally said with a sigh.

When they had gathered, I came to the position of attention, held up my right hand, and said, "I do solemnly swear that I will support and defend the Constitution of the United States against all enemies, foreign and domestic; that I will bear true faith and allegiance to the same; and that I will obey the orders of the President of the United States and the orders of the officers appointed over me, according to regulations and the Uniform Code of Military Justice. So help me God. I'm sure everyone's forgotten the Oath of Enlistment."

"It don't mean shit," Hernández stated.

"What do you mean?" I snapped at him.

"It don't mean shit 'cause we ain't been born yet!"

I had to stop and think about that. The oath was taken and would be obeyed for the duration of the enlistment, which was why the oath was given before every reenlistment. A true soldier would carry the oath throughout his life. Hernández was wrong, and right, up to a certain point.

"It appears that I lost sight of what we're supposed to be doing. At seventeen hundred hours, we'll have dinner together in the barracks. We'll discuss our situation and make a decision on whether to leave or stay. Until then, think about it. Fall out."

After everyone had dispersed into small groups, I noticed the shooters on the north wall had not resumed shooting. Sutter came to me, pointed to his radio, and turned it off. I did the same.

"Thanks for getting me back on track," I said.

"You didn't answer my question."

"Do you mean are we doing the right thing? 'The evil that men do lives after them; the good is oft interred with their bones.'"

"I hate that about you; giving obscure answers from history," Sutter stated.

"Actually, that was Shakespeare. But if you want history; 'He who refuses to learn from history is doomed to repeat it.'"

"Damn it." Sutter slowly smiled and shook his head.

"Since you asked, am I doing the right thing?"

"You mean, giving us a choice? Considering where and when we are…yeah, I think so."

"What're you going to do?"

"The same as you," Sutter said.

"Let's pack our gear and get outta here."

"What?" he exclaimed. Completely deadpan, I looked at him. When I raised my eyebrows, he said, "I thought I misread you."

"Run from a fight when I know details of what'll happen, and when? You've got to be joking. As soon as everyone has made up their minds, I'll give those who are staying a briefing on what to expect while we're here. The rest can pack and leave after dark."

"Have you considered the history of this place?"

"You know I've researched—"

"Why is there no mention of us?" Sutter interrupted.

"What do you mean?"

"Us. You, me, the squad, our weapons, the truck over there. You'd think something about us would appear in the history of this place."

"You're right. There's nothing about us being here that I've ever read. There's gotta be a way back before we change too much history."

"You want to get back and correct the history books," Sutter stated.

"I need to get everyone home in one piece first."

There was a sudden commotion on the west wall, followed by shouts for Colonel Travis and Sergeant Major Williamson. Sutter and I ran to the west wall, and when we climbed a ladder to the scaffold, Santa Anna was riding on horseback with some of his officers near the riverbank.

"He's got a pair of balls the Jolly Green Giant would be proud to own. What are you doing?" Sutter asked when I unslung the rifle from my shoulder.

"How far out do you think he is?" I looked intently at Santa Anna on his horse.

"I make it about three hundred fifty meters," Sutter observed.

"He's out of range," Travis noted. "Crockett could make the shot."

"Yes, sir, but he's not here." I suspected Crockett was with the Scotsman when I heard the sounds of a fiddle and bagpipes coming from the barracks area.

Putting years of training and experience to use, I steadied myself and my rifle on the wall, got the sight picture, lead the target, and corrected for gravity and wind—all with slow, steady breathing. Breathe in, half out, gently squeeze the trigger. In the moment between breath and surprise of the rifle's report and recoil, Santa Anna's spirited horse tossed its head and pranced sideways. A moment later, man and horse fell to the ground.

"You shot the horse," Travis said matter-of-factly, lowering the binoculars I'd lent him.

Santa Anna briefly struggled to get his leg out from under his horse, then got up and ran to his mounted officers. Using them as a shield, he pulled one man off his horse, mounted, and rode headlong back to the bridge, with his officers riding hard to catch up. The Mexican officer, who was suddenly on foot, looked briefly at the wall and then ran as fast as he could toward the bridge.

"Santa Anna's horse is down. Does that mean the battle's over?" Sutter was smiling with a toothy grin.

I slung my rifle on my shoulder, and silently walked away from the embarrassing scene with the certainty I'd never hear the end of it.

When I got off the scaffold, someone shouted, "Colonel Travis, Mexican soldiers are moving to the north!" Travis walked along the scaffold to see for himself until another soldier shouted, "Mexicans are moving to the south!"

"Sir, it's not an attack!" I shouted at Travis. "Santa Anna's sending troops to surround us as a show of force. They'll camp out there at night and stand in formation during the day."

"You knew about this and didn't tell me?"

"Yes, sir. Like I said, I know a lot about what Santa Anna's going to do."

"Sergeant Major Williamson! Set more men on the walls!" Travis shouted.

"Yes, sir!"

***

At sunset, I was walking toward the west wall in anticipation of the Mexican scouts crossing the footbridge when gunfire got everyone's attention. I heard fifteen muskets fire before I could get on the scaffold. Everyone was pouring powder and ramming lead balls down barrels when I looked over the wall and saw Mexican soldiers running back across the narrow footbridge or splashing through the river. One soldier was lying on the ground, unmoving, like Santa Anna's horse a short distance away. After one more shot I saw another soldier fall off the bridge into the river. I went to Crockett, and he said, "Yup, the last one was mine, just like you said."

"You're a better shot than I am. I have to report to Colonel Travis. Would you like to join me?" I sadly looked at Santa Anna's dead horse.

"You need not worry about shooting Santa Anna's horse," Crockett said, demonstrating an intuitiveness I didn't know he had.

"It's not what I wanted. If I'd shot Santa Anna today the siege would be over, and his officers and men would be going home."

"If he shows himself again, we will shoot him together." Crockett nodded his head in agreement with his own words.

When Crockett and I reached Travis's headquarters, I saw Hernández walking toward the barracks with a group of Tejano volunteers. When he saw me, he shouted, "Hey, Webber. The Mexican army has surrounded us. What now, Alamo genius?"

Crockett scowled at Hernández's comment, then said, "Are you gonna to let him talk to you that way?"

"I'll deal with him later." I knocked on Travis's door and walked in.

"This ain't no good," Crockett said when we saw Travis watching Hernández through the unshuttered window.

"I've heard much about that man." Travis rapidly tapped his index finger on his table as he continued to watch Hernández. "What can you tell me about him?"

"Private Manuel Hernández came to our company about three months ago and has demonstrated a lack of discipline ever since. He's difficult to motivate, and hard to train. He has no respect for most people, and will manipulate a situation against anyone to keep himself out of trouble, or to get his own way."

"I've heard about another who came with you; Sanchez."

"Private Juan Sanchez came to our company about seven

months ago. He was a good soldier until he became friends with Hernández. Now they think and act alike. His attitude changes noticeably when he's separated from Hernández, which is not often."

"They are your men. You will keep them under control."

"Yes, sir. Do you have problems with any of your men?"

"I leave the discipline of the men to the sergeants."

"They fight with them when they have to," Crockett added.

"Tell me you're joking." I smiled, looking at Crockett, then Travis.

"A fight keeps the sergeants respected, and keeps discipline among the men," Travis said.

"Is that why the sergeant major is so big?" I asked.

"To my knowledge he's never lost a fight," Travis said seriously. "You were right about the skirmish over the new footbridge. What will happen tomorrow?"

"Santa Anna will send soldiers across the bridge to the southwest to try and take the huts along the south road. You might want to prepare your men for the weather, because it will rain tonight and tomorrow morning. It'll get colder, and then freeze tomorrow night."

"Do your men have positions on the walls to go to?"

"Yes, sir. We'll man the walls under your command."

"You will command your men. Good night, Sergeant Webber. Crockett, stay a bit."

I saluted Travis before I left his headquarters. I wasn't looking forward to the meeting with the men, because I may have made a mistake by letting them choose what they wanted to do. I might be standing on a wall by myself tomorrow.

When I walked into the barracks I took a visual headcount, and then said, "Does everyone have their dinner?" Sergeant

Wright tossed an MRE to me before I sat down on my bunk. "Gentlemen, I think we can agree this is 1836, and it comes with a lot of unknowns we may never get the answers to."

"Like what?" Sutter asked.

"Like, how'd we got here? I don't know. Will we get home? I don't know. Were we deliberately put here, or are we here by some weird cosmic event? I don't know. As the ranking NCO I'm supposed to have the answers, or at least know where to get them. I must be having a blond moment, because I just don't know. If anyone has a clue, now's the time," I offered, looking around for a response. "Anyone? Sergeant Sutter? Private Hernández?"

"That's the first time you've asked me for anything, and I got nothing," Hernández said.

"Here's an answer I have; I didn't ask to be put here. What I know for certain is we're here, in the past, with a decision to make." I wanted to draw a line on the floor, but I let the thought go.

"If we decide to leave, will you let us go?" Sutter's question actually surprised me.

"I've already decided I'm staying. If you or anyone else wants leave, it's your decision."

"If we want to go, can we take ammo and MRE's with us?" Thompson asked.

"I'll make sure you get your share, except for grenades. We'll need them here. You'll have to pack and carry everything you want to keep and leave at night so you'll have a fair chance of not being seen by the Mexican army surrounding us. If you're killed walking out of here, destroy your rifles so the Mexicans can't use them against us." I suppressed a smile, waiting for a reaction to my deliberately misspoken words.

"If we're killed, how can we destroy our rifles?" Carpenter

finally asked. Confused looks were slowly replaced by laughter.

"I've listened to some of your bullshit about this place, and you've said messengers rode in and out all the time," Hernández interjected.

"I know what you're going to say. In this time, a horse and saddle are like a car in ours. Ask around and see if they can spare any horses but remember this—horse thieves are shot on sight; no police, no courts. As far as the truck is concerned, those of us who stay might need it in case we have to move to another firing position."

"Do you think my people are gonna let you leave?" Hernández asked.

"If it comes to that, I'm betting the shock value of a five-ton truck roaring out the gate in a cloud of diesel smoke, while they're dropping like flies from grenades and automatic rifles, will be enough to plow through them." Heads were nodding in agreement.

"Do you think we'll get back home?" Carpenter said, looking at his cell phone.

"Again, I don't know. I'd like to think if we stick together and see this through, something or someone will let us go home. Until then, we have to follow our conscience. Are there any more questions? No? Who's staying with me?" All but two hands rose with me. "Outstanding. What about you two?" I said, indicating Hernández and Sanchez.

"I'm not sure whether I want to stay and watch you get killed trying to be the hero of the Alamo or leave and hear about it later." Hernández was at his sarcastic best.

"What about you, Sanchez?"

He looked at Hernández before he said, "Yeah, me too."

"Make up your minds before the Mexicans have a chance to

consolidate their positions and catch you sneaking out of here."

"I don't think so." Hernández gave me a sly look, making me wonder what he had planned.

Having received their decisions, I got up and left the barracks. Sutter followed me out, and said, "I thought I knew you."

"How so?"

"Letting the men drink on duty and giving them a choice instead of orders."

"We have to adapt to the unique position we're in, so I gave them the choice because they deserve a say in what happens to them. As far as drinking's concerned, it's the social interaction of the time; like the Internet and cell phones are in ours." I looked at a group of men, staggering and laughing as they shared a bottle of whiskey. "They're social all right and couldn't care less if a cannonball knocks their heads off." I secretly wished I could hoist a bottle myself.

"They'll be sleeping well tonight," Sutter said.

"Why don't you go have a drink and get some sleep?"

Boom! Boom! Boom!

"Sleep—with all this racket? Not likely. What're you going to do?"

"I'm going to post Ruiz on guard duty. Then I'm going to have a talk about the future with Travis, Dickinson, and Crockett."

"This is Ruiz. Where do you want me?"

"Go to the southwest corner, next to the big cannon, and use your night vision goggles to watch for movement from the bridges."

"How long should I stay there?"

"The meeting shouldn't last more than an hour. I'll relieve you when I'm done."

Just as I walked past Travis's shuttered window, someone

walked out his door. My unexpected presence startled whoever it was, and I had to fend off a flurry of punches, several bouncing off my body armor and helmet. Hearing the scuffle, Travis came outside and separated us. After a gruff apology, the soldier went on his way. I was none the worse for wear, but I wasn't sure about him. Punching my armor was completely ineffective, and my helmet was hard on knuckles.

"I heard you let your men decide to stay or leave," Travis said when we walked inside.

"Yes, sir. According to history, on March fifth you do the same for all your men after a courier returns and reports reinforcements aren't coming. There's a story about how you gathered all the men together in front of the church, took out your saber, drew a line in the dirt, and told them that those who would join you and die for freedom should step across the line. All but one crosses the line. By that time, you'll have about one hundred seventy men ready to fight. The rest will be in the hospital."

"It's not going to be enough." Travis shook his head. "Maybe I should have abandoned this place to Santa Anna."

"Sir, before we get too deep in this discussion, we should wait for Captain Dickinson and David."

"Staff Sergeant Webber, ten people are crossing the bridge to the southwest."

"Roger that. Keep an eye on them. If they turn toward us, let me know."

"Yes, Staff Sergeant."

"Can your men see in the dark better than we can?" Travis asked.

"Sir, I'm sure you'd like another demonstration. Webber is offline." When we walked outside, I lowered the night vision goggles and turned them on, and said, "You'll see different shades of green." I took off my helmet and gently placed it on Travis's head.

He slowly turned his head around, and then took a few steps with his arms stretched out in front of him.

"Sir, the night vision goggles take whatever light is available and makes it brighter so you can see at night. Ask PFC Ruiz to talk to you."

"PFC Ruiz, can you hear me?"

"Sir, this is PFC Ruiz. Can you see me?"

"Where are you?"

"I'm to your right, on the south wall."

"Can he see me? Can you see me?"

"I see you, sir. What am I doing?"

I couldn't see Ruiz, but I knew he was waving because Travis waved back.

"You say an attack will come tomorrow?" Travis asked.

"Yes, sir. From the south, late tomorrow morning."

"What is that on your face?" I heard Crockett say from the darkness.

"Sergeant Webber is letting me use his helmet with these... things over my eyes. I can see in the dark as well as I can see in the daytime. Captain Dickinson, I see you coming."

"How could you see me when I couldn't see you? What is that on your face?"

"Sir, can I have my helmet? I'm sure the captain and David would like to try it."

Travis looked around a bit more before he removed the helmet. After letting Dickinson and Crockett use the helmet for a while, we went into the warmth of Travis's headquarters and pulled up crude chairs and boxes to sit on.

"Gentlemen, the colonel wanted me to relate what I know about the future. Right now, delegates are meeting at the Washington-on-the-Brazos, discussing a Declaration of Independence from Mexico, and they will formally sign the declaration on March third. This fact is known by Alamo historians in my time. I also want to relate something else, but I wanted to include the two of you."

"Why just the two of us?" Crockett asked.

"The future has been changing since we arrived, so I'll relate history as I knew it before we came here. Colonel, the Alamo is a pivotal battle in the history of Texas. For thirteen days with one hundred eighty-eight men, you stand against Santa Anna's force of over two thousand four hundred soldiers."

"I do not have one hundred eighty-eight men," Travis said.

"Right now, it's closer to one hundred thirty, and some of those are in the hospital. But Santa Anna doesn't have two thousand four hundred soldiers yet. They're still arriving."

"I hear something you ain't saying. What is it?" Crockett asked intuitively.

"I was hoping to work my way up to this, to make it easier to hear, but there's no way to do it. Before sunrise on March sixth, Santa Anna will overrun this compound and kill every man inside." I looked at Travis's slave, who was standing in the doorway to Travis's bedroom. "Except you, Joe. You'll fight beside the colonel, and despite being shot and bayoneted, you'll live and leave here as the only man to survive the battle inside these walls."

"Yes, suh. Very much obliged, suh," Joe said, casting an uncertain glance at Travis.

I was on a roll, finally able to give my knowledge to an interested audience.

"Captain Dickinson, history records that you, Lieutenant

Bonham, and Gregorio Esparza will be killed while fighting near the cannons in the church."

"I've been a soldier for many years. It's a soldier's duty to fight and, if necessary, die; and I'll do that when it comes," Dickinson said fatalistically. "But what of my wife and daughter, what happens to them?"

"Suzanna and Angelina will leave here unharmed, under Santa Anna's protection. Suzanna's account of what she saw is required reading for anyone who wants an accurate, albeit emotional accounting of what happened."

"Suzanna can't read or write."

"She told the story to others who wrote for her. There will be other survivors, mostly women and children, couriers who didn't or couldn't come back, and those who ran rather than fought."

"Who ran? Who didn't come back?" Travis was annoyed by the historical suggestion of uncommitted men in his ranks.

"Sir, on February sixteenth, you sent Lieutenant Bonham to search for reinforcements. On second thought, he'll return on March third. There were others, but the most notable is Captain Juan Seguin. You will send him as a courier to General Houston—he will order Seguin to remain with him. Despite Houston's orders, he will gather his own reinforcements, but will return here too late to help."

"Are there others?" Travis asked.

"Private Louis Rose."

"Rose? I do not know everyone—"

"History knows him as a French soldier of fortune that was not ready to die for Texas independence. There are others, mostly couriers, but I don't remember them all."

"Captain Dickinson and I share the same duty. But what happens to me? Is there an accounting of my death?" Travis asked.

"Yes, sir. Historical accounts differ only slightly, but all agree you'll be among the first to die on the north wall."

"How? How will I die?"

"You'll fire your pistol and the double-barreled shotgun into soldiers massed at the base of the north wall." I pointed at the shotgun leaning against a wall. "When you're reloading, you'll be killed instantly by a shot to the head."

"What of me?" Crockett asked.

"Until 1975, your story is one of bravery beyond measure." I instantly regretted relating that bit of history.

"What happens in 1975?" Crockett said, jumping on the date.

"Nothing of significance," I said, scrambling to dig my way out of the hole I found myself in.

"Sergeant Webber, what happens to David?" Travis asked.

"Captain Dickinson, Suzanna said she saw David's body against the church, surrounded by many dead Mexican soldiers."

"Sergeant Webber!" Travis said in a no-nonsense tone.

"Sir, I wanted Suzanna's account to be heard and understood. In 1975, an uncorroborated document called the De La Pena narrative tells a different account of the final battle. In his account, Lieutenant Colonel José Enrique De La Peña wrote…ah, look, I don't want to tell you what he wrote."

"Tell me. I want to know what was written about me," Crockett said gently.

"On the morning of March sixth, an attack along the south wall and palisade will be a diversion to keep the colonel from concentrating his men on the north wall, where the main attack will come with three battalions of infantry. Until 1975, the accepted account was that the Mexicans breached the north wall and swept through the compound, killing all one hundred eighty-eight defenders before sunrise. Here's where the accounts differ. One obscure account says about twenty men, David included, went over the palisade and ran east. All but six were killed by cavalry patrols. The six who were brought back, David included, were executed in front of the church. In Colonel De La Pena's account, he says the surviving volunteers abandoned their positions on the north and west walls to join David in front of the church. All but six were surrounded and killed. When Santa Anna rode into the compound, General Manuel Castrillon asked for clemency for the prisoners of war. Under Santa Anna's direct orders and observation, they were executed. In a final act of barbaric disrespect, the bodies of all the defenders were stripped, mutilated, and then stacked and burned."

"No matter what account I hear, we all die. It's all for nothing," Dickinson said.

"No, sir. It's not for nothing. By keeping Santa Anna here, you give General Houston time to consolidate his army. About two months from now, in a place called San Jacinto, General Houston defeats Santa Anna in an eighteen-minute battle, killing over six hundred Mexican soldiers and capturing the coward Santa Anna."

"Santa Anna is no coward. He proved it this afternoon," Travis said.

"No? When he was captured in San Jacinto, he was dressed in a private's uniform. Soldiers loyal to him unintentionally gave him away, and he was brought before General Houston, who gave Santa Anna and his men the mercy denied to those who died here."

The silence and foreboding surrounding us was thick enough to cut with a knife.

"Gentlemen, that's history as it is known where I came from.

I would offer 'Victory or Death,' but you already wrote that in your letter to General Houston. Tomorrow, we have a chance to change history as it was written in my time. Colonel, I have complete confidence in my men and our weapons, and that gives us the chance to live. Sir, I'll return to my men and go over tomorrow's preparations."

Without waiting for questions or dismissal, I stood, saluted Travis, and walked out. I didn't get a return salute, but there was not much of that here.

"PFC Ruiz, you're relieved," I said over my radio.

"Thank you, Staff Sergeant. I was listening to your meeting. Can we talk with the radios off?"

"Meet me at the well."

When we arrived, we turned off our radios and I asked, "What's on your mind?"

"I've heard that if a man knows he'll die tomorrow, he'll find a way to make it happen."

"They're not going to die, not if I can help it. And neither are you."

"I've seen you in your dress greens uniform, and I'd like to know, how'd you get your Purple Heart?"

"Combat in Afghanistan," I said, not wanting to review that situation.

"Tell me how you got it, please."

"Why is this important to you?"

"I'd like to know."

"We were on mounted patrol in a town when we were ambushed. We dismounted our vehicles and took cover. When Sergeant Sutter was advancing to another firing position, he was hit in the leg. When I was recovering him, I was hit on the right shoulder. It was a solid hit that knocked me over, broke my collar bone, and numbed my right arm. I switched arms and continued to drag him to safety while the squad gave us cover. It's no big deal."

"How can you say it's no big deal?"

"My body armor protected me."

"I've heard you go off on Hernández when he complained about it being too heavy to wear," Ruiz said with a grin.

"Which is why I get annoyed when I get complaints from anyone about it being too heavy. I've seen this armor save lives. You saw it save Snyder's life."

"Battalion legal questioned me about Hernández's complaints of the armor being too heavy and how you handle the complaints. I told them you were acting out of concern for his safety, and the safety of the squad."

"If you told them the truth, I couldn't ask for more from anyone."

"I hope it did some good."

"It did. Charges against the NCOs in the company have been dropped. Go to the barracks, have a drink, and then get as much sleep as you can. Tomorrow is going to be a busy day. Leave your radio off for tonight and have everyone else turn theirs off as well."

"Thanks, Sarge."

After he walked away, I said under my breath, "No; thank you."

I walked to the place where a cenotaph honoring the fallen Alamo defenders would be unveiled in San Antonio's Alamo Plaza in 1938. My mind's eye saw the spire where a naked man, the Spirit of Sacrifice set in carved marble relief, was rising from flames with his arms raised to the sky. I repeated the honorarium found at the base.

"'They chose never to surrender nor retreat, these brave hearts with flag still proudly waving perished in the flames of immortality that their high sacrifice might lead to the founding of this Texas.'"

With a sigh, my breath fogging in the cold evening air, I walked to the barracks hoping the whisky wasn't gone before I got there.

CHAPTER 4

DAY THREE – THURSDAY FEBRUARY 25, 1836

When my watch woke me at 0430 hours, I really didn't want to rise and take charge of the "last chance squad," as Sutter had put it. Instead, I lay listening to the rain, enjoying the sounds from the warmth of my sleeping bag. With a sigh, I finally rousted myself out of bed and dressed. When I was ready, I shouted, "Stand To! First Squad, Stand To! Everybody up!" I went around, kicking the bunks of those not moving, while the grumbles and shouts from sleepy Alamo defenders who weren't involved tried to quiet my racket. When the squad was up, or at least sitting on their bunks, I noticed Hernández and Thompson were still bundled up like hamsters against the cold. I stood between them and dead lifted the bunks by their frame rails, dumping the sleeping contents on the floor.

"Goddamn it; who in hell do you think you are?" Hernández shouted, looking like a worm as he squirmed around in his sleeping bag. Thompson looked confused when he unzipped his bag, but when the pleasantry of sleep had cleared from his mind, he recognized me as I stood glaring at him. He couldn't get to his feet fast enough.

I waited patiently until Hernández finally unzipped his bag, then I helped him up by his shirt, and quietly said in his face, "Stand To with everyone else."

"The captain will hear of this abuse!"

"I truly hope so. And be sure to mention that it's you and your mouth that made everyone Stand To."

"This is mass punishment!"

"You bet your ass it is. Get dressed."

When I returned to my bunk, Sutter said, "Tough night. Cannons firing, balls pounding the walls, Stand To."

"Do you have a complaint, Sergeant Sutter?" I said snappishly.

"Stand To does cut into sleep time. Yeah, yeah, so do the cannons." Sutter's sleepiness made him somewhat less tactful than usual.

"They stopped firing for a while, just after the heavy rain started. I slept pretty good after that," I said, listening to the calming rain again.

"What'll happen today, oh mighty and industrious leader?" Sanchez said.

"It's illustrious leader, not industrious; although it does work," Sutter said.

"First Squad, listen up! Break out your wet weather gear and long johns. It'll quit raining sometime before 1200 hours, and then the temperature will fall all day and freeze tonight. Santa Anna will begin moving his infantry after sunrise, and they'll be mostly using the Brown Bess musket. It's British built, smoothbore, with a maximum effective range of about one-hundred meters. In the hands of an experienced soldier, it can fire an astonishing three to four rounds per minute," I said, bringing tired laughter from the squad. "The Brown Bess fires a 75-caliber ball, but they can load two or three 36-caliber balls on top of it, making a shotgun effect. They'll come across the bridge from the southwest to try and take the huts along the road to the south. Sergeant Wright, open the grenades, and give each team nine. Use three of yours against the soldiers across the river, and the rest against the cannons in Bexar that are about four-hundred meters from the wall. When you've fired your grenades, move toward the southwest corner near the eighteen-pounder cannon, and use your rifles against soldiers on the west side of the huts. My team will take nine grenades and use them against the infantry if they come up the road. Pay attention to your radios. I may have to make adjustments on the fly. Everyone take an MRE and eat it when you can. You know the drill; keep your heads low to present a small target aspect to the Mexican infantry and watch your fields of fire. Gentlemen, as long as we're a team, there's nothing to worry about. Since we're here, we'll show them what we can do. Let's kick ass. That's what we're going to do; we're going to kick some ass. Are we a team?"

"Yeah."

"Are we a team?"

"Yeah!"

"What are we?"

"We're a team!"

"What are we going to do?"

"Kick ass!"

"Yeah! Total bad asses! Get your ammo, turn on your radios, and move to your positions. Let's get it done, people. Corporal Taylor, stay here. If a call comes for ammo, take it wherever it's needed. Sergeant Wright, a word before you leave," I said.

After ammo and MREs had been distributed, and the squad had left the barracks, I pointed to my radio and performed a throat cutting motion. Sergeant Wright reached up and turned his radio off, as I did mine.

"Are you aware of the problems Hernández and Sanchez are causing in the company?" I asked.

"Mostly rumors, confirmed by what I've seen and heard over the past couple of days. You're taking a lot of shit from them; a lot more than I would," Wright candidly admitted.

"According to McFadden, I have to. I can do nothing except take their crap and report the incidents to McFadden only. Mac has taken them to the first sergeant and the captain many times. I think they believe they can get away with anything because the captain's Hispanic."

"Sounds like Mac's looking out for you."

"Don't let that thought out. Hernández would see it as a sign of weakness, and I've enough problems keeping him in line without getting into more trouble because of him."

"I've also heard Hernández has something on the captain, and he's holding it over his head."

"That sounds like the rumor mill working overtime again; rumors probably started by Hernández himself. When I set the fireteams I gave you Sanchez, but he won't give you any problems. He's almost a soldier when he's away from Hernández. When the shooting starts, make him fire all three of his grenades to verify the range to the cannons in Bexar. I'll manage Hernández. Let's go."

"Not yet. I have to question the use of the open mike on the radio," Wright said.

"As NCOs, we're supposed to keep the men informed. VOX allows them to hear what's going on, and gives us a measure of control, because we can hear what they are saying."

"You don't need to tell them everything, and they don't need to hear everything. And, from what I've heard, Hernández has been talking to the Mexicans in here and—"

"*Tejanos*," I said.

"What?"

"They're called *Tejanos*. During this time in history, Mexicans in the region along the San Antonio River called themselves *Tejanos*. At this time, there were three separate and distinct regions of—"

"Instead of a history lesson, let's work on my concerns," Wright interrupted. "You may not have noticed that Carpenter opens his phone a lot."

"I've noticed. He misses his family, and we won't criticize him for it. As a money saving measure, he moved his family back home, which I think was a mistake."

"That's not what I was going to say. Hernández brought a couple of Mexicans—"

"*Tejanos*."

"...*Tejanos* into the barracks yesterday and had Carpenter play music on his phone. Hernández is using their religious superstitions and accusing you of witchcraft. I've heard they believe it's black magic, and you're the reason."

"You heard this? Do you speak Mexican?"

"I heard it from Ruiz, and they don't speak Mexican—they speak Spanish."

"Consider this. There's only one country that speaks Spanish, and it's not Mexico. There's only one country that speaks English, and it's not the United States. Think about it and get back to me."

"Uh-huh. Watch your back, mister wizard." He smiled and turned his radio on as he walked away.

I followed him into the plaza, where Sutter was waiting.

"Yes, Sergeant Sutter?"

Sutter pointed to his radio and turned it off, as did I again.

"Why didn't you give Hernández and Sanchez to me?"

"I want them separated from each other; and I want them on the wall defending our position, not dead under it." Sutter responded with a wicked grin. "The firefight should bring everyone in line," I said.

"I think Hernández is all mouth, and he'll fold under fire."

"I'll be watching him. I've already briefed Sergeant Wright about Sanchez."

"Have you considered what'll happen if we beat Santa Anna today?" Sutter asked.

"What do you mean, if we beat him? What's your point?"

"You said Santa Anna split his army in Mexico, and sent general…what's his handle?"

"He sent General Urrea, along with about fourteen-hundred soldiers, along the coast toward Goliad."

"Yeah, that's him. If we beat him, he might send for Urrea, and we'll be in for a lot of trouble."

"What're you worried about? We have the tactical advantages of weapons, and a defendable position," I said.

"'Fixed fortifications are a monument to the stupidity of man,'" Sutter said.

"I knew that was coming; General George Patton said it. He also said, 'anything built by man can be destroyed by him,' and that worries me. Santa Anna has rifled howitzers on the way here that can easily punch through the walls, but they won't get here until at least March seventh. We'll have to deal with them when they arrive."

"You should force a fight with Santa Anna, and beat him while he's not prepared," Sutter suggested.

"I'll keep your thoughts in mind. Let's get to it." We turned on our radios and walked to our positions on the walls.

Sutter's comments raised concerns in my mind. Everything I'd learned about Alamo history and the predictability I depended on would disappear after today, but I took comfort in the fact we were trained to adapt. The only constant from now on was the weather, if it was accurately recorded.

***

While we stood and chowed down on rain soaked MREs, the cold, blustery winds made it miserable to stand on the scaffolds; not so much for the squad, because we were prepared for it, but everyone else was not. The cloth ponchos and wide brimmed hats many of the Alamo defenders were wearing did little to keep them dry, or warm.

A young man yelled from the base of the ladder, summoning me for a meeting in Travis's headquarters.

"Sergeant Webber, what will happen today?" Travis asked when I walked in.

"Sir, I need you to remember, this is history as I knew it before we arrived here. Historians from my time are not certain how many men Santa Anna will send up the south road. It could be as few as twenty riflemen trained as snipers, or as many as four-hundred infantry." The mention of so many infantry started mutterings from the assembled officers. "They want to take the huts along the south road and set up another cannon battery closer to the wall and destroy the gate."

"How many men will I lose this day?" Travis asked.

"None, but history records one Mexican was killed and several wounded. That count could change when we use our grenades against Santa Anna's infantry, which will assemble out of range of your muskets. One of your men will be killed during a skirmish at the huts tomorrow, if it occurs."

"If it occurs? You said you know what happens."

"Santa Anna will lose some of his best infantry today, and history as I know it will change in a big way. What will Santa Anna do in response? You can't know the mind of your enemy like you know your own, but what would you do in his position if you lost a large number of your men in one battle against so few…rebels?"

"I would call for reinforcements," Travis said.

"Santa Anna split his army when he crossed the Rio Grande River. I think he'll make General Urrea speed up his march to reinforce him. Urrea's moving toward Goliad with about 1400 soldiers as we speak."

"Colonel Fannin is in Goliad, and he doesn't have enough men to stop Urrea. I've got to warn them," Travis said.

"Despite your letters for his help, Fannin will not join you. In early March, Fannin's scouts will inform him of Urrea's approaching army, and he'll abandon Goliad and his Fort Defiance. He'll be caught in the open and tricked into surrendering. Fannin and most of his command will be murdered."

"Murdered? If they surrender, they must be treated as prisoners of war," Travis said.

"Remember, Santa Anna has permission from his government to kill all the pirates he encounters. He's ordered Urrea and all his other generals to do the same. Some of Santa Anna's generals will try to change his mind, but most of the people he encounters will be killed by direct orders from Santa Anna."

"Urrea has about fourteen-hundred men, and Santa Anna has about twenty-four hundred. Reckon we're gonna do a whole lot of shootin'. Do we have enough powder?" Crockett asked.

"Sir, to conserve powder and other supplies, I suggest you fire only one of your smallest cannons at the northern Mexican battery to keep them occupied. You should also fire the eighteen-pounder at Bexar, but only at night," I said.

"Why?"

"To keep Santa Anna and his men from sleeping—like he's doing to us."

"I don't know where he's headquartered," Travis said.

"He has a tent in front of the San Fernando Cathedral, but he spends his nights in the cathedral itself. You already hit it with the eighteen-pounder just after we arrived."

"Captain Dickinson, send the order to the cannons to conserve powder and shot beginning tonight."

I glanced at my watch and said, "Sir, it's nearly time. I'd like to join my men on the walls."

"I'll join you there later."

"Yes, sir. I'll be on the south wall." I saluted Travis before I left the room.

On my way back to my position, I said, "First Squad; movement and activity report. North wall, report."

"Cannon battery preparing to fire again. Approximately one-hundred infantry standing in formation to the west of the battery," Breckenridge said.

"East wall, report."

"Approximately thirty cavalry moving from south to north at two hundred fifty meters. One hundred infantry standing in the open at three hundred meters," Sutter said.

"West wall, report."

"About one hundred infantry standing in formation across the river. To the southwest, infantry have been moving across the bridge at a double-time from west to east," Wright said.

"South wall, report."

"Infantry gathering in formation at the road intersection four hundred meters to the south," Thompson said.

"How many infantry?"

"About two hundred, with more approaching from the bridge."

"First Squad, listen up! According to history, the attack will come from the south only. No other walls will be attacked by infantry but keep your eyes open in case they decide to change. The Mexican cannons will continue firing during the attack, so keep your heads down. Use three grenades, one at a time, against the cannons. Then concentrate the rest on the infantry. If your position doesn't have cannons within grenade range, fire them at your discretion. Gentlemen, this is what we're trained for. Stand by, and watch your fields of fire," I said, and climbed the steps to the scaffold over the gate.

While we watched, the infantry stood in formation along the roads' intersection, while several soldiers weaved in and out between huts, advancing toward the wall.

Keeping our heads low over the top of the parapets, Hernández visibly cringed every time cannons fired. When we were taken under sporadic fire from sharpshooters from in and around the huts, a near miss splattered adobe rubble in Hernández's face. He dropped and balled up on his side, trying to make himself as small as possible.

I shook my head, and then said, "First Squad, fire at will."

The M203 grenade launcher makes a peculiar sound when fired, and I heard a "thoomp" from my right, followed by several more in rapid succession. Thompson fired a grenade at maximum angle, landing just behind the massed infantry at the road intersection, making a "choom" sound when it detonated. The explosion opened a large hole in the Mexican lines.

"Thompson, wait until they fill the gap in their lines, and then hit them again," I said.

Thompson didn't fire again. He looked stunned at what

his grenade had done to the soldiers out there. He dropped his rifle, knelt, and bowed his head, leaning against the parapet, apparently in prayer. He was finished with the fight.

"Sutter, what's your status?" I said as I relieved Hernández and Thompson of their ammo.

"Cavalry and infantry dispersing toward the tree line to the southeast."

"Sutter, Hernández and Thompson are out of action. Send me one shooter from your position."

"This is Taylor. I'm on my way."

"Negative, Doc. Stay put. They're not hurt," I said.

"This is Sutter. I'm coming to your position. Snyder, you're in charge of this wall. Report any change in enemy movement."

When Sutter arrived, I shouted, "Bury Hernández until we're done here!"

"Gladly!"

"No! Secure him, keep him safe!" I said, before he could act negatively on my order.

With a look of disappointment, Sutter secured Hernández by putting a knee on his balled-up figure, then opened fire with his rifle.

I'd experienced the fog of war before, but this was exceptional. Smoke from flintlocks and cannons was thick, obscuring our targets as it drifted across our front in the breeze. Travis suddenly tapped me on the shoulder and said something that was lost in the roar of battle. When the smoke briefly cleared, I saw sharpshooters beside a hut taking unhurried, deliberate aim. I jumped up and tackled Travis, knocking him off his feet just as a burst of smoke and gunfire billowed from muskets next to the huts. At the same moment my helmet was struck hard, violently snapping my head sideways. When I flopped on Travis, my helmeted head slammed against the wall. I struggled to get up, but Travis kept pushing me off balance when Sutter shouted, *"Medic! Man down, south wall!"*

"I'm okay," I said over a peculiar humming in my ears.

Travis rolled me onto my back and stood up in the line of fire again. While I lay on the scaffold, I shook my head to try and clear it then crawled to the wall, recovered my rifle, and fired at the riflemen poking their heads and muskets around the huts. I had to keep squeezing my eyes shut to clear my vision before each shot.

When Taylor arrived and stood over me, I reached up and pulled him down by his belt.

"Sarge, where're you hit?" Taylor shouted from a kneeling position.

"I'm all right! Get off the wall until the shooting stops!"

"Where're you hit?" Taylor shouted again.

"Get off the wall!" I shouted back.

"Sutter, where's he hit?"

"Helmet!" Sutter shouted between shots.

Taylor was leaning around me, examining my helmet to see where I was hit, until I again shouted, "Get off the wall!" and gave him a push with my boot to reinforce the order. He still didn't comply and remained by my side.

***

After about an hour of constant rifle and cannon fire, the noise suddenly stopped.

"First Squad; movement and activity report. North wall, report."

"Cannon battery is inactive. No one is attempting to load it. Remaining infantry moved out of range to the west," Breckenridge said.

"East wall, report."

"No activity except for wounded infantry. Cavalry and infantry have moved south, and then turned west toward the bridge," Snyder reported.

"West wall, report."

"Infantry have withdrawn from the river bank. To the southwest, infantry moving across the bridge from east to west. Cannons in town have been hit, but are being manned to fire again," Wright observed.

When the air cleared of smoke, I reported, "To the south, infantry and sharpshooters are withdrawing west toward the bridge. All clear!"

"We did it. We beat the shit outta Santa Anna!"

"Whoo-hoo! That's what I'm talking about!"

"Come and get it! I got lots more!"

"Knock it off, people. Does anyone need a medic? Sound off if you need a medic! Team leaders, keep an eye on enemy activity. Hernández, get off the wall!" I shouted while Sutter helped him up by his belt and half dragged him down the steps.

When I got to the bottom of the stairs, I got in Hernández's face. Before I could say anything, Hernández shouted, "Hey, I ain't got no damned death wish! We shouldn't even be here!" He was obviously recovered from his lack of activity on the wall.

"Yeah. One of my grandfathers fought with Santa Anna. I might kill him," Sanchez said when he joined us.

"That's a paradox, isn't it, Sanchez? How can you be born if you kill a relative in your own past? Since you're still here, your grandfather's still alive, if he's even here."

"I'm tired of your bullshit!" Hernández shouted.

Ignoring Hernández, I said, "Sanchez, consider this. Now that you're here, it's possible you're your own great, great grandfather. Try figuring that one out."

I mentally prepared myself for an assault from the two of them, but the hum in my head became a buzz that was getting louder, making it difficult to concentrate.

"*Usted mierda estúpida*," Hernández said.

"You're the only stupid shit here!" Sutter said, and stepped up beside me with Thompson in tow.

"I'm a stupid shit?" I asked. "The first sergeant told me the captain's going to start discharge proceedings on you. If we weren't going to the range, you'd be facing the battalion commander by now. Who's the stupid shit now, Hernández?"

"What about me? How come I'm not going with him?" Sanchez asked.

"The captain thinks you're a better soldier than Hernández." I was watching Hernández, fully expecting him to jump at me.

"Manny, what do we do?" Sanchez's face displayed a mix of confusion and fear.

"They can't do nothing."

"When you're dishonorably discharged, your green cards are revoked, and immigration will be waiting at the door to deport you. I wouldn't call that nothing," I said.

"*Usted estúpida bastardo*!" Hernández shouted.

Thanks to Sergeant Wright's warning, I was ready. With my left arm I was quick to deflect Hernández's fist coming straight for my nose, and countered with a swift, but carefully aimed right cross between his helmet and neck fragmentation armor. Landing squarely on his jaw, my fist's impact spun him part way around. When he tried to recover, I kicked his legs out from under him. The activity raised the volume of buzzing in my ears, and I think I was trying to do something when Sutter suddenly wrapped his arms around me and pushed me back.

"You're going to pay for this!" Hernández shouted, and

wiped blood from his mouth on back of his glove.

"Shut up or I'll finish what you started!" Sutter shouted, struggling to keep me away from Hernández.

"What is happening here? Why are you holding Sergeant Webber?" Colonel Travis shouted as he approached.

"I've resolved a breach of discipline," I said as I squirmed out of Sutter's grasp. The rifle sling was hung on my forearm and I placed it back on my shoulder.

"He hit me! You saw him hit me! Travis, I want him court-martialed!" Hernández shouted when he got to his feet.

"It doesn't sound resolved to me," Travis said with a steely-eyed gaze at Hernández.

When an officer and a burly sergeant stepped up and flanked Travis, Sanchez retreated to the well. Hernández looked around, and then said, "Yeah, that's right. All you Anglos stick together."

"Take him to the jail," Travis ordered.

"Sir! I need everyone in my squad to help defend the garrison."

"He showed cowardice before the enemy, and struck a superior officer," Travis stated.

"He's no officer! He's just an NCO!"

"I'm a non-commissioned officer who's been appointed over you! Get that into your thick head," I said, turning to Travis. "Sir, he has problems with authority, but I can handle it. I request you leave him to me."

"He's your man," Travis said, turning to Hernández. "But if I see any further disobedience or cowardice from you, I will have you shot where you stand! Do you understand me?"

Hernández nodded his head and then looked down at his boots, finally realizing what I said about disrespecting Travis and being shot was true.

"Thank you, sir." I saluted Travis as he walked past us, shouting for his men to open the gates and burn the huts along both sides of the road.

"This changes nothing," Hernández stated defiantly.

I was about to jump in his face again, but Taylor got between us and said, "Take your helmet off."

"Doc, I'm okay, okay?"

"Doesn't sound like it to me," he said, watching my eyes. "Any dizziness, headache, or nausea?"

"No." I was already bored with an examination I knew was coming.

"Stand still. Look at my finger. Follow it with your eyes only," he ordered, watching me for any unsteadiness until he shined his flashlight in my eyes. "Pupils are reactive, but unequal. Any ringing in your ears?"

"No…does buzzing count?"

"It does. Are you having problems with your vision?"

"No, why?"

"You're slow blinking. Looks like you have a concussion. Go to the barracks and get off your feet."

"Doc, I've got things to do." I examined my helmet for damage before putting it on again.

I watched Hernández talking to Thompson and Sanchez by the well. They kept glancing at me before Thompson threw up his hands and walked away.

"Sergeant Sutter, make sure he gets to his bunk. Sit on him if you have to. I'm going to help the wounded," Taylor said.

"There aren't any!" I shouted when he walked away.

Reluctantly I was walking toward the barracks when Sutter tapped my arm to get my attention. He turned off his radio, as did I.

"Sarge, you should've let the colonel put him in jail. At least we'd know where he was, and it would keep him out of trouble."

"I kept him out of jail because I want him to make another mistake in front of Travis. Then whatever happens is on their heads, not mine. Were you listening to what Hernández said in the meeting where I let everyone make a choice to stay or leave?" I asked Sutter as we walked toward the barracks.

"Yes, of course."

"Did you hear what Hernández said?"

"What did he say that got your attention this time?"

"His comment about his people not letting us leave. We can't be in a position where we have to be suspicious of each other. If we're going to survive this, we've got to be a team, trusting each other."

"Hernández is always talking shit. You know that."

"Now I have to watch him more closely than ever."

"You were going for your rifle. Would you have shot him?" Sutter asked.

"He's been working my last nerve for a long time."

"That's not an answer."

"It's not the answer you want to hear." I tugged at my earlobes, hoping to quiet the buzzing in my ears.

"When we get back and he's discharged, he won't lose his green card," Sutter said.

"He won't lose his green card because he doesn't have one. He became a citizen when he joined the army, so he won't be deported either. The best we can hope for is a general discharge, which gets him out of the squad and out of our hair."

"Was it a good idea to tell them about the captain's intentions?"

"With the thought in his head, he might run the first chance he gets. If he does, I'm not stopping him, and neither are you." I admonished Sutter by shaking my finger at him.

"While we're here, we're at war with Santa Anna, right? In war, deserters are shot. If he runs, can I shoot him?"

"No. Soldiers killed by friendly fire are hard to explain."

"Who says it has to be friendly?"

"Let it go, Sergeant Sutter."

I heard someone shouting my name and saw Sergeant Wright waving his arms over his head from a scaffold on the west wall.

Sutter and I turned our radios on. "What's wrong, Sergeant Wright?"

"Did you send Hernández and Sanchez out of the compound?"

"Negative." I looked at Sutter, who shook his head.

"They're outside the gate, walking on the road."

"Hernández? Hernández, report," I said halfheartedly.

"¡Vete a la mierda!"

"Hernández told you to fuck off," Sutter translated for me.

"I don't give a damn what he said. Sanchez, you're flirting with desertion. Return now and it'll be forgotten." When I didn't hear a response, I said, "Sergeant Wright, do you see them?"

"They're running toward the bridge."

"This is Ruiz. I have them in my sights. Can I take a shot?"

Frankly, it surprised me to hear anyone, besides Sutter, offer to shoot them. Sutter flashed me two thumbs up. Sometimes I couldn't tell whether he was joking or not. I slowly stroked the three-day old stubble on my chin with my thumb and forefinger, trying to look thoughtful and wise. Sutter was shaking his head because he knew me, and in his mind it wasn't working.

"They've started weaving. Can I take a shot?" Ruiz asked.

After a few more moments of thoughtful chin stroking, I said, "Negative; save your ammo." I looked at Sutter and said, "Maybe Santa Anna's troops will shoot them when they cross the bridge."

"I don't hear any shooting." Sutter intently listened for gunfire. "You should've let Ruiz take a couple of shots."

"It wasn't necessary."

"Do you realize what they can to do to us out there? They still have ammo and grenades."

"Do they?" I dug into my thigh pocket and showed him eight clips and five grenades I'd taken from Hernández and Thompson. "First Squad, listen up. Clear your weapons and clean them before it gets dark."

"What about Hernández and Sanchez?" Sutter said.

"They don't have to clean their weapons."

"That's not what I meant. They're going to join Santa Anna."

"I hope so," I said with a genuine smile.

"What? Why?"

"Santa Anna has no respect for the welfare of his soldiers. He reputedly said, 'What are the lives of soldiers but so many chickens?', or something to that effect. The way Hernández shoots his mouth off, Santa Anna will have a lot less patience with him than I do."

"Santa Anna might pump him for information, like Travis does to you."

"Yeah, you're right. We'd better rekey the radios."

"Do what?" Sutter asked.

"Manually rekey the frequencies on the radios. You've never done it?"

"I've never even heard of it."

"It's procedure when a radio's been captured. I'm sure they're listening for crosstalk right now."

"Their batteries will run out in a few hours," Sutter observed.

"What if they carry spares, like we do?" I asked.

"We're talking about Hernández and Sanchez, right?"

"We don't know what they have. Wait a minute…Sergeant Wright, did Hernández and Sanchez have their packs?"

"Negative."

"They left everything behind. Sergeant Wright, what about Sanchez's grenades and clips?"

"Sanchez fired all his grenades and was firing his rifle after we moved to the south wall."

"Sergeant Wright, locate and inventory all twelve clips from your position, empty or not, and figure out how many rounds Sanchez might have left."

"Wilco. I'll need all the empty clips to reload. Put them on my bunk."

"First Squad, meet at the truck to recharge the radios and night vision goggles. Before you do, recover your empty clips and turn them in to Sergeant Wright."

"Do you want to post guards on the walls?" Sutter asked.

"No, it's over for now. The recharge will take a couple of hours, so make sure everyone stays with their equipment. While they're charging, I'll show you how to rekey the radio."

"Roger that."

"Sergeant Webber, I put you on bed rest," Taylor said when he stopped in front of me.

At the same time, Travis walked to us from the gate and said, "Sergeant Webber, meet me in my headquarters immediately."

"Yes, sir. Sorry Doc, duty calls."

"I'm going with you."

"Sergeant Sutter, you're in charge. Make sure everyone gathers at the truck and recharges their equipment."

"Sergeant Webber, you and Corporal Taylor should turn off your radios until you can recharge them," Wright said over the radio.

"Webber and Taylor are offline." I nodded to Taylor, and we turned off our radios.

When I thought about it, Wright's suggestion that we turn off our radios was a good idea. The squad didn't need to know how I may be punished for tackling Travis.

When we walked into Travis's office, Crockett, Williamson, and Dickinson were already there. I'd noticed Travis always took off his hat indoors, but this time he'd kept it on when he sat behind his desk.

"Webber, stand there. What were you doing when you knocked me down?" Travis's voice was stern and hard, like the first time we spoke.

"Sergeant Webber saved your life by taking a bullet meant for you!" Taylor forcefully interjected.

"He's been shot? Where?" Travis's face suddenly reflected concern as he looked me over.

"He was hit in the helmet."

"Do you need a doctor?"

"No, sir, I already have one," I said, when I was finally able to speak for myself. With my radio off and other background noise quiet, the buzzing in my head was distracting until iron balls thudded against the walls from the Mexican cannons firing from Bexar again. "Sir, you exposed yourself to riflemen about thirty met…yards from the wall. I knocked you down to protect you."

"You said I will die on the north wall," Travis snappishly reminded me.

"I also said history is changing. You could've died today on the south wall if I hadn't pushed you aside."

"Sounds like he saved your life," Crockett suggested while Travis's index finger impatiently tapped on his table.

"Sir, if we're to keep this garrison from falling into Santa Anna's hands, we need your leadership to continue." I silently agreed that Hernández might be right about my bullshit, some of it anyway. But if bullshit was substituted with the word diplomacy, it sounded better.

"Maybe you did save my life." Travis's voice softened as he took off his hat.

"We thank you for it," Crockett said, further calming the situation by saving Travis from the potential humiliation of a thank you.

Mexican cannons pounded the walls again. Through Travis's open window, we saw a round strike the wall of the hospital above the barracks.

"Sir, we need to silence those cannons before someone gets killed," I said.

"Captain Dickinson, how can we do this?" Travis asked.

"Spike the cannons," Dickinson stated matter-of-factly.

"Sir, I'd like to get Sergeant Sutter involved with this." I turned the radio on again. "Sergeant Sutter, report to Colonel Travis's headquarters."

Sutter approached at a trot, and then knocked on the door before he let himself in.

"Radio off, Sergeant Sutter."

"Breckenridge says the northern cannons are being manned again and will be ready to fire in a few minutes," Sutter reported when he turned off his radio.

"Captain Dickinson, please explain in detail how can we knock out a cannon," I said.

"The touch hole of the cannon is plugged flush with an iron spike, and it cannot fire until metal boring tools are used to remove the plug. You should force a couple of cannonballs down the barrel with—"

"Couldn't they just roll them out again?" Sutter interjected.

"Not if you wrap the cannonballs with rags and force them in tight with the ramrod." Dickinson's voice snapped with annoyance at the interruption.

"We can get all the rags we need from dead Mexicans," Sutter said, unflustered by Dickinson's growling.

"Why block the barrel?" I asked.

"Once they clear the touch hole, they'll try to set fire to the rags in the barrel with hot pokers to burn the rags out. If they can't get the balls out that way, they'll load powder through the touch hole and fire the cannon. If they're jammed in tight enough, it could explode the barrel at the touch hole. I know what size spikes you need, so I'll make them. I was a blacksmith for many years before I came here."

"It'll have to be a night operation," Sutter suggested, his face lighting with anticipation.

I looked at Travis, who had said nothing during the exchange.

"Sir, what do you want us to do?" I asked, belatedly realizing we'd had left him out of the planning.

"It sounds like you already have it planned."

"Sir, I'll need eight men to volunteer for this mission. I'll put my men on the north wall, and they'll guide us around the sentries using their radios and night vision goggles. Once we take the cannons, the volunteers can spike them. When it's done, we'll run back to the compound while my men provide cover fire. We won't be able to silence the cannons in Bexar. They're surrounded by too many soldiers."

"How can my men follow you in the dark without torches?" Travis said.

"With these." I took off my helmet and showed him two

rectangular patches sewn onto the helmet band. "These are called cat eyes. They glow in the dark, and your men will follow us by watching these."

"They don't look like they're glowing to me," Travis said as he closely examined them.

"Sir, do you have a blanket we can use for a demonstration?"

"Joe, fetch me a blanket."

"Yes, suh."

While Joe went for the blanket, I unscrewed the red lens from my flashlight and shined the bright light on the cat eyes. When Joe returned, I placed the helmet on the table and helped Joe cover Travis with the blanket. I almost laughed as he squirmed around under the blanket, watching the glowing cat eyes watching him. Travis was speechless when he pulled the blanket off.

"Before we go out tonight, I'll have my men assemble—"

"Not tonight!" Taylor interjected.

"What do you mean, not tonight? Look, Doc—"

"Don't 'Look, Doc' me. A concussion doesn't clear up in a couple of hours. It can take days, even weeks to heal."

"I don't have time to argue." The buzzing, which had almost gone, ramped up in my ears again.

"You're right; we don't have time to argue," Taylor said, suddenly shining his flashlight in my eyes. "Your pupils are still not reacting equally, and I'll bet the buzzing in your ears has returned, louder than before. You'll not take a chance of collapsing out there. Change your plans."

Not being a doctor, I wondered if blood pressure had something to do with my suddenly deteriorating condition, because I could hear the blood pounding in rhythm with my heartbeat, even over the buzzing in my ears. I felt the need to squeeze my eyes shut to clear my vision again when I said, "Okay,

Doc, you win. Sir, we'll plan the mission to spike the cannons for tomorrow night."

While Travis watched and listened, I noticed his forehead furrowing. He may have been confused by our verbal exchanges; I was certainly annoyed by them.

"Webber, who's in charge of your men?"

"I am, sir."

"Corporal Taylor gave you an order. An order that you agreed with."

"Yes, sir."

"Is this the kind of leadership that exists where you're from? A soldier who is subordinate to you gives you orders that you follow?"

"Sir, you're correct. As a staff sergeant, I outrank Corporal Taylor by two pay grades…that's two steps in rank. In our time, a doctor has the authority to give orders, even to generals, when it regards their health. If necessary, they can relieve them of command."

"He said he's not a doctor," Travis observed.

"No, sir, he's not; but he is the ranking medical soldier assigned to my squad. Under our current conditions, I'm required to follow his medical orders, and he has a point. If I collapse while leading a mission outside the walls, my men will endanger themselves to get me, just as I would for any of them. We never leave our soldiers behind." I hoped my somewhat inaccurate information would compel the colonel to stay out of my squad's training.

"I see," Travis said, nodding his head. "Corporal Taylor, what are your orders regarding Sergeant Webber?"

"I want him to go to his bunk and stay there. I'll continue to evaluate him while I perform my other duties."

"Sergeant Webber, follow his instructions and go to your bunk. Corporal Taylor, how is Colonel Bowie progressing?" Travis said.

"Sir, it's been only three days, but he's showing signs of improvement. He's breathing easier and sitting in his bunk. If we could get him to stop drinking the whiskey his men keep bringing him, he might improve faster."

"We'll go see Bowie. He's slow with appreciation, but I'll see to it he gives you your just due," Travis said, rising from his chair.

"Turn on the radios," I said when we started for the door.

Travis and Taylor stopped to make sure Sutter and I were walking toward the barracks before they continued on to see Colonel Bowie.

"I think Travis wants to adopt our medic," Sutter said.

"I heard that," Taylor commented over the radio.

Sutter looked over his shoulder at the pair when Taylor held Bowie's door open for Travis.

"I'm not so sure his popularity extends to the doctors." I looked up at the hospital balcony on the second floor of the barracks. "He could help them, if they'd let him."

"Let's get you in bed before Taylor's popularity with Travis runs us over," Sutter said sarcastically. "I'll take your helmet and charge the radio while you're resting."

"Before I go to my bunk, I'll show you how to rekey the radios. Charge my night vision goggles for me as well."

After demonstrating rekeying the radios, I realized it was much too early to be in bed, despite Taylor's order. When I walked to my bunk, I heard horses gallop away. I remembered it was Juan Seguin and Antonio Cruz taking a dispatch to General Houston. I would've liked to have met Juan Seguin, but he wouldn't return with reinforcements in time to help us.

I picked up an MRE, and with full intention of eating it, I lay down just for a few moments.

My last memory was the MRE, sealed in its thick, brown plastic bag, slipping from my fingers onto the floor.

Chapter 5

Day Four – Friday February 26, 1836

I woke to find myself hanging upside down, tied by my feet. I looked to see a rope attached to nothing, going upward out of sight.

"What in hell's going on?" I shouted.

"¡Silencio!*" someone shouted, and I was struck on the back of my head.*

When I woke again, I was upright, tied to a post, surrounded by feted, decaying bodies. Blood was everywhere – men, women, and children, bodies riddled with bullet holes, some missing limbs, others burnt beyond recognition. I recognized them as those we'd killed – I recognized them because I'd seen them in the destroyed buildings. They hadn't stood a chance. They had no chance.

"Webber, look at those you murdered."

"Hernández? What in the hell are you doing?"

"You murdered them, Webber, and you're going to pay," Hernández said, and butt stroked me in the stomach with a musket.

Suddenly I was facing down, gasping for breath with my arms pulled taut by ropes secured to the walls. My feet weren't tied, but somehow they stuck to a wall.

"This is General Hernández." Santa Anna spoke without a hint of a Spanish accent as he sat in a chair, taking a sip from a fine china cup. "He says you committed murder. How do you plead?"

"I don't answer to this kangaroo court!"

"Guilty as charged." Santa Anna took another sip from his cup. "Sentence is death by firing squad. General Hernández, carry out the sentence."

In the blink of an eye I was outside, not tied up. When I tried to move, my feet were rooted to the ground. I looked to see an army of impeccably dressed Mexican soldiers standing at attention in a semicircle in front of me, with muskets at their sides.

A tall, gaunt Mexican officer walked to me and said, "Do you want a blindfold?" I wanted to grab him by the throat, but my hands were stuck in my pockets. "No? You should write down your experiences. They will be useful in the future," he said, and then walked away.

Hernández raised a sword and shouted, "Preparar!" *The entire Mexican army brought their muskets to the ready position.*

"Puntería!" *The army of muskets lowered and aimed at me.*

"Fuego!" *I tried to drop to the ground, but I was already there.*

***

The boom of the eighteen-pounder cannon ripped a scream from my lips as I struggled, desperately trying to get up and run, but was wrapped in my sleeping bag.

"Sergeant Webber! Sergeant Webber, are you all right?"

I looked around in abject terror and confusion. "Taylor? The barracks. I'm in the barracks in the Alamo."

"Yeah." Taylor flashed his flashlight in my face. "Open your eyes."

"No! I have a headache," I said, knowing the light would be painful if I did.

"Open your eyes!" I was right; it hurt like hell. "Your pupils are equal and reactive. Pulse is good. Here, take these for the headache," Taylor said after rummaging around in his small medical bag.

"Thanks," I said, reaching for my plastic canteen.

"Doc, is he okay?" Sutter asked.

"Looks like lingering effects from the concussion. They are just lingering effects, aren't they?" Taylor asked, eyeing me suspiciously.

"Why are you asking me, Doc? You should know. Next time, remind me to die instead of getting shot in the head." I struggled to pull my sleeping bag off, made all the more difficult by a throbbing headache and my rifle still slung over my shoulder in the bunk with me.

"Sounds like you had a nightmare," Sutter said.

"I don't have nightmares."

"Okay. Where'd you think you were? Let's have the X-rated version."

"I was Santa Anna's prisoner, and Hernández was a Mexican general."

"Heaven help us." Sutter rolled his eyes toward the ceiling.

"Santa Anna spoke English, and Hernández was in charge of a firing squad the size of an army, and they shot me."

"Fortunately, it was just a dream."

"A dream that was too vivid."

"Was it an omen?" Sutter said, trying not to smile.

"Gimme a break, will ya?" When I was able to sit on my bunk, I put my head in my hands. "What time is it?"

"It's 0310."

Boom! A solitary cannonball thudded against a wall somewhere.

"Just one? There'll be a cavalry charge from the south today, so get everyone up at 0600 hours. If I don't get up, dump me out of the cot; that's if the sergeant major doesn't beat you to it."

"What about Stand To?" Sutter asked.

"Our problem child changed the situation for us."

Not relishing the thought of sleeping again, I tried to get comfortable when I pulled the sleeping bag over me.

***

Much too soon, Sergeant Major Williamson walked into the barracks carrying an oil lamp, shouting and kicking bunks, getting everyone up as he worked his way down the barracks. When he came back, he wasn't satisfied with my movement. He kicked my bunk again and said, "Webber, you're late for a meeting in the colonel's headquarters."

"Yes, Sergeant Major." I made the mistake of ignoring him and immediately fell back to sleep.

"Webber, get up!" the sergeant major shouted. My booted feet were hanging over the foot of my bunk until he kicked them into the air.

"Yes, Sergeant Major," I said, struggling to sit on my bunk, hoping he'd leave sooner than later.

When I saw him waiting, I slowly got to my feet. He grunted and walked out, leaving the door open to a cold breeze.

"No, no, no, no," Sutter insisted, grabbing me by my shirt when I was about to sit on my bunk again. "Stay up, go outside, walk around."

"I have to get dressed."

"You are dressed."

"Close the door!" someone shouted.

The cold breeze helped wake me like a slap in the face. The longer I stood, breathing deeply in the breeze, the better I felt until a sudden gust of wind forcibly pushed me backward.

A hurricane wind whipped and snapped at my body as I sat, leaning out the door of a helicopter. I looked at the squad seated beside me and gave them a thumbs up. We were ready for the rapid insertion into a hot landing zone. As we dropped and flew low to the ground, we unbuckled our seat belts in anticipation of a hasty exit. The pilot gently bounced to a landing and as one we jumped out, allowing the pilot to quickly leave. After we took cover, the anticipation was excruciating as we cautiously scanned windows and doorways, waiting for some unfortunate enemy to fire at us. Nothing. We knew they were there, but what were they waiting for? Then, we saw a child crawling on all fours through a doorway. This was the kind of tactic we were trained to look for; the enemy using our compassion to expose ourselves. The child stood up, grew, and grew, ten, twenty feet tall, filling out into a giant. "Oh, hell no!" I shouted when I opened fire on the apparition in front of me. She strode forward, kicking walls over on the squad and then reaching down, grabbing and throwing men many meters away. Impervious to my rifle fire, she turned toward me. I had only enough time to slam another clip into my rifle before she reached for me. Laughing, she picked me up, her grip squeezing the life out of me. When she opened her mouth and moved me toward it, I struggled to one handedly fire my rifle into her mouth; her hot, fetid breath….

Suddenly I was outside the barracks, breathless and sweating in the cold breeze. The crushing pressure on my chest was gone, but not the impossible images in my mind. A massive headache, struggling to burst my head open, nearly blinded me with pain as I hurried back inside, slamming the door behind me. I watched the door, reluctant to tear my eyes from it, fearing the giant child would burst through at any moment. I suppressed my trained instinct to raise my rifle if the monster tried to get in.

"What's wrong, Sarge?" Wright asked.

"It's cold out there," I said with a forced smile. "What's for breakfast?"

"How about Mediterranean chicken?"

"Toss it."

Wright let the MRE fly like a Frisbee to land on my bunk.

"Everyone, listen up. It's cold outside, but it'll warm up to about sixty degrees by this afternoon, so plan for it. Sergeant Sutter, get them motivated. I've a meeting to get to."

Cautiously I opened the door and peeked out, looking around before I stepped through.

When I arrived at the headquarters, the sergeant major followed me in. Travis said, "It's good of you to join us." I wasn't sure if it was an oblique reference to my tardiness or directed at the sergeant major.

"Yes, sir, I apologize. Thank you for waiting." Admittedly, my mind was not yet fully functional. I needed coffee, lots of coffee.

"Sergeant Major Williamson, did you find out who deserted last night?" Travis asked.

"None of the regulars, sir. There are at least nine *Tejanos*, but I don't know their names yet."

"Sergeant Major, those men are public enemies," Travis declared angrily. "I want you to keep a close watch on the rest of the *Tejanos*. If they try to leave, bring them to me. If they get over the walls, shoot them."

I knew of the desertions from an obscure historical reference, but they were not spoken of in the hallowed halls of the future Alamo. And from what I'd read in Alamo history, Travis did condemn the *Tejanos* and treated them somewhat unfairly as a result. Those who remained behind the walls when the Alamo fell fought and died as bravely as everyone else.

"Webber, I've heard talk that we are being helped by

witchcraft."

"Sergeant Major, that sounds like a superstitious excuse for cowardice; probably started by Hernández himself."

"I saw two of your men walk out the gate yesterday," Travis said.

"Who?"

"Hernández and Sanchez."

"What?" I said, feigning surprise. "Did you try to stop them?"

"Hernández told me you sent them to guard my men while they burned the jacales. The last time I saw them they were walking on the road."

"Sir, I gave no such order. Do you recall the discussion we had about them? Lying to a superior officer and desertion are examples of what they'll do to achieve their own ends. It wasn't completely unexpected, but I have to ask; how many more of your men are going to leave?" I asked, secretly happy that Travis thought he'd had a hand in their departure.

"Webber, I've been impressed by the discipline of your men, your rifles, and the other things you have. We beat Santa Anna yesterday because of the grenades your men used on his soldiers. Now, two of your men are out there with Santa Anna, ready to use their rifles and grenades against us!" Travis' voice rose to a shout, tinged with fear.

"Sir, you have good reason to be concerned, but I assure you they don't have any grenades. They do have about twenty rifle rounds between them, but neither of them can shoot worth a damn so they're no more of a threat than Santa Anna's men are. Frankly, sir, I'm glad those two are gone, but I'm surprised nine left you. By the way, you left a cache of about fifty muskets hidden in Bexar. Since my men don't know where they are, your deserters will take Santa Anna to them."

"No, they won't. None of the regulars deserted, and they were the only ones who know where we left them," Williamson grumbled.

"Are there going to be any more desertions by your men?" Travis asked me.

"Sir, there's always a chance that someone will suddenly decide to run. Among my men, I'm confident we've seen the end of it."

"No, we haven't." Sutter's voice over the radio stopped me in my mental tracks.

"Uh, sir, what are my orders of the day?" I said, anxious to leave and find out who had left the squad. I couldn't think of anyone else who'd want to leave, but I had my suspicions.

"What will happen today?" Travis asked.

"Sir, after yesterday's battle, I can't give accurate advice because history has now changed for all of us. If yesterday's battle had not occurred like it did, there'd be a cavalry charge from the southeast this afternoon, but I don't expect it now."

"Put your men on the walls and wait for the cavalry charge."

"Yes, sir." With a hurried salute, I left the headquarters at a trot.

When I burst into the barracks, Sutter said, "Thompson won't be joining us for breakfast."

"Where is he?"

"He volunteered for guard duty last night."

"I scheduled Wallace for guard duty."

"Thompson told me he wanted to do it, and I made the change."

"Without clearing it with me?"

"Yes," Sutter said confidently.

"I'm listening." Whenever Sutter changed my instructions,

he had a good reason; or at least he thought he did.

"Yesterday, Ruiz told me he overheard Thompson talking with the Mexican volunteers—"

"*Tejanos.*"

"Okay, *Tejanos*. He didn't want them to sound the alarm when someone approached the west wall."

"Let me guess; Hernández and Sanchez."

"I waited up until Thompson came in and started rummaging around. Then I followed him to the west wall, where he was talking to them. I tackled him and took his ammo, and the ammo he was going to drop to Hernández and Sanchez. There was a struggle, and he...kind of...fell over the wall," Sutter said, looking at me like he'd done something wrong.

"Oops."

"That's it? Oops?"

"Please, continue." During his efforts to explain what had happened without getting into trouble over it, I genuinely tried to suppress a smile.

"He left his rifle leaning on the wall, and I told him I'd shoot all of them with it if they came back." Sutter handed me the rifle he'd hidden under his sleeping bag. "I thought you might want to give it to the colonel."

"No, he'd want to know where it came from. Sergeant Wright, keep this locked up until Taylor gets back."

"*Leave it locked up. I won't need it,*" Taylor said over the radio from the hospital.

I saw Ruiz standing nearby, listening while Sutter gave his report.

"What do you want, Ruiz?"

"I know what you're thinking, Staff Sergeant."

"Do you?"

"Yes, Staff Sergeant. I'm not one of those. I thought Sanchez and Hernández might leave, but I didn't know Thompson was one of them until I overheard him actually say it."

"Why did you inform Sergeant Sutter instead of me?"

"Sergeant Sutter is the assistant squad leader, and he's in charge while you're wounded."

"Just as you should have. I keep an eye on everyone in the squad, and I've noticed you've always kept your distance from those two. I've never considered you to be…one of those, as you put it. Just so you know, after your last evaluation, I recommended you for promotion, and Mac agreed with me."

"Thank you, Staff Sergeant. I thought of Thompson as a religious friend, but now, I know differently."

"What's your opinion of him now?" I asked, greatly interested in his answer.

"He was misguided by his friendship with Hernández."

"Like Hernández and Sanchez, he abandoned all of us. I heard you say you wanted to shoot Hernández and Sanchez. Would you shoot Thompson if you had to?"

He hesitated before he said, "I don't know."

"It may come to that, so think about it and be prepared just in case. Okay people, we've got work to do. I've told Colonel Travis that any one of you is better than twenty of his best. Now we get to prove it again. With the loss of Hernández, Sanchez, and Thompson, I have to modify the fireteams. I'm short a man. Who wants to come to my fireteam?"

"I will," Ruiz said, jumping at the opportunity.

"You're with me; team one on the south wall. Team two, Sergeant Wright and Private Wallace, on the west wall. Team three, Corporal Breckenridge and PFC Carpenter, on the north wall. Team four, Corporal Barnes and PFC Snyder, on the east wall inside the church. I need eyes in the tower, so you two switch off on your own. Sergeant Sutter, I want you to float between the walls. Sergeant Wright, make sure everyone has four full clips before we get on the walls, and fire at targets of opportunity. Ruiz, why did you want to join my fireteam?"

"You're a survivor. You've been there, and my best chance of surviving all of this is to stick with you," he said loud enough to be heard by the squad.

"I gave you the chance to leave."

"It's like you said, where would we go?"

"Sergeant Webber, you're supposed to be on bed rest," Taylor said, interrupting us when he walked into the barracks.

"Doc, I'm feeling much better. Do you want to shine the light of truth in my eyes again?"

Before I could blink, Taylor's light was blinding me again. "You know the drill. Stand still, follow my finger tip. Uh-huh, pupils are equal and reactive today. Put your hands over your ears. Any ringing or buzzing?"

"What? I can't hear you."

"Get serious. Is there any ringing, or headache?"

"No. I got plenty of sleep last night; a lot more than I wanted."

"You're rested, but not recovered. Before you finalize your plans for tonight, know that you're not going out. I have the colonel's ear in this matter, so don't argue."

"I'm going to get lazy if you don't let me do something," I said, regretting telling Travis about the power of military medicine, and a doctor's ability to wield it.

"You? Lazy? Not going to happen. A few more days of rest, and you'll be back to your usual, grumpy self," Taylor commented.

"What do you mean, grumpy?" And with that, I decided

to brief the squad on the mission. "Listen up, people, we have a mission. We're going out to disable the three cannons to the north. I've been told it's easy to do, but we're going to have some volunteers go with us. By us, I mean Sutter and I will be going."

"Why disable the cannons?" Taylor asked. "They can't shoot through the walls."

"Santa Anna is using his cannons as a psychological weapon, because he knows sleepy soldiers are ineffective fighters. We know what it's like to function when we're tired because we train for it. If we deny him the use of his cannons, we tell him we can do whatever we want, even when we're tired."

"If we take away his toys, it gives us the psychological advantage," Sutter agreed.

"Sergeant Webber, you won't be going," Taylor said firmly.

"I have to."

"We've been over this. I won't let you jeopardize yourself, or the mission."

"Damn-it-all, Taylor," I said with a resigned sigh. "Sergeant Sutter, you're in charge of the operation. Who do you want to take with you?"

"Sergeant Wright, can you spare Corporal Barnes?"

"Yes!" Barnes exclaimed.

"Apparently I can," Wright said with a confused look at Barnes.

"This operation will be a hit and run. Sergeant Wright, I want the squad on the north wall fully armed with grenades and a basic load of ammo. Sutter and Barnes will lead two assault teams of Alamo volunteers provided by Colonel Travis. I'll have the east entrance opened and the teams will leave through there and sneak up on the sentry pits to the east of the cannons. When the teams are in position, we'll fire a flare. The flare will be the signal for the assault teams to take out the sentries from the east on their way to the cannons. Sergeant Wright and the squad will fire grenades on the cannons and knock out the gunners. Sutter and Barnes will go through the cannon battery and hold position between the Mexican bivouac area and the cannons and give cover fire as needed while the volunteers do their work. You should have about ten, maybe fifteen minutes before the Mexicans can get organized enough to move on you. After yesterday's pounding, there shouldn't be many troops left in the bivouac area to the northwest. We'll keep our eyes open for troop movements in your area. Any questions?"

"A straightforward op. It should be easy," Sutter said, confident with the plan.

"Corporal Barnes, you're leading a team on your first combat mission. Any questions?"

"I've been hoping for something like this since I was in basic training."

"Sergeant Wright, issue the ammo and grenades to the squad. Give five magazines each for Sutter and Barnes, no grenades."

"No grenades?" Sutter asked.

"We'll keep the Mexicans off your back. Make sure the batteries in your equipment are fully charged before you get some rest. Everyone else, go to your positions until dark and wait for instructions," I said, suppressing a sudden surge of dizziness.

Taylor followed me as I walked as steadily as I could to my bunk, but I betrayed my condition when I flopped on my side with my legs hanging off the bed. I was one handedly struggling with my blanket when Taylor helped get my legs on the bunk and covered me with my blanket.

"You have a headache, ringing in your ears, dizziness, and nausea that clears up when you lie down."

"Yeah, how'd you guess?"

"I'm trained to know."

He was right. The longer I lay on my bunk, the better I felt.

"Doc, I've got to keep moving until the operation is over. Do you have anything in your bag to get me though the next few hours?"

"You've already proven to yourself that rest is the only effective treatment. Sutter and I will go to Travis and—"

"No! The operation will go on as planned, and I'm not staying in my bunk while I have men outside the walls."

"I was going to say that we'll go to Travis and get his approval to go out as planned, but after midnight. While you're on the wall, you can observe, advise, and take it easy."

"Thanks, Doc. Make sure everyone else gets some rest as best they can. Since we're going out late, it's going to make for…a long…night," I said, and promptly fell asleep. Actually, I think I fainted, but Taylor didn't need to know.

Chapter 6

Day Five – Saturday February 27, 1836

Exactly at midnight, Sutter woke me. "It's time. How're you feeling?"

"Truthfully?" I asked as I lay on my bunk, checking myself out.

"Is there any other way to be?"

"I feel good. Not perfect, but good." I rolled up to sit on the edge of my bunk.

"You have to take it easy," Taylor advised as he stood nearby, watching me.

"Come on, Doc, the colonel's waiting."

"He can wait. We've got plenty of time."

"Look, I'm up, no problems; okay, Doc?"

"You will not fire flares. Have someone else do it."

"Corporal Taylor, I'm perfectly capable of firing my weapon."

"The grenade launcher kicks harder than the rifle. If a recoil knocks you in the head, we'll have to carry you off the wall before the operation is over."

"Do you have any good news for me?"

"If you take it easy, you'll fully recover."

I continued to sit on my bunk, digesting what Taylor had said. Based on what I'd experienced thus far, I couldn't think of a reason to doubt him.

"All right, I'll take it easy," I said, slowly rising to my feet. "Let's get going."

When we arrived at Travis's headquarters, he was waiting outside with Captain Dickinson, Sergeant Major Williamson, and eight volunteers.

"Good evening, sir. Are the volunteers sober and ready to go?" I asked.

"They're ready," Williamson stated. "Sober is another matter."

"They must leave their muskets and pistols behind," I said, noticing they had them in hand.

"I will not send them out unarmed," Travis said firmly.

"They won't need them. They need free hands to spike the cannons and jam cannonballs down the barrels. My men will cover them from the wall."

"I keep my knife." A volunteer unsheathed his knife and held it up.

"Keep your knives. You'll need them to cut rags from Mexican uniforms for the cannonballs," I said, unwilling to argue with someone who had a very large blade in hand. "You four follow Sergeant Sutter. You four follow Corporal Barnes," I said, guiding the volunteers by their arms.

"There ain't enough light to see without torches," a volunteer said.

I looked up at the moon, which was just past half full, and the approaching clouds that would shortly obscure it.

"You'll follow them by watching these." I took off my helmet and pointed at the two rectangles on my helmet band. "They're called cat eyes, and you can see they glow in the dark. After you take the cannons, you can use the torches already out there. Once the cannons are spiked, we'll cover you when you run back here. While you're out there, follow orders from Sergeant Sutter and Corporal Barnes. They'll be in contact with us on the wall."

"Sergeant Webber, burn the limbers and caissons," Dickinson said.

"Burn the what?"

"A limber is used to pull a cannon or caisson. A caisson carries powder and shot. There are three cannons, so you'll have six limbers and three caissons to burn."

"Did all of you hear that? While you're spiking the cannons, Sergeant Sutter and Corporal Barnes will move west of the cannons to make sure none of Santa Anna's soldiers sneak up on you from their camp. Who has the spikes?"

"I have 'em," a volunteer said.

"Wrap them in rags to keep them quiet until you get to the cannons. As I understand the process, you'll need a hammer."

"I gave them two. Bring my hammers back," Dickinson said to the volunteers.

"Let's move out. Sergeant Wright, we're walking to the east entrance. What do you see out there?"

"Stand by, north cannons ready to fire. Everybody down!"

Boom! Boom! Boom! Two cannonballs slammed against the north wall—the third soared over our heads and bounced across the compound into the south wall.

"All day we've seen the cannons fire, then they reloaded and sat around for a while before firing again. Now that it's dark, they're staying with the guns," Wright reported.

"Sergeant Wright, we're at the east entrance. Confirm sentry locations."

A distant bugle sounded a staccato of notes.

"Checking…. There are no sentries between the wall and the cannons. Three sentries located fifty meters east of the cannons. Three more sentries located fifty meters northeast of the cannons. Three soldiers are moving from west to east…stand by. I've just located another sentry pit due north of the cannons."

"Didn't you see them before?" I asked.

"Negative. They're located just over the rise. Three soldiers are now moving from east to west toward the bivouac area. The soldiers might be a shift change."

"Can you reach the pit with a grenade?"

"They're about four hundred meters out. I'll take them myself."

"Everyone, listen to me. No talking until you take the cannons. As quietly as you can, take your teams to about fifty meters…fifty yards from the sentry pits. We'll be watching from the walls, and if we see any problems, we'll call a retreat. Ready, Sergeant Sutter?"

"Ready."

"Corporal Barnes?"

"Ready, Sarge."

"Keep low and keep silent. Good luck. Move out." With a sigh reflecting my desire to be with them, I watched the teams silently fade into the darkness.

Suspicion over what Hernández, Sanchez, and Thompson might be doing began gnawing at the back of my mind. They knew me well enough to anticipate what I might do.

"Sergeant Wright, send two shooters to the south wall and report movement."

"Ruiz, Snyder, double time to the south wall." Two shadows ran past me as I walked up a ramp.

The distant bugle sounded again, different notes this time.

"First Squad, keep a close eye on the northwest bivouac area. When we pop flares, don't let anyone get at the teams from there. Colonel, would you like to fire the grenade launcher?"

"Yes, I would."

"Assault teams, the sentries have not seen you. Keep low and keep moving," Wright said.

Again, a distant bugle sounded.

"Colonel, I'm loading a flare for you. I'll let you know when to shoot it straight up."

"Straight up?"

"Yes, sir, it will light the entire area."

We waited until the teams were in position. When movement around the Mexican cannons ceased, Sergeant Wright said, *"Cannon battery is ready to fire, stand by."*

Boom!

"Assault teams, move in!" Wright shouted as he fired his grenade, arcing it over the cannons, exploding just beyond the crest of the distant rise.

Boom! Boom!

"Colonel, fire that flare straight up!"

When the flare popped overhead, I recovered my rifle from Travis.

The distant bugle sounded again.

Grenades from the squad killed the cannon crews as rapid rifle fire from Sutter and Barnes quickly cleared the sentry pits when they ran past, followed by the volunteers. Under the flare's flickering light, I watched Sutter and Barnes run through the battery and take up kneeling positions to the northwest. The metal ringing of hammers sounded as the men pounded on spikes were disabling the cannons, while the remainder of the teams ran with torches to burn the limbers and caissons.

A few minutes later torches weren't needed to see, because the wooden limbers and caissons were well alight. The volunteers were running back toward the cannons, and for good reason. One by one the caissons exploded, sending fireworks-like pyrotechnics in all directions.

I was going to tell Wright to recall the teams when we heard Sutter shout over the radio, *"Infantry moving in from the northwest!"*

"Assault teams, abort mission! Retreat! Abort mission!" Sergeant Wright shouted.

"Back to the walls! Run! Run!" Sutter and Barnes shouted as they ran past the cannons, gathering up the remaining volunteers.

Bugles sounded, and every Mexican cannon in Bexar fired at the walls. The advancing soldiers shouted, "*Viva la Republica*! *Viva Santa Anna*!" and began running as a mob toward the walls.

"Infantry moving in from the south!" Snyder shouted.

It was wrong; it was all wrong! The massed attack that had originally defeated the Alamo was happening seven days early, and we weren't prepared for it.

"Cavalry advancing over the rise from the north!" Wright shouted.

"Wright, fire your grenades on the cavalry until the teams are in! First Squad, fire grenades on the infantry!" I shouted as I loaded and fired another flare.

Wright opened fire with grenades on the rapidly advancing cavalry. Explosions that didn't immediately kill man and beast, caused survivors to shy away into other horses and stumble to the ground, tripping other horses and tossing their riders.

I looked for the assault teams and spotted the eight volunteers running headlong toward the walls. Sutter and Barnes performed an overlapping withdrawal, providing cover fire from a kneeling position while they ran past each other. They remembered their training while protecting the volunteers and their own retreat.

"Assault teams, signal when you're in!" I shouted.

We loaded and fired grenades in quick succession into the massed infantry, opening gaping holes in their advance while cannons on our parapets fired, ripping into bodies and cutting off legs when iron cannonballs bounced through them.

"Taylor, go through the church and give me a report from the east!" I said.

"Going to the church!"

"South wall, report!" I shouted.

"We've slowed them down! Keep flares in the air!" Snyder reported amid the rapid popping of M16s and the click-bang of muskets.

I fired another flare, angling it toward the south, and then shouted, "Sutter, status!"

"Almost there!" He shouted over a short burst of automatic rifle fire.

"Sutter, we're in! Last leg!" Barnes shouted.

"Uh, damn! Damn it!"

"Medic! Man down!" Wright shouted. *"Barnes, get back to the wall!"*

"Like hell!" Barnes shouted when he ran to Sutter, lifted him on his shoulders, and then ran out of my sight next to the wall.

"Taylor! Report!" I shouted.

"No activity to the east. I'm on my way to you," he said breathlessly from the running around I'd sent him on.

"We're in! Medic! Where's the medic?" Barnes shouted.

"For shit's sake, I'm all right. I just got the wind knocked outta me," Sutter grumbled, reassuring me he was okay.

"Sutter, where're you hit?" Taylor shouted as he was running.

"My back," Sutter painfully said.

"Automatic fire! Sweep the infantry in short bursts! Barnes, get up here!" I shouted and fired another grenade.

"Ammo! I need ammo. Loading last clip!"

"Ammo! Last clip! Loading last clip!"

"Those on last clip, single fire!" I shouted.

"Last clip! Single fire!"

"We're going for ammo!" Sutter shouted.

"What? Wait!" Taylor started to argue, but in the flare's light I saw Sutter get up and run along the barracks wall, with Taylor in close pursuit.

"South wall, what's happening?" I shouted.

"Infantry turned! They're running north along the river!" Snyder said.

"Ruiz, do you have any grenades left?"

"We got a can full."

"Fire one grenade over the northwest corner at maximum range!"

"Grenade!" Ruiz shouted, followed by a thoomp.

"Incoming! Danger close!" I shouted, and yanked Travis and a volunteer off their feet by their belts. Alerted by the proximity of the incoming grenade, the squad pulled and pushed other defenders down before ducking behind the parapet themselves.

I couldn't have asked for a more accurate shot. The grenade exploded barely ten meters from the outside corner of the wall, clearing ladders in the area and laying out solders who had bunched up while loading muskets and waiting their turn on the ladders. Most importantly, it cleared away the unarmed Mexican berserkers whose sole purpose during the attack was to use axes to chop holes through weak spots in the adobe walls.

I was loading another flare when a ladder landed on the wall in front of me. With musket in hand, a Mexican soldier climbed up, followed by two others. Slamming the breech closed on my grenade launcher, I jammed the barrel of my M16 into his eye, causing him to fall off the ladder, taking the others down with him. I fired the flare into the air, and then fired my rifle on automatic spraying short bursts, sweeping the soldiers massing at the base of the wall.

"Ammo coming up the ramp!"

When I turned, Snyder was running up the ramp with the ammo cans he'd brought.

"You left Ruiz alone?" I asked.

"He's holding the wall with the other guys. They're keeping the infantry pinned in the burned-out huts, and away from the walls. Infantry is still moving this way along the river. I'll bring more ammo," Snyder said as he handed me clips.

"Negative! Leave the ammo here! Go back to the barracks and get more ammo for yourselves and stay with Ruiz! Go!" I picked up the cans and quickly distributed the desperately needed clips to my men along the wall.

"Ammo coming up the ramp! Damn!" Sutter shouted breathlessly.

"Sutter's down!" Taylor said, and I turned to see he'd stopped to help Sutter.

"Taylor, bring the ammo up here!" I shouted as I buttstroked a Mexican in the face before running down the ramp. "Taylor! Ammo! Now!" I shouted, affording myself the briefest look at Sutter, who was motionless, face down on the ramp. I grabbed two ammo cans and ran up the ramp, dropped one off with Sergeant Wright, opened another, and gave clips to anyone who needed them.

"Taylor, where are the grenades?"

"Here!" he shouted from beside me.

"Take a can to Wright, then help the wounded!"

The Mexican infantry repeatedly charged the walls but were driven back, only to be spurred forward again by shouts and whipping from their officers. Time and again they kept coming. We were killing them in droves; they knew it, they saw it, but they kept coming. Why did they keep coming? Charge after charge, they kept coming!

***

An eternity of eternities passed before the tempest of battle tapered off to occasional musket fire. When I fired a flare to survey the area, I was relieved to see no evidence of soldiers massing for another assault. Exhausted breathing pulsed through my radio, followed by the almost contagious sound of someone retching. I felt my stomach sour when someone else puked their guts out. Turning my attention closer to the walls, ghastly was the only word befitting what the flare's flickering light revealed. Heaps of bodies lay at the base of the wall, while some of the wounded crawled away. Others used muskets and each other like crutches as they hobbled off. I'd hoped to never again hear the sounds of the wounded screaming in agony, or the pitiful moaning and crying of the dying.

The day was ours, but at what cost? Dreading my next duty, I said, "First Squad, listen up. Sound off when your name is called. Wright."

"Here."

"Sutter."

"This is Taylor. Sutter's down. He needs a stretcher."

"I don't need no damn stretcher. I need to catch my breath," Sutter growled.

"Breckenridge."

"Here."

"Barnes."

"Here."

"Carpenter."

"Here."

"Wallace."

"Oh shit!" The sound of him puking was enough for me to know he was okay.

"Ruiz."

"Here."

"Snyder."

"Here."

"First Squad, check yourselves. Does anyone need a medic? Sound off, does anyone need a medic? Everyone get fresh clips and go to your assigned positions on the walls. Before you leave, get any ladders you can reach and bring them inside."

With unexpected difficulty, I had to brace myself against the wall to get to my feet and pull a ladder in. "Doc, I've got a stretcher for Sutter."

"I don't need it!" Sutter's irritated voice gave me a small measure of relief.

"Doc, what's his condition?"

"His armor stopped two shots in the back. He might have broken ribs, but I won't know until he lets me examine him."

"Let him go to his bunk. We need you up here."

"At least I'm not arguing about it, like some people I know."

"Get to your bunk, Sergeant Hard Ass," I said, as a concerned smile tugged at my face.

Our last parachute flare had burned out overhead, leaving only the flickering light from torches tucked into metal brackets attached to the walls. Flames from the limbers and caissons, which had been backlighting the Mexican infantry, were reducing to smoldering embers. I pulled down my night vision goggles and looked around for any wounded I could help. I almost fell from the side of a ramp when I saw Travis lying in a heap on the ground.

"Medic! Travis is down! Taylor, over here!"

"Where?"

"Use your goggles. Over here, to your left." I waved to get his attention, and then pointed at Travis's location.

Taylor arrived at a run and knelt beside Travis.

"Where's he hit? Is it a head shot? C'mon, Doc, do something!"

"Stand back, damn it! It's hard enough to work in the dark without you all over me! He's breathing, good pulse, there's no wound I can see with these goggles. Let's move him to his headquarters."

"Why not the hospital?"

"I have him, not you! Get some help, and a stretcher."

"You, you, come with me." I dragged men to Taylor's position. "Doc, tell 'em what to do. I'll get a ladder."

By the time I returned with the ladder, Taylor and the men I'd selected were already carrying Travis into his headquarters. When I reached the door, I thanked them when they filed out.

"Doc, can I help?" I asked when I looked into Travis's bedroom.

"Go help somebody else until I figure out what's wrong with him."

"I think it's my fault."

"I'm shocked. How'd you manage it?" Taylor said sarcastically while he continued to examine Travis.

"When Ruiz fired the grenade over the northwest corner, I knew it'd be close. I pulled him back and he must've fallen off the scaffold."

Taylor began examining Travis's extremities. "Uh-huh; yeah, just as I thought. He'll be okay, but you'll explain to him why he has a broken arm, and maybe a concussion."

"Aww shit. I'm gonna catch hell for sure. First Squad, listen up. We're taking responsibility for the walls. When you get to your positions, send as many men as possible from your areas to take the wounded to the hospital. Use your night vision goggles and watch for any movement coming toward the walls. If you see any, sound off and shoot."

Before I left Travis's headquarters, I recovered my binoculars from his desk, lowered my night vision goggles, and searched the scaffolds for any wounded I could find, and to locate Travis's hat. He was easier to find when he was wearing his hat.

***

For as tired as we were, no sleep was to be had by anyone. Not even the silence of the cannons, whose constant bombardment had plagued us over the past four days, could seduce anyone to sleep. Moonlight peeking between passing clouds enticed musket fire from the walls, shooting at Mexican soldiers who were struggling to get away from the battlefield. Repeated shouts to hold fire went largely unheeded. In moments of quiet I could hear the difference between the angry pop of an M16 rifle, and the distinctive click-bang of a musket. I was proud to note that none of the squad fired on the battlefield wounded.

Amid the sporadic shooting, shouts to help our wounded continued to galvanize the exhausted Alamo defenders into action. When we hurriedly made our way around the scaffolds, I couldn't believe how numb my mind became when we pulled the dead from the wounded and took them to the hospital. Maybe it was fatigue, or the numbness of my mind, but I couldn't wrap my head around what the so-called doctors were doing to their patients. Whiskey and laudanum flowed freely into the wounded while the surgeons worked. They acted more like carpenters than doctors as they sawed off arms whose bones had been broken by musket balls. Other still conscious but not yet drunk or drugged men were held down, screaming and writhing in pain, as doctors moved from patient to patient with bloody, unwashed hands, shoving fingers into bullet holes and moving them around, blindly searching for imbedded lead balls. If that wasn't enough, long and thick tweezer-like instruments were used to pull out deeply imbedded lead balls, followed by a finger pushed into the bullet hole to stop bleeding. Those more fortunate fainted from the treatment, or were so affected by the laudanum, it left them painlessly happy. Subsequent trips to the hospital had me leaving that house of horrors as quickly as I arrived with a patient.

***

Dawn brought no comfort when night finally faded. In the slowly brightening sunrise I used the binoculars to count how many high-ranking Mexican officers were among the dead, knowing they'd be easily identified by their bright, colorful uniforms. I counted five officers among the dead; two of them were with the cavalry. I was tempted to go out and see if Santa Anna was among them, but discretion was the better part of valor. I shuddered when I looked at the dead and dying piled up at the base of the wall beneath me. I knew those men who were still alive and made it back to town would get little medical treatment, because Santa Anna had left most of his medical corps behind when he began his campaign against Texas. I climbed off the scaffold with a dull sense of emptiness haunting my purpose. Desperately trying to clear the images of the Mexican dead and scenes in the hospital from my mind, I found Taylor walking out of Travis's headquarters.

"How's Travis?"

"I've set and splinted his arm, and bandaged a cut on his head. Joe is a great assistant. He followed his orders without question. He's agreed to get me if there's any change in Travis's condition. How do you feel?"

"I'm okay."

"Hmm," was his only comment when he shined his flashlight in my eyes.

"Doc, that's getting tiresome."

"I guess what you needed was something not in my bag."

"What's that?"

"A dose of combat," Taylor said, too flippantly for my current state of mind.

"Hey! If I could've talked my way out of this mess, I would've."

"I had to look in on Bowie because he kept yelling at the top of his voice."

"If he's making that much noise, he must be getting better."

"He's pissed off because he wasn't strong enough to join the fight. To prove he was ready to fight, he stood up and downed a whole flask of whiskey right in front of me. We had to catch him before he hit the floor."

"Sounds about right for him." I had to smile at the historical implications of Bowie's drinking. "Have you been to the hospital yet?"

"Yeah, I've been up there. Those barbarians want to practice their own brand of medicine and ignore what I can do for them. I could save many of them, but they won't let me try," Taylor said, frustrated by his inability to help. "I've been told to help outside, so I've set up a triage area next to the barracks."

"By yourself? I'll get some men to help you."

"I don't need them. I kept two men with me who helped carry the wounded to the barracks. Until there's room in the hospital, they're being made as comfortable as possible."

"I've no doubt those you've treated will live. We've cleared the walls of the wounded, but you might want to go around and check for any we missed."

"I've already checked everyone. The dead are being moved off the scaffolds, and the wounded are—"

"Being killed in the hospital," I finished for him.

"Some slower than others. Those who are dead, or soon will be, have an X on their forehead."

"You brought a magic marker?"

"It's in blood. We don't have body bags, so they'll need burial as soon as possible. We're lucky the weather's cold; it'll help keep diseases from spreading."

"And keep the bodies from stinking for a while. We should do something about the Mexican wounded outside the walls. I'll get with Travis—"

"He'll be out for a while," Taylor interjected.

"What did you do to him?" Taylor smiled and shrugged his shoulders. "Okay, I'll ask Bowie."

"He's useless; drunk off his ass by now," Taylor said disgustedly.

"Are any of the chain of command still alive?" I said, looking around. "There's Williamson; thanks Doc. Sergeant Major!"

"What do you want, Webber?"

"We've recovered our wounded, and they're being treated. Can I have some men to help the Mexican wounded?"

"Why do you want to help the Mexicans?" Williamson said tiredly, turning to stand in front of me.

"We should treat them like the soldiers they are. Wouldn't you want the same for your men?"

"Did you see the red flag in Bexar?" Williamson's voice was uncharacteristically soft-spoken, and it should've warned me of what was coming.

"Yes," I replied.

"Did you see the red flag?" he shouted, suddenly nose to nose with me.

"Yes, Sergeant Major!" I shouted back, snapping to attention.

"Do you know what it means?"

"Yes, Sergeant Major! No quarter! No mercy!" I shouted back, avoiding eye-to-eye contact with him. I didn't want to appear to challenge his authority, so I focused on an interesting scar on his forehead.

"You said the Mexicans call us pirates, murdering good people for no reason, and you want to help 'em? We got too many wounded to take care of, and too many to bury! Leave the Mexicans out there to bleed!"

"Yes, Sergeant Major! Thank you for the attitude adjustment, Sergeant Major!" He hesitated, looking as if he had more to say before he walked away.

"That was loud and clear. Sounds like he has a different morality than we do," Sutter said.

"He has a point. Looks like I'll need an officer to get anything done."

"Captain Dickinson went in the church a few minutes ago," Taylor said.

"Thanks Doc. Have you had a chance to look at Sutter?"

"I haven't forgotten about him."

"Doc—"

"Triage means the assignment of degrees of urgency to wounded or

ill patients. Sutter is in no danger of bleeding out or dying. When I've done all I can for those in triage, I'll check him again."

"I'll be there in a few minutes," I said, indicating I was going to be certain about Sutter's care. In my mind, my men came first.

I walked around and looked at those who had been carried from the walls and were laid on the ground, all with Taylor's bloody X on their foreheads. I saw an Alamo officer was among the dead. For reasons I couldn't explain, I wasn't repulsed when I saw much of his head had been blown away. I actually envied him as I offered a small prayer. I wished Thompson hadn't decided to run; prayers would've been a job more suited to him.

When I walked into the barracks, Sutter was sitting on his bunk, stripped to his waist while Taylor examined him.

"What's the word, Doc?"

"He has two contusions—one low on his left shoulder blade, and a larger one just below that. Looks like he was shot by the stacked, small caliber rounds you mentioned."

I walked around the bunk and said, "Sergeant Sutter, who gave you those humongous hickeys?"

"They're bruises, not hickeys; and in case you don't know, I'm cold sitting here."

"The armor's good for stopping bullets, but doesn't always stop bones from being broken," Taylor commented. "It's going to be painful to tell anything without an x-ray."

"Just get on with it!" Sutter said impatiently.

"Take a deep breath." Taylor pressed his fingers on Sutter's back.

"Son of a bitch! Damn it, man!" Sutter exclaimed as he exhaled.

"Did you feel any grinding where I pressed on your back?"

"No, but it hurt like hell!"

"I didn't feel any movement either, so they're probably either stress fractures or bruised. The best I can do is tape you up and give you some pills for the pain."

"How many did we lose?" Sutter said painfully when he straightened up on the bed.

"Just one of the squad was wounded."

"Who was wounded?" Sutter looked around when we didn't answer. "Never mind."

"I haven't tried counting the Mexicans, but I'm guessing hundreds, maybe approaching a thousand. They're piled up five and six deep against the north wall, and scattered across the fields to the west and south." Another unexpected shudder, that had nothing to do with the cold air, rattled me. "I don't know how many dead are among the Alamo people."

"Sixteen dead, thirty-two wounded, and it's all because they have to stand to load and fire their muskets," Taylor grumbled, shaking his head. "The way those butchers operate up there, many of the wounded won't make it. If shock doesn't kill them, they'll die from infection, septicemia, or a host of other blood transmitted diseases."

"Doc, you talk like all the wounded can't function. I'm sure some have minor—"

"I've already treated those with minor wounds. They're counted as wounded, and back on the walls. I could help many of those in the hospital, but they won't let me try to save them!"

"Okay, okay, I'll take your word for it." I defensively put my hands up between us. "I'll get with one of the officers and see what I can do."

"I guess I'm lucky to have you as my doctor," Sutter's voice strained while Taylor worked on him.

"Did you know that Taylor comes from a family of butchers?"

I commented slyly.

Taylor glanced at me, picked up on my lead, and said, "It's true; my father and grandfather are butchers. They cut and hack on meats of every kind. I worked with them for a while before joining the army."

I almost laughed at Sutter's wide-eyed reaction as he slowly turned his head to watch what Taylor was doing.

"You'll have to take it easy," Taylor said, rummaging around in his medical bag. "Take these, one every four hours for the pain. Sarge, help him get dressed and put his left arm in this sling. I'll check my patients in triage again before I go upstairs and see if they want my help yet," Taylor said, closing his medical bag as he walked out.

"Thanks, Doc," I said, and helped Sutter pull his shirt on. "You know, it's too coincidental that Santa Anna planned his attack at the same time we were out spiking the cannons."

"Someone in here must've told them about it. But we rekeyed the radios before we planned the mission." When I stopped helping him dress, he looked at my face. "Uh-oh, what's wrong?"

"I didn't rekey the radios when Thompson went over the wall. One detail; I missed one small detail and almost got everyone killed."

"You can't think of everything."

"I'm a non-commissioned officer, responsible for my men! I have to think of everything!"

"It wouldn't surprise me if Hernández and Sanchez had their hands in it." Sutter was unconcerned by my irritated shout, which he knew wasn't directed at him.

"I'm sure you're right. Last night, whenever I gave a command, I heard bugles. Santa Anna's army is trained to listen for bugle calls to communicate and coordinate movements."

"You should've gotten the Mexican in the jail to tell you what was happening," Sutter said.

"Something else I didn't think of."

"Hindsight is most accurate, and it's a good teacher. Speaking of hindsight, I heard Sergeant Wright suggest you change the radios from VOX to PTT. We should do it now," Sutter said firmly.

"Right. First Squad, listen up. Change your radios from voice-operated switch, to press-to-transmit. I say again, switch radios from Victor Oscar Xray to Papa Tango Tango as seen on your switchboxes."

When Sutter and I made the change to our radios, I heard, *"Staff Sergeant Webber, I want to come back."*

"Who said that?"

"Key the radio," Sutter said, struggling to one handedly drop his helmet on his head so he could also listen.

"I was used to VOX," I said, before keying the radio. "Who said that?"

"Me, Thompson. Hernández is dead."

"How do you know he's dead?"

"Santa Anna killed him about an hour ago."

"What happened?"

"When the attack failed, Hernández said he was getting out of town. We were separated, and I hid. I heard shouting when they caught him and brought him back to the plaza. I couldn't hear what they were saying, but whatever it was made Santa Anna pull his sword. He kept stabbing Hernández in the chest, but his armor kept the sword from sticking. When he figured out he couldn't kill him that way, Santa Anna cut his throat."

"What's your location?"

"I'm safe, and I'm not moving."

"Where's Sanchez?"

"I haven't seen him since yesterday. He must've bailed out on us."

"Thompson, I'm going to give you a chance to redeem yourself." Sutter frantically waved a hand at me. "Since you're already out there, you're going to be my eyes and ears. I want to know what Santa Anna is doing. I want troop numbers, movements, and Santa Anna's plans."

"How am I supposed to do that? My Spanish ain't that good, and he's looking to kill me."

"You should be shot for desertion and conspiracy."

"When you changed the radios, I had to tell Hernández what you were doing, or he was going to kill me and take my radio. He still has eighteen rounds he took from Sanchez. Look, I'm scared. I said it, okay? I'm scared!"

"Do what I ask, and I'll let Colonel Travis decide what to do with you."

I'll try.

"Don't try; do it! Conserve your batteries and turn off your radio. I'll be listening when you have something useful to say."

"Have you lost your mind?" Sutter exclaimed. "How do you know Hernández is dead and Sanchez ran off? How do you know they're not all working together?"

Getting a tight grip on my intolerance of the phrase I hated most of all, I sat on the bunk opposite him. With a sigh to sooth my patience, I said, "Sergeant Nicolas Sutter, there's not a man anywhere whom I would more willingly trust with my life. You know I value your input and you're right, we can't trust Thompson. His story doesn't sound true to me because he said they searched for him but didn't find him. The Mexicans aren't stupid."

"Santa Anna must've taken over all the buildings in town to

bunk his men, so there won't be many places Thompson can hide in," Sutter added.

"Hernández is alive and well."

"What? How do you know?"

"Never underestimate your enemy. I think all three of them are safe in Santa Anna's headquarters, either in the plaza or in the cathedral. Thompson said Hernández has eighteen rounds, and he said it like Hernández is still alive."

"And he wouldn't give his location." Sutter nodded in agreement.

"We've got to figure out what Santa Anna's going to do without Thompson's reports. Will Santa Anna try another sneak attack with the men he has left? Will he wait and send for Urrea and his army, or will he pack up and leave? I'd like to keep him here where we can contain him, and we have the advantage of good cover and firepower."

"If Thompson is working with Santa Anna, we told him about our plans last night and about our dead and wounded today, because the radios were on VOX," Sutter said.

Dark thoughts invaded my mind, brought on by our strategizing and highlighting the mistakes I'd made.

"I'm tired," I said quietly.

"Aren't we all?"

"No, it's not that. I'm tired of fighting, tired of being responsible, tired of blood on my hands." I looked past my hands at the floor, remembering a story told during a tour of the modern-day Alamo. The fighting on the last day was fiercest in these barracks, with blood running ankle deep on the floor. My mind's eye saw blood dripping from my hands and onto my dirty boots.

"Looks like I'm gonna get my second Purple Heart," Sutter

said, gently testing the movement of his arm in the sling.

"If command approves it," I said, not looking up from my mind's eye gaze at the blood, flowing like a river across the floor, getting ever deeper in my mind, threatening to drown me.

"I'll have to put an award star on my dress greens ribbon, and the medal we never wear."

"If you get it."

"Any regrets about Hernández?"

The slowly sinking feeling in the pit of my stomach hit bottom with a nauseating thud. "Of course I have regrets, but it's his own fault."

"Even though you suggested he leave."

"I gave everyone the chance to leave before all this started."

"You didn't try to stop him when he left, or to get him back."

"It was his decision to leave when…he…did…," I began to shout, but stuttered to a stop when I realized what he was doing. I looked up to see Sutter grinning from ear to ear. "You're a bastard, you know that?" I shouted and threw my inflatable pillow at him.

"I had to bring your mind back on track and pull you out of your funk," he said, and started laughing. "Oww, it hurts, it hurts." He held himself around his chest, rocking back and forth on his bunk. His laughter echoing in the barracks was so much out of place in our situation.

"Stop laughing and it won't hurt. Damn it, you're lucky I like you. I've got to see how much ammo we have left. How many rounds do you have?" I said, my sense of duty and purpose quickly returning.

"One full clip, plus what's in my rifle." Between his laughter and reaching for the rifle, his face reflected the intense pain in his back.

"Relax; I got it. It looks like fifteen rounds in here." I made the weapon safe before I put the magazine back in the rifle.

"I emptied and dropped three clips outside the walls," Sutter said.

"We'll get them later. Knowing you, you'll be on your feet in about an hour."

"Yeah, after these pills kick in," Sutter said with a groan as he lay back, struggling to get comfortable on his bunk.

When I finished the ammo inventory in the barracks, I walked around the walls and counted what everyone else had left.

"Is it as bad as I think it is?" Wright asked when I finished counting his and Barnes's.

"We've got three thousand one-hundred rounds, and fifty-three grenades so far. We used too many grenades…too many," I said, shaking my head. "Flares are gone, and I still have to count what's left on the north wall. Thank you for taking the time to load the clips and putting them in the ammo cans. If you hadn't, I don't think we could've survived the night," I said with heartfelt appreciation.

"There are some loose rounds I can load into the empty magazines. Did you count them as well?"

"No, not yet. Load them and give me the count later…later, not now," I said when Wright started to leave for the barracks.

"By the way, I get it," Wright said. "They speak Spanish in Spain, so they speak Mexican in Mexico."

"Who speaks English?"

"England. But what do we speak if it's not English?"

"We speak American."

"That's ridiculous," Wright said.

"We can debate it later," and we shared a tired laugh together. "Corporal Barnes, do you recall your remark to Sergeant Wright's order to return to the walls last night?"

"I said, 'like hell.' We don't leave our own behind."

"Uh-huh. Sergeant Wright, we have a case of disrespect to an NCO. What you think we should do about it?"

"Considering the situation, I think we should say thank you and move on."

"I agree. Thank you for retrieving Sergeant Sutter." I shook Barnes's hand. "But next time, think of something else to say, or just do it without comments."

"Do you think it's better to ask forgiveness than get permission?" Barnes asked.

"If Captain Ibanez was in a fair mood, I'm sure he'd file it under adapting to a situation; but I'd say, don't carry it too far," I said, turning to Sergeant Wright. "I want everyone to trade off and clean their rifles. We put a lot of rounds through them last night, and I don't want them jamming. I've already notified everyone except Carpenter and Breckenridge," I said, keying my radio. "First Squad, movement and activity report. North wall, report. North wall, report!"

When Carpenter and Breckenridge didn't respond, I looked for them through the binoculars at the far end of the compound and found them sitting, unresponsive. I scrambled down the ladder and sprinted toward the north wall. I feared the worst—that they had lied about their condition and had sat down to die.

"West wall, report."

"Soldiers moving toward the footbridge and fording the river. Looks like walking wounded," Wright said.

"Breckenridge, Carpenter, report.... Damn it all! South wall; Ruiz, are you all right by yourself?"

"I'm good. Looking south, cavalry and infantry moving west along the road toward the bridge. Some of the infantry are still hiding behind

the huts.... David says he's not dead."

I had to smile at Ruiz's report. "Tell the Mexicans to go home and tell those on your wall not to shoot them when they leave. East wall, report."

"All clear. No movement."

"Breckenridge! Carpenter!" I shouted after I ran up the ramp and kicked their booted feet.

"Huh? What?"

"North wall, report!" I shouted at the pair, even though I could see the situation beyond the wall.

"Yeah, okay. Shit! Movement, I got movement!" Breckenridge shouted, and they tried to take aim. Before they could fire, I pushed their rifles over by the handles.

"If you'd been awake, you would've seen they're wounded trying to get away. Show me your ammo; quickly, or I'll put you on burial detail. Switch your radios from VOX to PTT. Do it now! Keep your heads down while you do it." I keyed the radio and said, "First Squad, send one man from your position and pick up MREs and a blanket. When he returns, choose one to sleep in place for two hours. Sergeant Wright, team up with Ruiz and watch the south and west from the corner near the eighteen-pounder cannon. Ruiz, get an MRE and a blanket for yourself, and rest as best you can. Carpenter, go to the barracks. When you get back, clean your rifle. Move out, Carpenter! Breckenridge, after he gets back, clean your rifle, then you sleep first."

I appreciated that they were tired; we all were. But we had to stay awake in anticipation of another attack, however unlikely it may be in coming. After checking the remaining ammo cans and getting the final count from the south wall, I was on my way to the church when I caught Carpenter walking toward me with a blanket and MREs.

"Why are you walking? Get to your position! Move! Move!" I shouted and pounded the back of his armor with my gloved fist, motivating and chasing him until I was sure he'd run all the way up the ramp, knowing the exercise would help him stay awake. My sprint with him certainly helped me.

When I was finally able to go into the church, I found Captain Dickinson in the chapel.

"Sir, I'm happy to see you're alive. Are you wounded?"

"No, I'm not. Sergeant Webber, this is my wife Suzanna."

"Please, call me Elliot." I politely bowed slightly to her. "I apologize for not introducing myself sooner. And this young lady must be the pretty Angelina." I dropped to one knee in front of her. She shyly smiled as she backed into her mother, hiding her face in the folds of her mother's dress.

"Do I have you to thank for saving my husband?" Suzanna asked.

"No, ma'am. My men couldn't have stood against so many without the brave effort from everyone here. We're alive because of their courage, and their sacrifice."

"Thank you. Thank all of you," Suzanna said, taking her husband's hand.

"Unfortunately, it may not be over. Sir, according to Corporal Taylor, both sides need to bury their dead before diseases start spreading. We need to talk to Santa Anna, so he can recover his dead and wounded."

"We must get permission from Colonel Travis before we can send anyone. He might want to send Captain Martin to negotiate again."

"Sir, Colonel Travis fell off the scaffold and broke his arm. He's unconscious in his bunk. I'm sorry to report that Captain Martin is dead."

"Then we need to see Colonel Bowie. He might want to send Major Roth, or Captain Dimmitt."

"Sir, Colonel Bowie is too drunk to make decisions. Major Roth is wounded in the hospital, as is Captain Dimmitt."

"What about Captain Forsyth?"

"I'm sorry, sir, he's dead."

"Oh Almaron, I knew him," Suzanna said sadly, her eyes tearing.

"Sir, you and I should negotiate with Santa Anna."

"Almaron, please send someone else," Suzanna pleaded with her husband.

"Don't worry, ma'am. I'll take good care of him. Sir, we should bring David with us. Let's ask if he wants to come with us. By your leave, ma'am," I said, touching the brim of my helmet before leading the captain out.

"Why do you want to negotiate with Santa Anna? I don't believe burying the dead is your reason," Dickinson said.

"No sir, it's not the only reason. Mexican dead are piled so high against the north wall, another charge there could use the bodies to climb over the walls without ladders. We saw them picking up their dead and wounded after the fight the day before yesterday. I want them to see how many dead and wounded they have to pick up this time. It might break their morale, and end Santa Anna's campaign against Texas."

"He still has the advantage, despite his losses. He's not going to retreat, because it would destroy him as a general," Dickinson said.

"Sir, we've lost several of our own, but he's lost hundreds of dead and wounded."

"We have to offer an armistice to bury our dead without getting shot."

"An armistice?" I asked.

"Yes. We must reach an agreement to clear the battlefield of the dead and wounded. Both sides lay down their arms, and obey the terms agreed to. Do you use an armistice in your time?"

"We soldiers kill as many as we can to force an enemy to the negotiation table."

Dickinson regarded me with a puzzled expression, and then said, "Let's find Crockett, and see if he wants to go with us."

"Ruiz, is David still in your area?"

"*Negative. He said he was going to check his men.*"

"There he is." I pointed to the palisade. "David, we're going to meet with Santa Anna to negotiate an armistice. Would you like to join us?"

"I'm not fit to meet him. He killed one of my men, and wounded two others. I might shoot him instead of talkin'."

"I'm sorry for the loss of your men, but we need to negotiate an armistice. We'd like you to come with us," I said.

"*Sergeant Webber, they're carrying out three more dead from the hospital,*" Taylor said.

"Doc, get up there and help them. If they won't listen, let me know. We'll toss the so-called doctors out of the hospital, and you'll take charge."

"What is happening to the doctors?" Dickinson asked about the one-sided conversation he'd overheard.

"They're bringing out three more men who died up there."

"How many men have died?" David asked.

"There are nineteen dead, and twenty-nine wounded. Corporal Taylor has the medical training to help, but the doctors won't let him."

"It's Pollard. He believes he's the only doctor here. I'll remove him if he won't let your man help." Dickinson surprised me with his opinion of the surgeon.

"Doc, Captain Dickinson says he'll remove Pollard if he won't cooperate. When you talk to him, make sure he knows it."

"*Roger that.*"

"Sir, how do we tell Santa Anna we want to talk?" I asked Dickinson.

"We will fire a cannon to get his attention and wave a white flag from the wall."

"Won't that mean we're going to surrender?"

"Not as long as our flag flies up there." Dickinson pointed to the tri-colored flag flying over the church. "We'll need a white flag."

"I'll get it."

"Unload the cannon!" Dickinson shouted when he walked up the ramp.

After the men backed the cannon and rolled the cannonball out, they waited until I arrived with the flag, then Dickinson shouted, "Fire!" I'd never get over hearing that cannon roar.

"Sir, my men will cover us while we walk to the bridge."

"Walk? We'll ride. Horses run faster if we have to leave in a hurry," Dickinson said, and we walked down the ramp toward the corral.

"Sergeant Wright, I'm going to switch my radio to VOX. I want the squad to listen to the negotiations and have them tell those around them what's being said."

"*Roger that.*"

The horse I was given was cooperative despite my inexperience, but I still needed help saddling him. I made a mental note of the large teeth I worked around when I was shown how to put the bit in his mouth.

"Okay, how does it work?" I asked, looking at the horse

looking back at me.

"Have you ever ridden a horse?" David said, smiling at my discomfiture.

"Yeah, a pony when I was a kid."

"You mount the horse from his left side. Put your foot in the stirrup, pull yourself up, and swing your leg over his back. To make him turn, pull the reins left or right."

When I settled into the saddle they trotted for the gate, but my horse stayed in place. I bounced up and down, twisting in the saddle to try and make him move.

David stopped at the gate and shouted, "What is wrong?"

"He won't move."

"Kick your heels in his side."

"Won't it hurt him?"

"Kick him!"

When I kicked him into movement, I heard shouting from the hospital. I wanted to stop and see what was going on, but I was totally out of my element when my horse trotted out the gate, following the others. My two-handed death grip on a thick piece of leather where the saddle horn should have been kept me in the saddle while I was bounced around. David said to stand in the stirrups and let go of the leather I was hanging onto. Standing made the ride a lot smoother, but letting go of the leather swell, as David called it, was another matter.

When we arrived at the bridge, two impeccably dressed Mexican officers were waiting on horseback.

"I'm Captain Dickinson. This is David Crockett and Sergeant Webber."

"I am Colonel Almonte. This is Colonel Bartres. Where is Colonel Travis?" Almonte said in a thick, Spanish accent.

"He's unwilling to meet with you under these conditions,"

Dickinson said.

"Where is Colonel Bowie?"

"I've taken the authority to speak in their stead." I liked the way Dickinson responded, not giving away the condition of our officers. However, no thanks to me, I thought they already knew.

"His Excelencia, Antonio López de Santa Anna, commands you to surrender if you wish to save your lives—" Almonte said brusquely.

"Wow! That's quite a command," I said, interrupting him with more bravado than I felt.

"You will immediately place yourselves at the disposal of His Excelencia, from whom you may expect clemency after some considerations," Almonte said.

"We will not surrender," Dickinson said.

"If Santa Anna wants to surrender, send him to our gate and we'll consider it," I answered before Dickinson could continue.

"We offer His Excellency an armistice so he can bury his dead and care for his wounded. Inform His Excellency of our offer and ask how much time he'll need. We will wait for His Excellency's answer."

Colonel Almonte spoke in Spanish to Bartres before he turned his horse and galloped to Santa Anna's headquarters.

"I know about you, Sergento Webber." Almonte said. "We killed one of your especial soldados from the future who tried to join His Excellencia's army. He is not as especial as you think he is. He died easily on the point of His Excellencia's sword, just as you will, and all the especial soldados you brought with you. We have two more of your especial soldados in His Excellencia's headquarters."

If this was Almonte's version of small talk, he needed to polish it with dinner and some whiskey, lots of whiskey, and a course in English as a second language.

"Who did you kill?" I feigned ignorance, trying to look sad at my loss.

"Hernández. We cut him to pieces and put his body in our *letrinas*."

"They dumped him in the crapper," Sutter said over the radio.

"Please don't tell them I'm still in town," Thompson moaned plaintively over the radio.

"When your other two especial soldados watched what we did, they proved to be useful. They are telling all about you, and how to kill you."

"I didn't see any others leave. Who are the other two?" I said, still feigning ignorance.

"Thompson is one. The other refused to give his name, calling himself a *soldado* in the army of the future."

Pretending increasing anger, I said, "Before this battle is over, I'm going to catch Santa Anna, and when I do, I'll treat him like the pirate he says we are. Before I blindfold him with his own red flag that's flying over the cathedral, I'll piss in his face; then I'll slowly hang him. When he's dangling at the end of my rope, kicking out the last of his pitiful life, the last sound he'll hear will be his own band playing *'El Degüello'* for him."

David leaned over to me, and whispered, "That is not how we get their cooperation."

"I don't want their cooperation. I want Santa Anna dead," I said, loud enough for Almonte to hear.

"His Excellencia will not enjoy what you said." Almonte looked a bit fearful, probably at the thought of what he had to repeat to Santa Anna.

Having made our respective positions clear, Almonte said, *"Don Benito*—the famous person of minor importance in your own country."

"Who in hell is *Don Benito*?" I asked.

"It's what the Mexicans call me," Crockett said.

"Learn something new every day," I commented.

"His Excellencia will be glad to kill you and all your men, but I ask you to *abandonar Mission de San Antonio de Valero* and save all your lives—except you." Almonte pointed at me, regarding me like a dangerous insect needing to be squashed.

"Almonte, are you asking us to leave without a fight? Let's all go ask Santa Anna about your request. I'm sure he'd be glad to hear about it from you," I said.

The shock over my suggestion to meet Santa Anna directly was obvious on Almonte's face. There was no more talk while we uncomfortably waited for Batres to return with Santa Anna's answer. I carefully scanned the area with my binoculars for snipers, and more importantly Thompson, who was a better shot than Hernández or Sanchez. Bartres returned at a gallop and tightly reined in his horse, skidding to a stop beside Almonte and speaking to him in Spanish.

"His Excellencia accepts your offer of an armistice. He will require four days."

"Four days? Just to pick up the dead and wounded? Captain, that's too much time. Give him two days!" I exclaimed.

"Thank His Excellency and tell him we accept his offer of a four-day armistice," Dickinson said, ignoring me.

"Captain, you've got to put limits on what they do," I said.

"What limits do you think there should be?" Dickinson snapped at me.

"They don't need to bring muskets. Make them remove the dead during daylight, and they all must be back across the bridge before sundown."

"These things are understood during an armistice."

"Are they?" I asked, turning to Almonte. "Are they understood?"

"His Excellencia is an honorable man."

"Yeah, like hell he is." I heard faint laughter from the Alamo walls.

"Colonel Almonte, you can begin picking up your dead and wounded immediately. Webber, we're done here." Dickinson and Crockett turned their horses and trotted toward the Alamo.

Instead of leaving with them, I said, "Almonte, when you see Santa Anna, tell him I'm the one who shot his horse out from under him. I missed him then. Next time, I'll have *Don Benito* with me, and together we won't miss again. Be sure to tell him I'm looking forward to pissing in his face."

Seeing Almonte's face cloud over at the reminder, I was unwilling to turn my back on either of them. I continued to watch them as I struggled to turn the horse and kick him into an uncomfortable trot, laying low over the horse's neck until I rode through the Alamo gates.

"All hail Staff Sergeant Webber; the master negotiator returns!" Sutter shouted from the scaffold on the south wall when we rode through the gate, bringing laughter from the men on the walls.

I looked around to see some of the squad raise their hands in the air and repeatedly bow, imitated by a few of the Alamo defenders.

"Webber, what's happening?" Dickinson said, looking around.

"Sir, my squad is joking about my negotiation skills."

"I didn't see you present any such skills to Almonte."

"No, sir. First Squad, shouldn't you be watching the

Mexicans?" I shouted, and they turned to watch over the area again.

"Sergeant Webber, it was disrespectful the way you spoke to Almonte," David said when we dismounted our horses.

"I deliberately disrespected Santa Anna by poking—"

"*Hot mike! Sergeant Webber, hot mike!*" Sutter shouted over the radio.

"Damn it, I like VOX," I mumbled under my breath, belatedly remembering Thompson might relay the information to Santa Anna, if he was working with him. I switched the radio to the push-to-talk setting again.

"If we can keep Santa Anna here, where we have the walls for protection and the firepower to keep him at bay, we'll be in a much better position to beat him."

"Santa Anna is not going to fall for something like that," Dickinson said.

"Sir, we lost almost a third of our men last night. We need reinforcements, and we need them badly. According to history, General Houston is camped near Gonzales with about three hundred-fifty men. He's not ready for Santa Anna's army, no matter how many Mexicans we kill if we lose."

"We must send a messenger to President Jackson. We need him to send the men he has in Louisiana to help us." Dickinson was still not convinced we could beat Santa Anna.

"Sir, Jackson can't get involved because he's bound by treaties with Mexico, and we're in Mexican territory. We have to send messengers to Fannin and Houston and tell them the Alamo has held against Santa Anna. We must convince them to come here and reinforce us, and we have only four days to do it."

"Colonel Travis must make that decision," Dickinson said.

I keyed my radio, and said, "Doc, what's Colonel Travis'

condition?"

"I haven't heard from Joe, so I assume he's still asleep."

"We have to wake him."

"If you can wake him at all, he'll be groggy."

"Even better. Join me in Travis's headquarters."

"Negative. I'm treating the wounded in the hospital."

"Are you educating them in proper medical procedures?"

"Roger that. I've met resistance, but they're listening."

"I heard shouting earlier. What happened?"

"I almost had a riot when I used whiskey to clean hands and medical instruments."

"Let me know if you need any help. Sergeant Sutter, meet me in Travis's headquarters."

"Sergeant Webber? Four riders – "

"Thompson? You have to speak up. I can barely hear you."

"I can't. Four men just left Santa Anna's tent and rode out of town in a hurry."

"Roger that."

"When can I come back?"

"I'll get back with you after I report to Colonel Travis."

"Does he have to know about me?"

"Keep observing, and report anything else you see and hear. Webber, out." When Sutter arrived, I said, "I should let you rest, but I need you."

"It's cool. Whatever's in those pills is workin' real good."

"Are you taking them according to Taylor's instructions?"

"Yup. Just one every four hours. Feelin' no pain." He gave me a huge, toothy grin.

"When did you take your last pill?"

"About a few minutes ago, I think."

"It hasn't been an hour since your last one."

"Isssat why I'm feelin' buzzy?"

"Gimme the pills. Give 'em up!" He reached into three different pockets before he found the pill bottle. "I'll give these to Taylor, and he'll give them to you. Try and keep your head screwed on while we're here." I held the door open for Dickinson and Sutter when they walked into Travis's headquarters.

"Hello, Joe. How's the colonel doing?" I said.

"He be sleeping, suh."

"We need to talk to him. Can you wake him for us?"

"Yes, suh. Colonel Travis, suh. Colonel Travis, youse have visitors. Please wake up."

"Where am I?" Travis said sleepily, looking around.

"Sir, you're in your headquarters," I said.

"The battle! What happened?"

"Sir, you won. Santa Anna retreated after nearly three hours of fighting."

"We won? I have to see," Travis said, struggling to seat himself on his bunk. When he tried to stand, he groaned and sat back down.

"Sir, please take it easy. You fell off the scaffold, hit your head, and broke your arm. Corporal Taylor treated your injuries."

"I have to see what happened. Help me up. Help me up!"

Joe and I helped him to his feet, but he was so unsteady we guided him to his desk, where we insisted he sit.

"I must know what happened. Captain Dickinson, can we stand another attack?"

"With Webber's men maybe, but we still need reinforcements."

"How many men did we lose?" Travis asked, his voice shaking with concern and worry.

"Sir, we lost nineteen dead and twenty-nine wounded. I don't have an accurate count of how many Santa Anna lost, but I estimate nearly a thousand dead and wounded," I said.

"How many of my men are wounded but can still fight?" Travis asked.

"Sir, I don't know exactly. My men are manning the walls, letting your men get some rest while the cannons are quiet."

"I lost over a third of my men. How can we stand against Santa Anna now?" Travis said, suddenly looking tired and worn out.

"Sir, we need help," Dickinson insisted. "You must send couriers to General Houston and Colonel Fannin, telling them the Alamo has held against Santa Anna, but we need reinforcements."

"Where is Major Roth?" Travis said, reaching for his quill.

"Sir, Major Roth and Captain Dimmitt are in the hospital," I reported.

"Where is Captain Martin?" Travis said, not looking up as he wrote.

"Sir, Captain Martin and Captain Forsyth are dead."

Travis's shoulders slumped as he paused his writing. He sighed, dipped the quill in his inkwell, and started writing again. "Where is Sergeant Major Williamson?"

"He's very much alive, sir," I said, remembering our encounter.

"Captain Dickinson, find the sergeant major and send him to me."

"I'll do it, sir." I keyed my radio. "First Squad, locate Sergeant Major Williamson and send him to Colonel Travis's headquarters."

"This is Carpenter. I gave the sergeant major your message."

"Sir, the sergeant major's on his way."

"Webber is the reason why Santa Anna is still here," Dickinson said. "He might have left after last night's battle, but he's still here."

"What did you do?" Travis said to me.

"I sent a message through Colonel Almonte, promising to catch Santa Anna and piss in his face before I hung him."

"How did you talk to Almonte?" Travis asked.

"We arranged an armistice," Dickinson said.

"Without my order?"

"Yes, sir."

"What were the terms you arranged?"

"For the next four days, Santa Anna will pick up his dead and wounded, and take them back across the river. We'll bury our dead outside our church during the armistice," Dickinson said.

"Four days? That's too much time," Travis insisted.

"Sir, we'll be watching their movements," I said.

"Sergeant Webber, why did you say you're going to hang Santa Anna?"

"Sir, we need to keep Santa Anna here. I felt that if I insulted his authority, he'd want revenge. To get revenge, he'd have to stay here."

"If he had gone, we would be safe from further attacks," Dickinson said.

"But no one else would be," I said. "I agree that he could've left us alone, but he could've taken the remains of his army north to locate General Houston. General Urrea is advancing on Goliad right now with about fourteen hundred men, and several cannons. Despite Colonel Fannin's position behind his walls, which are shorter and not as thick as ours, he can't possibly stand against those odds with just four hundred men."

"We did, with one hundred twenty men," Dickinson said.

"My men and I brought weapons from the future, and these

walls are thick. Fannin has no such advantages. For his own protection, we must convince him to reinforce us here. Neither Fannin nor Houston can stop Santa Anna by themselves. We have to get Houston to come here with his three hundred fifty men, even though they're mostly untrained. If we can get everyone to come here, we'll have over eight hundred men to defend the walls. With our consolidated force, we can make Santa Anna fight here. We can defeat him here, instead of letting him run loose to kill everyone he sees."

"Sergeant Webber, men are crossing the bridge to the southwest," Wright reported.

"How many?"

"They're still crossing, but it looks like about fifty so far."

"Are they armed?"

"Not that I can see. They're bringing wagons as well."

"Are the wagons covered?"

"I can't tell. I'll let you know when they get closer."

"Have the men stand ready but hold their fire. Keep me posted."

"Roger that."

"What is happening?" Travis said.

"Sir, men with wagons are crossing the bridge. Santa Anna may be honoring the armistice."

"I don't trust 'em." Sutter was weaving as he stood beside me.

"Have a seat, Sergeant Sutter," I said.

"Not tired."

"Sit, before you fall down," I ordered, kicking a box towards him.

"Sssanta Annie might get sssurrea to be here. Maybe, he's goin' round zoliad." Sutter slurred and stumbled over his words, looking like he may tumble off his box at any moment.

"Is he drunk?" Travis asked as I tried to quiet Sutter.

"No, sir. Our medic gave him something for his pain."

"What happened to him?"

"He was shot twice in the back when he retreated from spiking the cannons. His body armor stopped the bullets, but he may have some broken ribs."

"He should be in the hospital," Travis said.

"Yes, sir. Sergeant Sutter, go to—" While I was telling him to go to the barracks, he slowly closed his eyes, and with a groan, tumbled off his box. I checked him, but he'd passed out.

"Sir, despite his condition, he has a point we should consider. I have a report that riders left Bexar, heading south. They might be couriers going to Urrea with orders for him to come here. It's also possible Santa Anna has ordered his heavy cannons to speed up their march. Those cannons are twelve pounders, howitzers large enough to blast straight through the walls. If that's so, all the more reason to get Fannin and Houston to join us. If Urrea's coming here, we'll have a chance to defeat Santa Anna's combined army."

"I see. Captain Dickinson, I'll send couriers to—" Travis was saying when Sergeant Major Williamson suddenly burst into the room without knocking.

"Webber, I have reports saying many of my men are listening to you over me and the officers! You think you're in charge here, but you're not!"

"Sergeant Major, it's not my intent to override anyone's commands."

"I agree with the sergeant major," Travis said. "You may think you're acting in the best interests of my men, but I'm in command here."

"Yes, sir. That has never been in dispute."

"Sir, if you're sending couriers to Fannin and Houston, Webber should not go to Goliad. He will not be able to convince Fannin to join us," Dickinson said.

"He's convinced us of who he is, and that makes him the best man we can send."

"But he has no skills at diplomacy."

"Diplomacy and knowledge work together. Sergeant Webber, what do you know about Colonel Fannin?"

"Sir, Colonel James Fannin is a partially trained military officer—"

"What do you mean by partially trained?" Travis interrupted.

"History indicates he enlisted in the Military Academy at West Point, where he was academically deficient and often absent from classes. He spent two years there before he resigned and went to Florida to help his sick grandparents. He spent a short time as a judge in Georgia. He married Minerva Fort, and has two daughters."

"He knows Fannin better than either of us," Travis said to Dickinson. "Webber, I want you to send someone to General Houston's camp. Who can you send?"

"I'll send Sergeant Wright."

"Can he convince General Houston to join us?"

"I trust him. I'd send Sergeant Sutter, but he's in no condition to go anywhere." I looked at Sutter, who had blissfully passed out on the floor.

"Captain Dickinson, I'm sending you and Webber to Goliad. Sergeant Major, select someone who knows the area to go with them. Captain Dickinson, prepare—"

Shouting from the walls interrupted Travis.

"Sergeant Wright, what's happening?" I said, keying my

radio.

"A Mexican soldier just ran to the gate. He says his name is Esparza, and he's looking for his brother."

"Sir, a Mexican soldier is at the gate," I said.

"Let him in. We need to question him," Travis said as he looked at the gate through his window.

"Sergeant Wright, Colonel Travis says let him in."

"Wilco. There are fifty men with four uncovered wagons. They don't have weapons."

"Roger that. Keep a close eye on them. Muskets are lying around that they could pick up and use."

The gates opened, and Jose Esparza ran to embrace his brother.

"Francisco Esparza says he wants to join his brother in the garrison. He says he wants to fight against Santa Anna," Wright said.

"Sir, the Mexican wants to join us. He claims he's the brother of Jose Esparza."

"Send him to me," Travis ordered.

"Yes sir. Sergeant Wright, escort Francisco Esparza to Travis's headquarters. Make sure he's not armed."

"Roger that."

"He's on his way, sir."

"Sergeant Webber, prepare yourself for the ride to Goliad," Travis ordered.

"Sir, should I stay and hear what Esparza has to say? I can help with—"

"Be on your way, Sergeant Webber."

Yes, sir."

"We'll leave before sunrise," Dickinson said to me.

"Yes, sir." I saluted Travis and started to walk out.

"Webber, do not leave him there." Travis pointed to Sutter

on the floor.

"Yes, sir." I lifted Sutter's unconscious body onto my shoulders and left Travis's office.

Taylor was watching us from the balcony of the hospital, wiping his hands on a relatively clean rag.

"What happened to him?"

"He's passed out. He took too many of the pills you gave him. I've recovered the pills and I want you to dispense them."

"I thought he was better than that."

"He is!" I said, glaring at Taylor until he retreated into the hospital.

After depositing Sutter's unconscious body on his bunk, I covered him with a blanket and started packing for the trip to Goliad. I thought about how history portrayed Colonel Fannin and realized convincing him would not be easy. His self-confidence, bordering on arrogance, got most of his command killed. History recorded that he was the last to die after watching his unarmed men being shot, any survivors bayoneted. Words might not be enough for Fannin. Shotgun diplomacy might work, but shooting a colonel would look bad, and I didn't want to have to fight my way out of there. I had to think of another way to convince him to reinforce us.

I climbed the ladder to the west wall and met with Sergeant Wright.

"I've made arrangements to send you to General Houston's camp to convince him to bring his three hundred fifty men here. I'm going with Captain Dickinson to Goliad to get Colonel Fannin and his four hundred men. We'll sneak out before sunrise tomorrow."

"What about the squad?" Wright asked.

"Sutter can't ride a horse with his injuries, so I'll leave him in charge."

"If anyone can convince Colonel Fannin, you can. But I'm not sure I can convince a general to do anything."

"When Houston hears we've held but we need his help, he should agree to join us. Use your rifle to convince him."

"Don't worry, I won't shoot him," Wright said with a smile.

"Thanks. I'll brief Sutter when he wakes up."

"I saw you carrying him to the barracks. What happened?"

"Suffice it to say he's feeling no pain." Wright didn't comment, but he smiled and shook his head. "We'll take as much ammo and MREs as we think we'll need."

"How far am I going?"

"I don't know. You'll have to ask those who're going with you. For me, it's about ninety miles to Goliad, so four MREs and four clips of ammo will be enough. I forgot to ask, can you ride a horse?"

"I've ridden a horse many times on my grandpa's ranch in Wyoming."

"Good. We'll meet with Travis at 0500 hours tomorrow for our final instructions. Go see Travis now, and find out who he's sending to Houston's camp. Then pack what you'll need and be ready to leave before turning in tonight. I'll walk around and let the squad know what we're doing. I don't want our plans getting out over the radio again," I said, checking my radio to verify I was not on VOX again.

CHAPTER 7

DAY SIX – SUNDAY FEBRUARY 28, 1836

With anxious anticipation, I rolled out of my bunk when the alarm on my watch woke me at 0430 hours. I was packing for the ride when Sergeant Wright walked into the barracks.

"Sarge, they say it's about seventy miles to General Houston's camp, so we're getting an early start. I've been told only a few people know General Houston's exact location."

"It's northeast of here; somewhere near Gonzales. Did you pack your wet weather gear, extra socks, ammo, and MREs?"

"I've got everything I need."

"Roger that. Keep your eyes open for Mexican patrols. Good luck."

When I finished dressing, I gently woke Sergeant Sutter.

"How do you feel?"

"My back hurts something fierce." He strained painfully when I helped him to his feet.

"Get with Taylor for your pills. I'm leaving you in charge of the squad."

"Why?"

"I'm going to Goliad. Travis wants to deliver messages to General Houston and Colonel Fannin to get them to reinforce us."

"I know how to manage horses. Sergeant Wright should take charge of the squad."

"Since you can't ride because of your back, I sent Sergeant Wright to get General Houston. He left a few minutes ago. Captain Dickinson and I are taking messages to Colonel Fannin. I've been told it's about ninety miles, so I expect to be gone about three or four days. I've already informed the squad of what's happening and that you're in charge. Maintain radio silence and keep an eye on the Mexicans while they pick up their dead. Stay close to Colonel Travis, and hold the fort," I ordered as I escorted him to the hospital stairs.

When I arrived at the corral, Dickinson was saddling his horse and pointed to the one I was to use. After a struggle getting mine prepared, we guided our horses to Travis's headquarters. When we walked in, we almost bumped into Sergeant Major Williamson and one other soldier who was already there.

"This is Sergeant Badillo from Seguin's Cavalry Company," Travis said. "He'll lead you to Goliad because he knows the area. Captain Dickinson, take this message to Colonel Fannin and make sure he reads it. Wait for his answer before you return. Sergeant Webber, I expect you will convince Fannin of who you are and have him come here."

"Sir, Fannin might not want to leave his fort, mostly because he has about forty men in his hospital who are unable to ride," I said.

"Convince him to come here. We need him and his men. Considering Bowie's improving condition, I could leave him in command and go with you myself; but your Corporal Taylor knows his medicine, and he's convinced me to stay here." Travis looked at the splint on his arm, grimacing when he flexed his hand.

"Sir, I left Sergeant Sutter in charge of my men until I get back. I told him to stay close to you, so he can relay messages if necessary."

"Good. Be on your way. Good luck, and bring Fannin back with you," Travis said.

When I started to guide my horse toward the south gate, Dickinson said, "Not that way. We'll go through the east entrance and turn north."

"Wouldn't it be faster going directly south?" I said.

"Santa Anna will have patrols out there, and he will have reinforced the area around him to keep us from capturing him," Dickinson said. "We'll go north for a while before turning southeast."

"After the last battle, he won't have many horses left for patrols." Dickinson looked at me, and was about to say something, but I said, "Okay, let's check with my men on the north wall and ask what they saw last night."

When we walked to the north wall, I handed the reins to Badillo and met Carpenter, who was on guard duty.

"Anything out there?"

"Nope. No sounds, no movement, nothing. Even the wounded are quiet."

"They're probably dead," I said, as an unexpected shudder rattled my body.

I used my night vision goggles to slowly survey the area. There was no discernable movement, but what surprised me most was that the cannon battery was unmanned. No effort was being made to repair the damage we'd done.

"We're ready to leave. If you see any movement at all, let me know until we go over the rise behind the cannons. If there's anything beyond that, I'll report our situation and you can cover us in case we have to come back in a hurry. If I don't report, assume we're on our way. We should be back in about three or four days. I'll make contact when we're within radio range again. Until then, maintain radio silence."

"Roger that. Good luck, Sarge."

"We'll walk the horses over the rise. I don't want the horses to trip over the bodies out there," Sergeant Badillo said before we mounted.

We guided our horses out the east entrance and walked them north. I intently watched the area with my night vision goggles and listened for reports of movement from Carpenter. Thankfully, none were forthcoming.

When we approached the unmanned cannons I shook my head, because Santa Anna must have consolidated his remaining forces so tightly for his own protection, he left these important pieces of battlefield equipment unguarded, even though they had been disabled. As we walked past them, I belatedly thought we should've had someone bring the cannons into the Alamo while it was still dark. That way, they couldn't have been repaired and put back into service. I could've reported to Carpenter, but Thompson's radio would hear it and know what we were doing. I hoped it didn't come back and bite me in the ass.

When we topped the rise, we saw the bodies of Mexican soldiers in a guard pit. I mentally complimented Sergeant Wright, because he'd dropped a grenade into the pit from four hundred meters away.

Sergeant Badillo suddenly spurred his horse into a gallop and we quickly followed. I had to admit, it was exhilarating riding headlong on the large animal. I was certainly getting much needed riding experience, but I didn't have the confidence to release my hand from the saddle just yet.

The phrase "riding a horse" was a misnomer. To ride, you're supposed to sit like you would in a car. To ride a horse, you don't sit; you stand in the stirrups, flexing your legs like shock absorbers as you speed along. I guess my legs were too short because I couldn't stand up, so I sat and bounded along in the saddle.

***

After about an hour of fast riding, Badillo slowed us to a walking pace, giving the horses a walking rest and the chance to catch their breath. To someone like me, who was unaccustomed to horse riding, my body was one mass of pain, but I kept it to myself. I took advantage of the break to turn off my radio to conserve batteries.

"If we can keep this pace, we'll be in Goliad before sundown," Badillo said.

"So soon?" I asked.

"We've already covered about twenty miles."

"I thought we'd have to camp somewhere on the way," I said, genuinely surprised by the projected speed and endurance of the horses.

"We'll continue the hard ride until we get to Goliad," Dickinson said. "After we deliver Travis's message, we'll water and feed the horses and rest overnight. We'll leave before sunrise tomorrow, and if all goes well, we could be back by tomorrow night." He reached into his pocket and pulled out what looked like a thick piece of bread.

"What's that?"

"Hardtack," he mumbled as he gnawed off a piece and

stuffed it back in his pocket. Apparently, hardtack didn't spoil even when left unwrapped in a pocket. I considered opening an MRE, but decided against it because of the horse bouncing me around.

***

The rest of the ride was uneventful, which surprised me. I constantly watched for Mexican patrols but didn't see any.

The sun was just above the horizon when we approached Fort Defiance in Goliad. Like the Alamo, Fort Defiance was a reinforced church. I hadn't studied this portion of the Battle for Texas Independence with as much intensity as I now realized I should have. I'd have to adapt with the knowledge I had.

We were watched, but not challenged by guards as we trotted through the open gate. We stopped and dismounted in front of a low building guarded by two riflemen.

"Sergeant Badillo, make sure the horses are watered," Dickinson said.

When we approached the door, one of the guards said, "No muskets in the colonel's office."

When Dickinson was disarming himself, one of the guards reached for my M16. I grabbed his wrist, twisted his arm behind him, pinned him against the wall, and said, "That's mine. You can't have it."

Normally I was confident with the things I did because I usually had time to think them through beforehand. When the other guard placed the muzzle of his musket against my arm, my confidence fled. During the seconds when the soldier thought he had me restrained and under his control, the brief respite gave me the moment I needed to think.

"General Dickinson, get this man under control!"

In my peripheral vision I saw the soldier holding me turn his head to look for a general. Steeling myself for the explosive click-bang I thought was sure to follow when I spun around, I knocked the musket away and kneed him in the groin. When he doubled over, I wrenched the musket from his grasp and quickly turned it on the soldier I'd pinned against the wall, then backed up to cover both soldiers.

"What is happening out here?" an officer shouted when he stepped out of Fannin's door.

"Major Mitchell, this man refuses to be disarmed." The kicked soldier groaned and pointed at me from his doubled over position.

"Sir, get your men under control." I kept the flintlock trained on the soldiers.

"What are you?" Major Mitchell asked, looking me over. "I don't recognize your uniform."

"Sir, I'll be happy to explain, but your men must be under your control first."

"Give me the musket," the major ordered.

I disarmed myself, sort of, by handing the flintlock to the major. I hoped the shorter M16, cross-slung across my back, wouldn't be immediately recognized as a rifle.

"Come in."

"Major, he still has— ahh…!" the soldier exclaimed when I twisted his arm as he reached for my rifle again.

"I told you, that's mine! You can't have it." I released his arm and pushed him away before quickly following Dickinson inside.

Sitting behind a rough desk I recognized Colonel Fannin from a picture in an Alamo history book I'd once read. At the time I saw the picture I remembered thinking he looked wimpy. The picture didn't do him justice, because he didn't look that way now. He looked more robust.

Fannin looked me over, and said, "Looks like another drunken fool trying to join my army. Who are you, and why are you here?"

"I'm Captain Dickinson, and this is Sergeant Webber. We have a dispatch from Colonel Travis." He reached into a pouch and presented a folded paper to Fannin.

Before Fannin opened it, he said, "If Travis wants me to reinforce him, I won't."

"You tried once, and gave up after only one day," I interjected.

Fannin scowled at me when he unfolded and read the dispatch. "So, Travis held Bexar. Why does he need my help? Perhaps Santa Anna is not as good a general as he makes himself out to be."

"During the attack, we lost forty-eight men," Dickinson said. "We might not be able hold against another attack without reinforcements."

"You're the Sergeant Webber Travis wrote about in this dispatch," Fannin said, looking at me and tapping the paper with his finger. "He says I should listen to you. Why should I?"

During our ride, I'd thought about contingencies during our visit, and I was as prepared as I was going to be.

"Sir, has Colonel Francis Johnson's patrol returned from San Patricio yet?"

"Francis? His name is Frank," Fannin said.

"Actually, sir, his given name is Francis White Johnson."

"How do you know I sent Colonel Johnson on a patrol?"

"Sir, Mexican General Urrea's advance units surprised Colonel Johnson's patrol near San Patricio before sunrise yesterday morning. Urrea's forces killed sixteen of Johnson's men, and took twenty-four prisoners. Johnson and five others escaped, and they will return here in a day or so. When he returns here, he'll tell you that all twenty-four of the prisoners had been executed, when in fact, they were taken to Matamoros and sentenced to death. But they'll be released in late March."

"You can't possibly know that unless you're a spy for Santa Anna," Fannin stated firmly.

"I assure you, sir, I'm no spy, but I do know the history of the fight for Texas Independence."

"Do you now? What are the names of the men who supposedly escaped with Colonel Johnson?" Fannin asked.

"I believe their names are Beck, Hufty, Love, Miller, and Toler." I hoped I'd remembered their names correctly.

Fannin looked at Major Mitchell, and then said to me, "How do you know this?"

"Sergeant Webber, think of another way to tell him!" Dickinson warned.

"Captain, there's no way to explain our unique situation except with the truth. Colonel Fannin, I'm from the future. And I can prove it, with this," I said, quickly unslinging my rifle from my back, holding it up for him to see.

"How did you get that musket in here?" Mitchell exclaimed. Fannin held up his hand to Mitchell, silencing him.

"I've never seen a musket like that. Give it to me."

"Sir, before I do, I'd like to demonstrate its operation. After you've seen its capabilities, I'll let you fire it. Will you agree to this?" I asked, hoping to gain his confidence, like I had with Travis.

"What kind of demonstration?" Fannin asked suspiciously.

"Sir, if you could get three of your best riflemen, I'll give you a demonstration you'll never forget, and I assure you, Colonel, I will embarrass your men," I said, not intentionally meaning to challenge Fannin, but I belatedly realized it came out that way.

"Will you now? I have the best riflemen in *Tejas*."

"Shall we see?" I asked, extending my hand toward the door.

When we walked outside, Fannin said, "Major Mitchell, get three men over here."

While Major Mitchell shouted for volunteers for the demonstration, I walked to a clear space against an adobe wall, picked up a rock, and scratched a large circle on the adobe. Then I paced across the compound to Fannin and said, "Sir, can your men hit that circle over there? It's about thirty met…yards."

Fannin gave me a look like I had just insulted his command. Then he said, "I could hit it with a rock from here."

"Yes, sir."

When three men with their muskets arrived, I said, "Colonel Fannin, do you have a pocket watch?"

"Yes," he replied, and pulled it out from his small watch pocket.

"I'd like your men to fire at that circle as fast as they can for one minute. Can they do that?" I realized I had to stop challenging Fannin. "Please have them load and prepare to fire. When they're ready, tell them when to fire and time them. When they're done, I'll show you what I can do with this," I said, cradling the rifle against my chest.

"Major Mitchell, are the men ready?" Fannin demanded.

"Yes, sir. They heard the instructions."

"Very well. Make ready! Take aim! Fire!"

The three men were experienced and accurate with their muskets as I counted the rounds fired. After one minute, Fannin called, "Hold fire!"

"Sir, from what I saw, all eleven rounds hit in the circle. I'll demonstrate my rifle now. I'll put twenty rounds in that circle in less than fifteen seconds." The look of disbelief on Fannin's face reminded me that I had to get hubris under control. It might provoke Fannin in a way I didn't want.

Fannin looked at his watch, and said, "Make ready! Take aim! Fire!"

True to my training and rifle capability, I unleashed the promised twenty rounds into the circle. After clearing the rifle and making it safe, I said, "Want to give it a try?"

Briefly stunned, Fannin looked at Major Mitchell, and said, "Give it to me."

When I held it out to Fannin, he snatched it out of my hand, looked it over, and said, "This is what held the San Antonio de Valero mission?"

"Sir, there are ten more rifles just like this one, with my men who are trained to use them. Colonel Travis is waiting for you and your men to reinforce him. When can I tell Colonel Travis you're going to arrive?"

Fannin gruffly threw my rifle at me and said, "Come inside."

"Sir, do you want to fire the rifle?"

"Inside, now!"

I wondered what was on Fannin's mind when Major Mitchell, Dickinson, Badillo, and I followed Fannin into his office. One thing was certain—the way he'd returned my rifle gave me a bad feeling. I didn't relish the idea of fighting my way out of the fort, but just in case things got out of hand, I covertly slipped a loaded magazine into the rifle and closed the colonel's door behind us.

Sauntering to his desk, Fannin said, "You can tell Travis I will stay here and defend my command. I will not abandon my men in the hospital, nor will I abandon the men I have on patrol. Travis will have to do what he can without me."

I removed my helmet and rubbed my short-cropped hair in disbelief. How could he throw away his life and the lives of all the men under his command like this?

"Sir, I understand your position. Like I said, I'm not drunk. I'm from the future, and I have knowledge of what'll happen to you and your men if you stay here. Do you want me to tell you what I know will happen if you don't leave?"

After a thoughtful moment, he narrowed his eyes at me and said, "Yes, tell me."

"What I'm going to describe will be called the battle of Coleto Creek. On March nineteenth, after receiving reports of the Mexican army advancing on your position here, you will order a retreat."

"What? I will never retreat!" Fannin shouted.

"You will attempt to transport nine cannon, more than five hundred spare muskets, and all the supplies and baggage you can pack into your wagons. You will travel about six miles before calling a halt to rest your animals. At about three that afternoon, Mexican cavalry will overtake you and your men. You will form a hollow square with your wagons, and place cannons in each corner for defense when General Urrea's main force arrives and attacks. After a battle lasting into the night, the Mexicans will lose about two-hundred killed and wounded. You will see nine of your men killed and sixty wounded. You will be wounded in the leg. The next morning, you will surrender your command to try and save your men."

"I will never surrender!"

"The Mexicans will bring you and the survivors back here, where everyone will be held as prisoners. General Urrea will send a dispatch to Santa Anna and ask for clemency for your men. Despite the appeal, Santa Anna will order Colonel Portilla, who is traveling with Urrea, to execute everyone. The survivors who can walk will be marched out of the fort, where they will be shot between two rows of Mexican soldiers."

"That cannot be true. Santa Anna must respect the law of war. Even he cannot execute prisoners."

"Sir, Santa Anna convinced Mexico's Minister of War, José Maria Tornel y Mendívil, to write what will be called the Tornel Decree. The decree states that all foreigners bearing arms against the government of Mexico will be treated as pirates and killed immediately without trial. Santa Anna is exceeding the decree by executing anyone, including his own countrymen, who are seen carrying a musket or pistol."

Fannin looked directly in my eyes, and after an uncomfortable pause said, "What else would you have me believe?" The tone of his voice gave me a subtle warning I didn't dare ignore.

"Sir, you will be forced to watch your men being killed. The sick and wounded who cannot walk will be executed where they lie. You will be taken to the courtyard in front of the church, blindfolded, and tied to a chair because you won't be able to stand. You will make three requests; you'll ask for your personal possessions to be sent to your family, to be shot in your heart, and to be given a Christian burial. Mexican soldiers will keep your belongings, shoot you in the face, and burn your body along with the bodies of your men."

Fannin leaned forward and placed his elbows on his desk with his right fist balled in his left hand, drilling me with his eyes. Having already made my decision about what I'd have to do when the conversation ended, I tightened my hands on my rifle.

"Sir, Colonel Travis trusts this man," Dickinson said, attempting to defuse the situation he also saw brewing. "I trust him as well. He has shown us that his men are well trained soldiers. They stood on the walls with us when we fought Santa Anna, and we won. But Santa Anna will not leave Bexar despite his losses during the battle."

"How many men did Santa Anna lose?" Fannin asked, not taking his eyes from mine.

"Sir, we estimate over a thousand killed and wounded," Dickinson said.

"Estimate? Did you go outside the walls and make an accurate count?"

"No, sir. Santa Anna still has a strong army in Bexar ready to kill anyone who moves," Dickinson reported.

"I do not believe you; either of you!"

"Captain Dickinson, we'd better leave. Travis will want the bad news as soon as possible," I said, realizing we'd lost any measure of control.

"You're not going anywhere," Fannin declared, standing and then leaning forward on his desk with his balled fists supporting him.

"Sir, we must get back to Colonel Travis and inform him of your decision," I said, already prepared for the worst possible scenario.

"You're not going anywhere! I think you're spies for Santa Anna! Major Mitchell, arrest these men and lock them up."

With a quick move, I hit the colonel solidly against his head with my rifle butt. As he fell unconscious to the floor, I trained my rifle on Major Mitchell.

"Major, don't make a sound, or you'll die where you stand," I stated as Mitchell slowly raised his hands.

"Webber, what are you doing?" Dickinson exclaimed.

"Sorry, captain. Badillo, gag and tie the major…do it!" While he was being secured, I said, "Major, I'm sorry about this. I would've liked to have Fannin's cooperation, but as you saw, he left us no choice. General Urrea will be here in a few days, and

I'm not going to rot in jail, only to be killed when Urrea arrives and overruns this place. Like I said, Johnson and five of his men will return in a day or two. When they do, you must be here when they report to the colonel."

"You killed the colonel," Mitchell said before he was gagged.

"No, sir, he's just knocked out. You must remind the colonel about what I said, and what Johnson will tell him. I hope the colonel will come to his senses and decide to reinforce Travis. If he does, have him approach from the northeast, not through Bexar. Santa Anna's army occupies the town with over a thousand men, with more on the way. Captain, let's get out of here while we still can."

Dickinson opened the door and strode out with false confidence. I chose to leave last, and before I closed the door behind me, I turned and said, "Thank you for your time, Colonel Fannin. I'm sure Colonel Travis will be disappointed with your decision." I hoped our calm exit from Fannin's office would give us the time we needed to peacefully leave the fort.

While Dickinson and Badillo recovered their weapons, I untied my horse's reins from a nearby post, mounted, and as casually as possible rode toward the still open gates. Dickinson and Badillo quickly followed, passing me at a gallop when we cleared the gates and disappeared into the gathering darkness.

After a short run, Dickinson shouted, "Slow down! Walk the horses so we can hear if we're being followed. Webber, why did you hit Fannin?"

"Did you hear what he said? Did you even listen? Before he read the dispatch, he said he wouldn't reinforce Travis. His reactions were those of an arrogant, overconfident officer. He's been given a command of his own, and because he's partially trained, he thinks he has something to prove. When he ordered our arrest, I had to act. I wasn't going to be in his jail when Urrea gets here."

"Travis might throw you in our jail," Dickinson predicted.

"I expect you'll give him an accurate report. Even then, I think Travis will be angry with Fannin because he won't help."

"Captain, if we stay on the trail, we can walk the horses all night. There's enough moonlight to see if we don't ride too fast," Badillo suggested.

"We'll keep moving. We have to tell Travis what happened as soon as possible."

CHAPTER 8

DAY SEVEN – MONDAY FEBRUARY 29, 1836

Being in the saddle all day yesterday, and then through most of the night, the rhythmic motion of the horse's walk had galled my knees and calves and made my back ache. The pain gave me a healthy respect for the men of this time who were adapted to their life here, as I was adapted to mine in the future.

When we stopped at a stream to water and rest the horses, I would have thought getting off the horse would be a thankful experience. Instead, it amounted to a monumental effort, beginning when I tried to dismount by swinging my leg over the horse's back. Failing that, I stood as high as I could in the stirrup and used my hand to help drag my leg over. With neither leg cooperating with balance, my hand slipped off the saddle and I fell to the ground with my foot caught in the stirrup.

"You're lucky the horse is tired," Dickinson said when he walked over to me. "If he started running, you would get dragged by him."

"Thanks for the advice. Can I have some help?"

"You're no horseman," Dickinson commented when he

removed my foot from the stirrup.

"This is not the kind of riding I'm used to," I said, relieved that I was completely off the saddle. I thought the horse was annoyed with me as well, because he turned his head and snorted at me before walking to the stream for a drink.

"How long before we get to the Alamo?" I said, realizing that lying on the cold ground was becoming increasingly comfortable.

"The horses are tired, so we'll continue a walking pace until sunrise when we can see where we're going, and then an easy gallop will get us there after midday," Badillo said.

"How long before the sun comes up?" I asked.

"About four hours. Get on your feet, or you won't be able to when we need to ride," Dickinson commanded, offering his hand to me.

With a groan from me, and a combined effort from Badillo and Dickinson, I was helped to my feet. Actually, it felt better to stand, where I was better able to stretch out my cramped muscles on straightened legs.

"Eat. You haven't had anything since yesterday morning," Dickinson ordered when he reached into his pocket for his hardtack.

When I opened my MRE, Dickinson went to my horse and made an adjustment on the saddle.

"What're you doing?" I asked.

"I'm cinching the buckles higher because the stirrup leather is too long for you. Stand in the stirrups when we mount again. You'll ride easier," Dickinson mumbled with hardtack clenched in his teeth as he made the adjustment with practiced hands.

When we finished our meals and the horses had drunk their fill, we took the reins and walked the horses along the road, listening for any movement. After about hour, we mounted and rode in the dark at the horses' walking pace. The adjustments Dickinson had made to my saddle were welcome, because I was able to stand and get some relief from some of the most painfully abraded parts of my body.

***

When the sun began to rise we were able to quicken our pace. When we passed huts and farms, I noticed there was a single light in only one window. Otherwise, they appeared to be abandoned.

"Captain Dickinson, we haven't seen any Mexican patrols, or anyone else for that matter, since we began our ride," I said.

"Good. We won't have to fight to get back."

"It could be bad. I think Santa Anna is consolidating his forces, pulling in patrols, having his officers push the scattered pieces of his army to get to the Bexar as soon as possible. There could be a big fight to take the Alamo; bigger than we can handle without reinforcements."

"We'll have time to prepare before he attacks, and I'm sure General Houston will join us. You said he has about three hundred fifty men. With your men, it will help."

"Sir, Santa Anna's last attack caught us by surprise."

"Seeing your men fight like they did tells me we can win against whatever Santa Anna attacks us with."

"Sir, in all honesty, we were extremely lucky we weren't overrun. When the ammo for our rifles runs out and our grenades are gone, our advantage will be gone with it. We'll have to learn to use muskets like everyone else."

"I'll have Sergeant Major Williamson teach you to use a musket; then you can train your men with it."

Something to look forward to—learning from the sergeant major who I was sure hated me.

***

It was late in the afternoon when we approached the area of the Alamo. We rode toward the northeast to avoid any Mexican patrols near Bexar, then we turned south to approach the Alamo. Despite the armistice I had been expecting gunfire, but there was none to be heard. The quiet worried me, because the Alamo could've been overrun while we were gone. I wanted to contact Sutter, but I had to wait until we were ready to approach the walls. No need to get shot by friendly fire with an unannounced, headlong gallop toward the walls.

Badillo stopped us and said, "Wait here." Dismounting his horse, he ran up a rise and then lay on the ground, crawling to the hillcrest. He carefully looked around for a few minutes, then crawled back down and ran to us.

"Captain, there are no Mexicans that I could see in any direction," Badillo reported, mounting his horse again.

"Did you see anyone on the walls?" Dickinson said.

"Yes, sir. The cannons we passed yesterday are gone, but the dead are still there."

"Sir, some historians from my time labeled Santa Anna as a murderous monster. Looks like he used the armistice to recover his cannons, but left his wounded to die."

"Badillo, can we get to the walls without a fight?" Dickinson asked.

"Yes, sir, but we should ride hard to get there."

"Wait! Let me contact my men to let them know we're coming." I turned on my radio and keyed the mike. "Sergeant Sutter, are you there?"

"Sarge? I'm here. Where are you?"

"Alert the north wall that three riders will come in through the east entrance."

"This is Carpenter. There hasn't been any activity to our north

since you left, other than Santa Anna moving the north cannons."

"This is Sutter. The east entrance is open. You're clear to come in."

"Roger that. Sir, they know we're coming, and they've opened the east entrance."

"Let's ride!" Dickinson shouted, and kicked his horse into a gallop.

We charged over the hill, riding hard and fast toward the wall. I looked around for Mexican cavalry to appear and pursue us, but none were anywhere to be seen. I almost expected the men lying on the ground to suddenly spring up and start shooting at us. It could be the type of ruse Santa Anna might use.

We made the turn, galloped through the entrance, and inside the safety of the walls. The entrance was hurriedly blocked when we stopped in front of Travis's headquarters.

"Badillo, take the horses to the corral. They've earned a rest and a feeding. Sergeant Webber, you will say nothing until I have finished my report to Travis. Do you understand?" Dickinson said when we walked to Travis's headquarters.

"Yes, sir."

When we knocked on the door and walked in, Travis, Williamson, and Sutter were there.

"Sergeant Webber, stand there! Do not speak! Do not move!" Dickinson said, jabbing his finger at the spot where I was to stand in front of Travis's desk.

I stepped up to Travis's desk and came to the position of attention, unmoving, unspeaking, head and eyes to the front. Sutter looked confused by the order, and I was sure he was wondering what I'd done this time.

"Fannin will not come to help us, and it's Webber's doing," Dickinson said.

"Sir, Fannin got your first message and tried—"

"Do you have a problem following orders...Sergeant?" Dickinson said to me.

"No, sir!"

"What happened?" Travis asked.

"When we arrived, Webber would not surrender his rifle as ordered by Fannin. He twisted the arm of a soldier who tried to take it. Another soldier nearly shot Webber until he took the musket from him. When we went inside Fannin's headquarters, I gave him your dispatch, but he said he would not help us. Webber demonstrated his rifle for Fannin, but he refused to believe Webber was from the future—"

"As did we all, at first," Travis observed.

"We tried to leave, but Webber knocked Fannin out with his rifle, and we had to leave in a hurry to get back here."

"Captain Dickinson, I thought you were going to give an accurate report to our commanding officer," I stated from my position of attention.

"You will not speak again!" Dickinson shouted, inches from my ear.

"Captain Dickinson, stand aside," Travis said calmly with a wave of his hand. "Sergeant Webber, what happened?"

Travis's order came in the nick of time, because I was primed to knock Dickinson out, but I forced myself not to follow the impulse. I'd clocked enough officers for one career, and I needed his cooperation. Besides, Sergeant Major Williamson was standing beside Dickinson, and he seemed to get bigger every time I saw him.

"Sir, Captain Dickinson's report is reasonably accurate. After the rifle demonstration, we went into Fannin's office. I told him about his future, and the future of his command. When I gave him the facts of his future, he lost his temper, accused us of being spies, and ordered Major Mitchell to put us all in jail. I was forced to knock Fannin out with my rifle and tied Major Mitchell up. We then left the fort without further incident," I concluded my very brief report.

"Curse him! I need him here." Travis banged a fist on the table with his uninjured arm. There was no mention of me or what I'd done, but I was certain I'd hear about it later.

"Webber must be shot for striking an officer," Dickinson said.

"Sir, Fannin doesn't believe what he's up against, and there's nothing we can do about his arrogance, which will kill him and all four hundred of his men. He tried to send men and supplies to you last month, but he abandoned the effort after only one day," I said.

"What are you going to do about Webber?" Dickinson asked.

"Webber, you can go—I will call for you later. And take Sutter with you."

When we walked out the door, we heard Dickinson start to say, "It's a mistake to let him…." The rest of his statement was muffled when the door closed.

"Did you really knock Colonel Fannin out?" Sutter asked as we walked toward the barracks.

"I had to or end up in jail."

"I can't take you anywhere. Is it because of your…?" Sutter started to ask.

"Because of what?"

"Nothing; just rumors."

"What rumors?" I was curious about what he knew, or thought he knew.

"I heard you have post-traumatic stress disorder."

"I've been diagnosed with a mild case of PTSD. Who told you that?"

"Mac mentioned I should keep an eye on you. He didn't say why, but he mentioned some things I should watch for, and if they happened, to report in detail to him. A little research made me suspect what you had. After all we've been through, I'm surprised I don't have symptoms too. What surprises me most is that my head isn't rolling on the ground right now." Sutter smiled weakly.

"That's one of several options still available to me. What happened with Santa Anna while I was gone?"

"Santa Anna was in a hurry to pick up his dead."

"How do you know he was in a hurry?"

"He brought four more wagons, and about a hundred more men to pick up and throw the bodies and wounded together in the wagons. They threw many of the bodies in the river. Just before dark, they ran back across the bridge. This morning he continued clearing bodies, but only on the south side. When he finished clearing the field, he gathered muskets and ammunition. I thought it was a violation of the armistice and I reported it to Travis, but he said not to shoot at them."

"It was probably a good idea not to provoke Santa Anna. After all, he's an honorable man." I noticed my sarcasm was not lost on Sutter when he smiled.

"We saw the cannons being moved from the north and set up across the river on the west side, and they've been working on them ever since. He also moved his other cannons closer to the southwest corner."

"When we came in, I saw bodies still piled up against the north wall. Did Santa Anna do anything about them?"

"No, he hasn't done anything about bodies anywhere except the south."

"What about Thompson?"

"I heard a few reports from him, but we didn't respond because you wanted to maintain radio silence."

"Good. Reports from him were probably bogus anyway. Any word from Sergeant Wright?"

"Nothing yet, but you're back early."

"We rode fast all the way to Goliad and back. We didn't see anyone coming or going; no farmers or ranchers, not even Mexican patrols."

"Can I assume Santa Anna is gathering his forces for a final push against us?"

"That's my guess. It sounds like he cleared the south field so he can attack from there without stumbling over bodies. Have any reinforcements come to help us when I was gone?"

"Four men joined us last night," Sutter said. "They said to expect twenty-five more tonight."

"Does Travis know they're coming?" I asked.

"I was with Travis when the new arrivals told him about it," Sutter confirmed.

"If memory serves—"

"It always does." Sutter interjected.

"There's going to be a storm tonight, so I doubt any reinforcements will get here. It's obvious Santa Anna's got something planned for us, despite the pounding we gave him."

"After you left there was talk you might get killed, and that led to talk about what would happen to us."

"I hope everyone knows I'm not indestructible."

"After you were shot in the head and walked away, they think you are."

"My helmet did its job. Do you think I'm indestructible?" I asked.

"I know you are," Sutter agreed with a smile.

"What about you? How's your back?"

"I want to apologize for my misuse of Taylor's drugs."

"No need to go there. How's your back?"

"I feel it when the pills wear off; but why are you limping?" Sutter looked at my slow walk.

"That horse ride was painful like you can't imagine."

"I don't need to imagine pain," Sutter said, carefully hunching his shoulders.

"Where's Taylor?"

"He's helping in the hospital."

"For as much as I don't want to go up there, I have to."

When I struggled up the steps on painful legs, Taylor was talking to a patient. When he saw me he smiled and said, "You're back early. How was your trip?"

"Fannin won't come," I said disgustedly. "I hope Sergeant Wright has better luck with General Houston."

"You said Fannin might not help. You also said you'd never come up here again."

"That brainless horse tore my ass up."

"If you're up here, I'm sure it did. Drop your pants and we'll see what the damage is."

The expression on Taylor's face said it all as he opened his med bag. Areas on the inside of my knees were rubbed raw, and my thighs and calves were bright red and blistered like a bad sunburn. Taylor sprayed something cold on them that immediately made them feel better.

"That's some good stuff. What is it?"

"It's an analgesic spray. This is an antiseptic," Taylor said, and applied another cold spray over the first. While my legs were partially numb, Taylor gently rubbed a salve on my wounds, and wrapped them in a light bandage.

"Flip over on your stomach. Uh-oh, I'd better check the horse's back."

"That damned horse is on the edge of getting shot," I stated caustically.

He applied the analgesic spray to my ass, and said, "It's not nearly as bad as your legs, but there not much I can do about it except tell you to sit as little as possible. See me every day so I can change the bandages on your legs."

"Roger that. Thanks, Doc."

***

I was resting on my bunk with my legs spread, planning what I would say and do when Travis called for me. I really didn't want to explain my actions to him, but it was necessary to detail the reasons why I'd clubbed Fannin.

Two uniformed soldiers walked in and said Travis wanted to see me. I knew I was in trouble when they ordered me to surrender my rifle. Hesitantly I gave my rifle to Sergeant Sutter and strode like a true bow-legged cowboy across the compound in the fading light of day.

When I knocked and entered Travis's office, Sergeant Major Williamson and Lieutenant Melton were there, sitting with Travis behind his desk that had been moved opposite the door. Beside them were two men with pistols in their belts. I knew this would be a serious meeting because Travis had his hat on.

"Sergeant Webber, stand there. This court-martial will determine your punishment for striking a superior officer; specifically, Colonel Fannin."

I was anticipating a conversation with Travis, but a court-martial? This was completely unexpected.

"Do you want an advocate to speak for you?" Travis asked.

"No, sir. The facts will defend me."

"Very well. We have heard testimony from Captain Dickinson and Sergeant Badillo. Tell us what happened."

"Sir, we entered Fort Defiance late in the day. There were guards outside Colonel Fannin's office demanding that we couldn't see the colonel with our weapons in hand. While Captain Dickinson and Sergeant Badillo were disarming themselves, one of the guards tried to take my rifle. I wouldn't take a chance that it might get lost or stolen, so I refused. I stopped one man from trying to take it from me and was held at gunpoint by another. I shouted for General Dickinson to get the man under control."

"Dickinson is not a general," Melton said. After a confused moment, he nodded and indicated I should continue.

"I disarmed both men and held them at gunpoint when an officer, Major Mitchell, relieved me of the musket and told us to go inside."

"Did anyone inside Colonel Fannin's office try to remove your rifle?" Williamson asked.

"No, Sergeant Major."

He grunted, and said, "Continue."

"In Colonel Fannin's office, Captain Dickinson gave him your dispatch. Before he opened it, he stated he would not reinforce you. When he did read it, he was impressed that you held against Santa Anna, and stated that Santa Anna might not be as good a general as he claims to be. Captain Dickinson reported our losses during the attack, and indicated we could not withstand another attack without reinforcements. Colonel Fannin was skeptical about everything Captain Dickinson and I said. I told Colonel Fannin that one of his patrols, led by Lieutenant Colonel Johnson, was surprised by General Urrea the day before we arrived, and they had been scattered with heavy losses. Some of the patrol escaped and would return to Fort Defiance with a report that several of his men had been captured and were executed. We had a rifle demonstration where three of his men fired eleven rounds into a circle in one minute. I put twenty rounds in the same circle in fifteen seconds."

"You embarrassed Colonel Fannin with your demonstration," Melton said.

"It's possible, yes, sir. When I offered my rifle to Colonel Fannin to shoot, he took it, looked at it, and threw it back at me. He ordered us into his office, where I offered to explain his future to him. He agreed to listen, and became angry when I did. He claimed we were all spies for Santa Anna and ordered Major Mitchell to arrest us and put us in jail. I knocked Colonel Fannin out with my rifle and ordered Major Mitchell to remain quiet while Sergeant Badillo tied and gagged him. I asked that Major Mitchell be available to Colonel Fannin when Colonel Johnson returned from his patrol. I asked that he remind Fannin of what I'd said about Colonel Johnson. We left Colonel Fannin's office, Captain Dickinson and Sergeant Badillo recovered their weapons, and we left the fort without further incident."

"I suspect Colonel Fannin had to counter his embarrassment by putting you in jail," Melton added.

"Sir, it was not my intention to embarrass him. It's just the way things happened."

"Lieutenant Melton, do you have any more questions?"

"No, sir."

"Sergeant Major Williamson?"

"No, sir."

"Guards, take him outside while we decide punishment."

The two guards followed me out and made me stand away from the door where I couldn't overhear what was being said.

My mind was whirling with what I had to do. I wished I'd set my radio to VOX so the squad could hear what was happening. I was certain that Sutter, with the squad in support, would back me up no matter what decision Travis made. But that was too fanciful, even for me. I'd struck an officer, and that was unacceptable at the best of times, future or past. I suddenly remembered a story my mother had told me about my dad, who had a knock down, drag out fight with his commanding officer, and he spent seven days in the stockade with loss of rank and pay. Like father, like son I guessed.

After painfully pacing for a lot longer than I wanted to endure, Travis shouted for the guards to escort me back in.

With guards at my back and the two others standing with their hands on their pistols, Colonel Travis said, "Stand there, Sergeant Webber. There are differences between your testimony and Captain Dickinson's. Sergeant Badillo's testimony follows yours more closely than Captain Dickinson's. This court-martial has considered Captain Dickinson's request that you be shot as a warning to others who attack a superior officer. Do you want to add anything to your statements that may sway the conclusion of this court martial?"

"No, sir."

"Because this court is split in its judgment, the majority will prevail. Because you struck a superior officer, I order you to be placed in jail for thirty days. I know you to be an honorable and trustworthy man, and I expect you will report for your sentence after we win against Santa Anna. This court-martial is now closed."

"Thank you, sir. Would you like to know what will happen tonight?"

"This is one of several reasons why I do not want him shot," Travis said to Williamson. "What will happen tonight, Sergeant

Webber?"

"History says there'll be a storm tonight with heavy rain and strong winds. Tomorrow, it will clear and turn cold. You might want to tell the men it's coming so they can prepare."

"Sergeant Major, inform the men. Make sure the horses are tied securely, and close and lock all doors and shutters. Sergeant Webber, you're dismissed." Travis took off his hat and leaned back in his chair.

It was dark when I walked across the compound and keyed my radio. I was ready to tell the squad about the storm, but instead, I walked to every man in the squad who were on the walls and sent them all to the barracks. When I arrived, I told them about the coming storm, face to face. I didn't want Thompson to hear about it over the radio and inform Santa Anna. I also told the men not to say anything about the storm to anyone else. I had unintentionally pissed Williamson off with radio messages to the squad, who were then telling his men what I'd said before he could notify them. Because Travis had looked at Williamson when I volunteered information about the storm, I knew Williamson had voted to have me shot instead of jailed.

Considering our situation with low ammunition, we'd be in deep trouble unless we got considerable reinforcements. The Mexicans having been beaten in battle and then ordered to stay and pick up their dead and wounded would have a huge effect on their morale. With the coming storm, Santa Anna would be in the cathedral where he'd be comfortably bunked. I knew his army didn't have what they needed to keep dry and warm against the rain and cold I knew was coming. No matter how well-trained soldiers were, they would begin to feel sorry for themselves when morale started a downhill slide. I wondered if the Mexican rank and file knew how Santa Anna felt about them; like so many chickens to be sacrificed for victory. One thing was certain—after their last attack, they had proved there were no chickens in Santa Anna's army. I must use every tool, every scrap of experience I had to keep my men out of harm's way for as long as possible.

CHAPTER 9

DAY EIGHT – TUESDAY MARCH 1, 1836

The storm hit with a violence I'd never experienced before. Even indoors the lightning was blinding, thunder shook the walls, and unbelievably heavy rain found its way through every crack in the tightly closed windows and doors. What bothered me most were the horses. Their panicked screaming mimicked the sounds of dying men. In anticipation of the storm I'd rotated every man in the squad, one at a time on the southwest corner, limiting them to one hour shifts beside the eighteen-pounder cannon. When we came back from our shifts, we were soaked to the skin despite the rain suits and boots we wore.

By sunrise the rain had finally ended, and the sky was clearing, but the weather had turned bitterly cold. My guess was it was near freezing, not helped by an icy wind blowing. Everyone was hunkered down close to the parapets trying to stay warm, occasionally peeking over the walls for any movement.

Before I set the squad on their daily watch, I made sure they were wearing dry clothes and their rain boots. The boots would keep their feet dry in the muddy quagmire the rain had created in the compound. I also encouraged everyone to use the ropes from their shelter halves to hang their wet clothes on.

***

As the day wore on I decided to warm the squad up a bit and had them do in-place exercises. I was not heartless, at least not totally, so I had everyone do the exercises on the scaffolds. There were those within our company who'd have delighted in having everyone down in the mud to do physical training exercises—after all, we were infantry. But it was well known in our company that the officers and senior NCOs would be down in the mud with us.

Sutter and I were checking the squad when a crackle of static tore across our radios, followed by a faint, unintelligible voice.

"Don't answer!" I exclaimed when I saw Sutter reaching for his radio key.

"It might be Sergeant Wright."

"If it is, we don't want to give him away with crosstalk Thompson or Hernández might pick up. I'll head over to the church to get better reception. If it is Sergeant Wright, we'll give him all the help we can to get him back here."

A few minutes later, distant gunfire from the east got our attention over the whistling wind. A burst of static tore across my radio; then I heard, *"Staff Sergeant Webber, are you there?"*

"I'm here. Where are you?"

"East! We have the Alamo in sight! We're being chased by a Mexican patrol! We have wounded!"

"Come straight in through the east entrance. We'll cover you."

"This is Taylor. I'm moving to the east entrance."

"Taylor, tell Pollard wounded are coming in," I said as I ran down the ramp.

"Already done!"

"First Squad, give me two on the wall at the east entrance; give me two on the wall in the corral. Sutter, Ruiz, go up the ramp in the church. Prepare to give cover fire to reinforcements coming in from the east! No grenades!"

I was running to Travis's headquarters when Travis, alerted by the commotion and gunfire, was leaving his office. I shouted, "Sir! General Houston's coming in the east entrance! I have my men on the walls ready to give cover fire when they're in range."

"Good. Come with me." We trotted to the east entrance as it was being opened.

The squad opened fire on the Mexican patrol following General Houston and his men, causing them to rein their horses to a stop. There was a bottleneck at the entrance when riders had to enter single file to get through the narrow opening. Those who were caught outside the walls turned their horses and fired on the Mexican cavalry, exposing themselves to Mexican pistol fire while protecting their comrades as they filed into the compound.

When everyone was safely inside, Sergeant Wright dismounted and walked to me.

"Sergeant Wright, do you need a medic?"

"Negative, I'm good."

"Report."

"We started out with about two hundred and fifty men two days ago. When we saw the storm coming, General Houston decided to camp and wait it out. Just as we dismounted, we were jumped by Mexican cavalry. We had to ride all night through the storm to stay ahead of the cavalry. A lot of men got lost in the dark."

"You got back safely with General Houston, that's what counts. Was it hard to convince him to leave his camp?"

"He's decisive to say the least. He read Colonel Travis's letter, then he sat with me and listened to what I had to say. When I demonstrated my rifle and let him fire it, he asked if there are any more of them. When I said there were ten more here, he told his men to break camp and prepare to ride that afternoon instead of waiting for morning," Wright said, concluding his report.

"I need Travis in the hospital," Taylor said over the radio.

"What's wrong?" I asked.

"Get him up here!"

Looking around, I found Travis talking to some of the officers who'd arrived with Houston.

"Sir, Corporal Taylor requires you in the hospital."

"I just heard General Houston is wounded. Find Lieutenant Melton and have him make room for Houston's men," Travis told me before he walked to the hospital.

While I was looking for Lieutenant Melton among the mass of men and horses, I spotted Sergeant Major Williamson. I told him what had to be done, and sent him looking for Lieutenant Melton. If Melton needed to bunk people with Williamson, who had his own private room in the barracks, I didn't want to be the one to tell him.

"Sergeant Wright, is there anything else to report?" I asked when I located him again.

"There are about seventy-five men and women following with supply wagons at least four days behind. We should send out some riders to cover them, and warn them about the cavalry."

"It might be a while before Travis leaves the hospital."

"What happened to Travis?" Wright asked.

"Nothing, but General Houston is wounded."

"He looked okay when we entered the gate."

"Taylor won't say how he was wounded over the radio. We'll

have to wait until we can ask Travis what to do about the supply wagons. You'll have to give him a report, so keep it as brief as possible. Until then, let's find out how many reinforcements we have."

When we were able to get the count among the horses and men milling around in the plaza, we found that seventy-three had made it into the Alamo with General Houston. The rest had either been killed by Mexican cavalry or got lost during the storm. I knew there were about three hundred fifty men in Houston's camp, and I hoped those who survived would eventually find their way here. To insure reinforcements wouldn't accidentally get shot, Wright and I spread the word around the scaffolds to watch for stragglers arriving at any hour of the day or night.

***

"Sergeant Wright, did you finish alerting everyone about the stragglers?"

"Everyone's been notified, including those who came with Houston. Many of Houston's men are on the walls with us."

"What about radio silence?" I asked cryptically.

"The squad's prepared to talk to everyone without radios when someone arrives."

"You brought seventy-three to help us. I couldn't get Fannin to leave his compound."

"The great negotiator couldn't convince a colonel to move? What happened?"

"I knocked him out."

"You knocked him out?" Wright asked incredulously. "That sounds like a story I'd like to hear."

"Fannin wouldn't believe we're from the future despite my rifle demonstration and some facts about one of his patrols that had not reported in yet. Instead of being reasonable, he accused us of being spies and arrested us. Before anyone could move, I clubbed Fannin and told Major Mitchell, who was with him, to keep quiet while he was being tied and gagged. Before we left, I made sure Major Mitchell reminded Fannin about what I'd said, and what the patrol would tell them when it returned. With facts from two sources in his ear, hopefully Fannin will want to save himself and reinforce us."

"I'm surprised you're still walking around. Striking an officer is a court-martial offense," Wright said.

"I've been court-martialed."

"Already? That was fast," Wright said incredulously.

"I've been sentenced to thirty days in jail, contingent on our victory against Santa Anna. You know, for all the research I've done, and all the wishing that I could be here, I'm getting tired of this place."

"That's something I never thought I'd hear you say," Sutter admitted when he approached us.

"Has everyone been notified about our reinforcement arrivals?" I asked.

"I've checked, and they're ready," Sutter confirmed.

"Let's get on the walls and—"

"Riders coming in!" Someone shouted.

"Where? How many?" I shouted back.

"At least twenty from the east!"

When challenges were issued and identities confirmed, twenty-four reinforcements who we were expecting to be delayed by the storm rode in. They claimed to have seen Mexican cavalry chasing small groups of men, running them down and killing them. It was hard to hear, but not unexpected. I'd read the Texians had respect for the Mexican cavalry and didn't want to challenge them in a one-on-one encounter, which was one of the several reasons why the Alamo defenders didn't leave when they had the chance.

Suddenly feeling a bit overwhelmed, I leaned against the parapet wall to take a break, and maybe rest my eyes for a few seconds. I spread my legs a little to ease the pressure on my bandages.

I found myself in a grove of trees, a cool breeze gently stroking my brow. I was walking, but to where I didn't know. Suddenly, dozens of horses ran through the stand of trees behind me, all black horses, red eyed, snorting fire as they ran toward me. I flattened myself against a thick tree and let them run past. Just when I thought it was over, one horse ran through the tree at my back and knocked me to the ground. It stood over me and said, "Get up," spraying my face with flames. I stood and started running, but the horse took me in its teeth by my belt. It held me off my feet and waited for the other horses to return, then it dropped me. "Get up" it said again, when another horse climbed on my back and screamed, "Run!" I ran with the horse on my back while the others laughed, spraying fire everywhere until I fell, unable to run anymore. "Time to die!" All the hell horses surrounded me and inhaled. Expecting the flame throwing horses to end me, I got up and ran….

"Sarge! Sarge! What happened?" Carpenter exclaimed as he stood over me.

Roaring headache aside, I was completely confused as I lay on the ramp, my normally squared away uniform muddied.

"Stand aside. I have him. Stand aside!" Sutter said when he helped me to my feet. "Come on, Sarge, let's go see Taylor."

"I don't want to go up there. He's busy."

"Taylor finished with General Houston over an hour ago," Sutter reported as we made our way across the courtyard.

I vaguely remember struggling against Sutter when he tried to get me to climb the steps to the hospital.

"Okay, okay. Let's see if Taylor will make a house call." Sutter seated me on the steps to the hospital and shouted for Taylor to come down.

"Sutter, what happened?" Taylor asked when he saw my muddy uniform and began a preliminary exam.

"I didn't see it for myself, but Carpenter said he started running around until he tripped and rolled down the north ramp."

"There's nothing physically wrong that I can see. It's possible you're still feeling the effects of the concussion, but is there something else I should know?"

"I think I had a flashback, but I've never been chased by hell horses before."

"Flashback? Have you been diagnosed with PTSD?" Taylor asked.

"A mild case," I enunciated, making sure he understood every word.

"There's no such thing as a mild case. Either you have it or you don't. Do you get any warning before you have an episode?"

"Like what?"

"Some people get what's called an aura. It's been described as an unusual feeling something is off, or an urgent need to get to safety."

"Not that I'm aware of. They just happen."

"What about the after effects. How long do they last?"

"Not long. I always have a headache, but sometimes, like now, I'm tired…and bored," I said, looking directly at Taylor.

"How many episodes have you had since we've been here?"

"Why all the questions?" I was annoyed by his invasion of my medical privacy.

"How many episodes!" Taylor repeated forcefully.

"Three!"

"Just one would be enough to send you to the psychiatrist for evaluation."

"I've already had evaluations. They said unless or until my flashbacks become violent, or interfere with my duties, I'm under observation, nothing more."

"Have you had a flashback before, during, or after the Mexican attack?"

"Which one?"

"Either."

"No. Not at all."

"Bullshit. You had a flashback the morning after you got your concussion. I should relieve you of duty, but I can't, not in our current situation."

"It's just as well, because I'd ignore you because of our current situation. I'm feeling better, so let's find Sergeant Wright and get with Travis. He'll want a report about what happened at Houston's camp. Doc, you can go back to the hospital and continue training."

"I don't need training."

"You're not training them?"

Taylor went back to the hospital without further comment.

We located Sergeant Wright and went to Travis's office to find him sitting in the dark.

"Colonel Travis?"

"General Houston was shot and has something Corporal Taylor called a sucking chest wound. Even with a doctor, I've seen men die very quickly from such wounds, but Corporal Taylor wouldn't give up. I watched him work; I watched him save General Houston. Thank you for bringing Taylor to us."

"Actually, sir, like the rest of my men, he was along for the ride. How's the general doing?"

"When Taylor was working on him his pain became visibly less, and when Taylor finished with him, he was easily talking with us. Taylor insisted the general lie on his injured side, saying something about inflating his lung."

"It's good news the general is doing so well. Would you like to hear Sergeant Wright's report from the general's camp?"

"Yes…yes!" Travis said when he reached for a lamp to light. "Sergeant Webber, have you been fighting with the sergeant major?" he exclaimed when the light came up and he saw my uniform.

"No, sir, I slipped on a muddy ramp. Sergeant Wright, report."

"Sir, the general read your letter, and when I let him fire my rifle, he asked if there are any more of them. When I said there were ten more here, he ordered his men to break camp and ride immediately. We left General Houston's camp that afternoon with about two hundred and fifty men. When we stopped for the storm, we were attacked by Mexican cavalry. We ran ahead of them during the storm, but they kept in contact with us all night until we got here," Wright said, concluding his brief report.

"Sergeant Webber, did you count how many men came with the general?"

"Seventy-three are inside the walls; four of those are wounded. It's possible many of General Houston's men are still alive out there, and hopefully they will make their way here. The twenty-four we expected the night before last are also inside the walls."

"Sir, there are at least seventy-five men and women following with supply wagons about four days behind. We should—"

"Sir, should we send out some riders to contact them, and

warn them about the cavalry? We can gather any men from General Houston's command we can find while we're out there. The men and supplies would make excellent additions to our defense," I concluded for Wright.

"Sergeant Webber, call for Captain Dickinson and Lieutenant Melton, and send them here."

"Yes, sir." I started to key my radio, but instead I said, "Sir, messages sent by our radios can be picked up by one of my deserters, and he can relay messages to Santa Anna. For the time being, I'd like to act as a runner and bring them here."

"Do it, quickly."

"Yes, sir. Wright, let's go." When we went outside, I said, "I had to cut you off in there. The sergeant major is pissed off about us informing his men by radio, rather than doing it himself."

Following Travis's instructions, Sutter, Wright, and I went to different ends of the compound and sent Dickinson and Melton back to him. Against my better judgment, I went to see Taylor in the hospital again.

"Hey, Doc; I'm here for a bandage change," I said, deliberately not looking around.

"Drop your pants," Taylor indicated, reaching into his bag.

When I dropped my pants, General Houston said, "Horse?"

"Yes, sir. That brainless horse is lucky I don't shoot it."

"I once had similar wounds, but I was more expressive with my choice of words," the general stated with a smile.

"Yes, sir." I couldn't help but smile back.

"Are you Sergeant Webber? Sergeant Wright spoke of you while he was at my camp. He claims you have a much better knowledge of the future than he has. When you're finished being bandaged, sit and talk with me."

"Yes, sir. But before I do, I must see to the needs of my men."

"I can see you're a leader who cares about his men. When you have seen to your men, return and sit with me. I'd like to hear about the future."

"Yes, sir."

When Taylor finished with my legs, I went to find Sergeant Wright. I had him load all the clips with our remaining ammo and divide them among the men, along with the remaining grenades. Even though I didn't have any basis for my bad feelings about tomorrow, I wanted my men prepared.

When I received my clips and grenades, I made sure Wright distributed the remaining ammo to the squad before I went back to the hospital. I saluted General Houston and then sat beside him, squirming to find a comfortable position on the stool I'd selected. When Taylor finished his rounds in the hospital, he joined us, and we had a long and serious conversation. Before I could excuse myself and go to bed, Taylor gave the general a pill for his pain. It wasn't long before he dozed off.

"He needed a break from you." Taylor smiled at me.

"Thanks, Doc. I needed a break from sitting," I said as I carefully stood.

I saluted the sleeping general before I left for my bunk.

CHAPTER 10

DAY NINE – WEDNESDAY MARCH 2, 1836

I was up just before sunrise and went outside to be slapped awake by frigid morning air. The baked clay eves were dripping with remnants of rain which had started and stopped during the night. I climbed the stairs to the south wall and was happy to have gotten up early. When I lowered my night vision goggles, I could see Mexican troops were crossing the southwest bridge, and I wondered why no one had raised the alarm. Even through my goggles the soldiers were hard to see because they weren't carrying torches. They didn't seem to be in much of a hurry as they casually streamed across the bridge.

Taking their lack of speed as a good sign, I notified everyone along the wall that Mexicans were gathering along the road. Initially I was met with skepticism because they couldn't see or hear them, but they agreed to watch more closely. I went back to the barracks and shouted, "First Squad, get up; everybody gear up!" I shouted, walking around shaking and kicking the squad awake. "Mexicans are gathering along the road to the south. You know the drill; take your MRE with you, but don't go to your assigned positions. I want everyone on the south wall." Despite grumbles in the now crowded barracks, others were getting up as well.

"Sarge, why do we have all this ammo? We've got a lot more than the basic load."

"Good question, Ruiz. Everyone listen up. The ammo you've been given is all we have left; there is no more. Don't fire on automatic—semi only—and be sure of your target before you squeeze the trigger. Don't use grenades except on command. If you run out of ammo before this is over, you'll be butt-stroking Mexicans off the walls instead of shooting them."

"Sarge, can we get some of those cloth bandoleers that came with the rounds?" Barnes asked. "It'll be easier carrying our grenades in those, rather than our pockets."

"Those who want the bandoleers, see Sergeant Wright. Get your MREs and let's get on the wall. Move it!" I shouted and grabbed a couple of the bandoleers for myself.

When I went through the archway and turned toward the wall, Taylor shouted from the hospital balcony for me to join him.

"Doc, I don't have much time. We've got Mexicans moving—" I started to say when I saw General Houston sitting on his bunk, with Colonel Travis and the sergeant major seated beside him. It surprised me to see Colonel Bowie there as well, looking considerably better than the last time I'd seen him.

"Sergeant Webber, I've been speaking with Colonel Travis about you," General Houston said. "He tells me you and your men are good fighters, and he gave me the details of your court martial."

"He should have been shot," Williamson grumbled.

"Sir, we were brought here with no known way back to our time. I gave my men the choice to stay or leave, and three decided to leave. Those of us who remain have the duty to defend this position as best we can." I stated briefly.

"It was a good decision not to have him locked up," Houston said to Travis.

"Colonel Travis, Santa Anna's army is lining up on the south road."

"Why wasn't I told before now?"

"Sir, it's dark, and they're moving quietly without torches. My men are on the walls watching them, and if there's any change, they'll inform me."

"Are my men on the walls?" Houston asked.

"Sir, men are already on the walls waiting for your commands."

When Houston started to get off his cot, Taylor said, "General, you will stay here until you're healed enough to move. If you get up before you're healed, you could die faster than I can save you," Taylor said, pulling out the doctor's all-powerful death card, used to gain compliance from a difficult patient. I tried not to smile, because it had been pulled on me before.

"*Sarge, cannons being towed across the bridge,*" Sergeant Wright said.

"Roger that. Colonel Travis, I've just been told that cannons are crossing the bridge. Sir, can the cannon at the south gate be turned to face down the road? It would counter the Mexican cannons being set up down there," I suggested.

"No, it would weaken the defense of the palisade."

"Sir, you could move one of the cannons from behind the gate to replace it. If the Mexicans get past the cannons outside the gate, one less cannon inside won't make much difference."

You could almost see his tactical mind working before he said, "I'll order the cannons moved."

When we started for the door, I could see frustration on the general's face at not being able to oversee the coming battle.

"It looks like Santa Anna is gathering his whole army," Travis said when we arrived on the south wall.

"Sir, before I came here, I studied the Battle of the Alamo, and even then, I was surprised Santa Anna focused his attack on the north wall. This compound's weakest at the palisade, because he wouldn't need ladders to get over it."

"Webber, I see you."

I keyed my radio, and said, "Hernández? How are you still alive? Thompson told me Santa Anna killed you."

"Look who's leading Santa Anna's army."

"You don't lead Santa Anna's army."

"Estúpido bastardo! Look who's in front."

"He called you a stupid bastard," Sutter translated for me.

"I knew that one," I replied sarcastically.

Through the binoculars I saw a two wheeled cart being pulled to the road leading to our gate. One soldier was holding the horse's reins, while another stood well away from the cart with a torch. Corporal Thompson, stripped of his armor and helmet, was tied to a post mounted in the cart.

I knelt and steadied my binoculars on the wall, then I could barely see what looked like kegs arranged around Thompson's legs.

Suspicious of what I thought I saw, I handed my binoculars to Travis and said, "Colonel, can you see what's in the cart in front of Santa Anna's army?"

"It looks like one of your men. Who is it?"

"It's Corporal Thompson, one of my deserters. But you need to see what's in the cart with him."

"Whiskey? Why would they give us...? No! Those are

powder kegs!" Travis exclaimed as he leaned forward with the binoculars, trying to get a closer view. "They're going to blast a hole through the gate!"

"That's what I thought. They've made a bomb, and Hernández expects me to hesitate and protect Thompson by not shooting at it."

"Sarge, it doesn't make any sense," Sutter said. "Hernández knows we can drop the horse with our rifles. Even if we miss, we can still stop it with a grenade."

Keying my radio, I said "Hernández, I see you've turned on the Reverend Thompson. I thought you were a religious man. You're going to hell for this."

"I made sure His Excellency positioned his men outside your grenade range, and when His Excellency gives the order, I'll watch you die. I told you I'd watch you die! I told you! When you're dead, I'll piss in your dead face."

"Hernández, you need to find something original to say," I said to my radio.

After a pause, Sutter said, "Sounds like he's going to ignore you."

"Let's see if I can change that with some disinformation." I keyed my radio and said, "Hernández, I have a message for the coward Santa Anna. Over the past two nights, we've been reinforced by over three hundred men from Colonel Fannin's army in Goliad, plus many volunteers from around the area. I led Fannin and his men here two days ago. Be sure to tell Santa Anna I called him a coward."

Through the binoculars, I saw Hernández lean over to the Mexican officer next to him, confirming it was Santa Anna.

"His Excellency says you don't have that many men."

"That didn't work," Sutter said.

"The number of men I suggested is in the back of Santa Anna's mind, where I wanted it to be."

"Psychological warfare," Sutter said with a smile.

With a smile I keyed my radio, and said, "Hernández, you've ignored your training again. I'll give you this one last chance to leave, so you'd better run while you still can!"

"*Vete a la mierda!*"

"He told you to fuck off," Sutter translated again.

"You're a joy to have around, do you know that?"

"Translating for you is the only time I can cuss at you and get away with it," Sutter said with a toothy grin.

Shaking my head, I said, "First Squad, gather around. Get low in case of snipers. Our training is always ongoing," I said, and I was greeted with the expected groans and grumbles. "What's the maximum range of the M16?"

"Thirty-six hundred meters," Barnes quickly replied.

"Right. What is the maximum effective range of the M16?"

"Five hundred fifty meters," Snyder said.

"Right again. Santa Anna's sitting on his horse at about five hundred meters. Can we hit him at that range?"

"Sarge, we've only fired at stationary targets, three hundred meters away," Wallace noted.

"Steady your rifle on the wall and aim high," Sutter stated.

"Private Wallace, how would you handle shooting Santa Anna at that range?" I asked.

"Me? I'd send as many rounds downrange as I could."

"Why?"

"Better chance of hitting him."

"Good answer! Everyone place your weapons on safe and load one, twenty round magazine."

"Won't they fight without Santa Anna?" Barnes asked.

"His army is made up of poorly trained conscripts. Some of them were trained how to march and fire a musket on the way here. There are a few hard-core volunteers and battle-hardened veterans who are loyal to the Republic of Mexico, but not necessarily to Santa Anna. They aren't prepared for the cold, so most of them don't want to fight."

"Since we've pounded him twice already, they might go home without a fight if Santa Anna's killed," Sutter said.

"That's what I'm hoping for."

"If we kill Santa Anna, won't one of his generals take over the army?" Barnes asked.

"Let's kill Santa Anna first, and see what happens."

Taking turns with the binoculars, I had everyone locate Santa Anna behind the formation. Several Mexican officers were in front, and I reminded the squad the officers frilled hats looked similar to Santa Anna's.

When everyone was certain of their target, Ruiz said, "Is that Hernández next to Santa Anna?"

"He's got a lot to answer for, so I want him alive if possible. Everyone spread out and take up a good, supported firing position. Remember, aim above Santa Anna's hat to allow for the round's gravity drop."

When everyone was settled and ready, I shouted, "Take your time, steady your shot. When Santa Anna goes down, fire at anyone with a fancy hat. On my command, twenty rounds, fire."

Under a hail of bullets, Santa Anna, Hernández, and several other soldiers in his area went down. Other officers quickly followed.

When the squad had expended their rounds, I scanned for Santa Anna and Hernández, but I didn't see them anywhere.

"Hernández, my man, are you still alive out there?" I said,

taunting him.

"Maybe we hit his radio," Sutter suggested.

"We're not that lucky. Snyder, take my binoculars and give me eyes in the tower. Try to locate Santa Anna and Hernández. Double check anyone being carried across the bridge."

"Sergeant Webber, the cart is out of range of Crocket's musket. You're good at shooting horses; you should do it," Travis said to me with a completely straight face.

"Sir, we have to wait until it starts moving. If we kill the horse now, they'll just replace it. We'll stop the cart long before it gets here."

I went to each of my men on the wall, and said, "Watch the horse and cart. When it starts moving, shoot the horse, and don't stop until it drops."

"What about Thompson?" Ruiz asked.

"Ruiz, make the decision. Do we all die to save Thompson, or does Thompson die to save all of us? Choose," I calmly said in his face.

Ruiz took an uncertain step back, and said, "It's not for me to decide who lives and who dies."

"Every time you pick up that rifle, you decide who lives and who dies. Sutter! Who lives and who dies? Thompson, or all of us?" I asked.

"It's a no-win for Thompson. Either he dies getting shot when we stop the bomb, or he dies from the explosion that would kill us all."

"Any questions?" I said to Ruiz, who uncertainly shook his head. "Prepare to fire at the horse, and don't miss."

Ruiz looked toward Thompson, then said, "I—I don't think I can. Thompson's one of us."

I keyed my radio, and said, "Snyder, do you have eyes on

Hernández or Santa Anna?"

"Negative."

"Get off the tower and bring me the binoculars."

"I'm coming down."

"Ruiz, get on the tower. The rest of us will do what's necessary. After the bomb goes off, you will fire at the Mexicans when they charge."

While I waited for Ruiz to make his way to the tower, we watched the Mexican lines continue to swell with more men from the town. I noticed some soldiers were crossing the bridge back to town.

Keying my radio, I said, "Ruiz, fire a grenade at the Mexican lines, and see if you can reach it from up there."

"If I fire at the center, I might kill Thompson."

"Snyder, get back on the tower and throw Ruiz off! Then give me one grenade on the left of the Mexican lines."

"Yes, Staff Sergeant!" Snyder shouted, and ran back to the church.

I eyeballed a quick count of Mexican soldiers along the road, and it didn't look like fifteen hundred men to me. Despite the number of men crossing the bridge back and forth, it looked closer to five hundred. Where were the rest?

"Carpenter, Wallace, double time to the north wall, on the corners, and report movement!" I shouted, and they scrambled down the steps.

Thoomp!...Choom!

"Looks like Snyder dropped the grenade short," Wright observed.

"Even so, it dropped about twenty soldiers. It's enough for Santa Anna to get my message."

"What's the message?" Wright asked.

"Our reach goes a long way," I said with a confident smile when we saw soldiers running away from the lines. They didn't get far, because cavalry patrols were cutting them down.

***

After an hour of tense waiting, a bugle sounded from the south. Another bugle responded from the west, and cannons in Bexar opened fire. Our eighteen-pounder responded, followed by the lighter cannons along our west wall. I was trying to locate the cannons that were being moved near the huts earlier when I saw a soldier run to the cart, light the fuse, and then run as fast as he could toward their lines. Another soldier whipped the horse, making it run along the road toward us.

"Kill the horse!" Travis shouted, pointing at the bomb rolling toward us.

"First Squad, kill the horse, kill the horse!" I shouted over the radio, and we began firing.

A few seconds later, the horse fell to the ground about a hundred meters in front of the Mexican lines. The sudden stop pivoted the cart upward, and then it slammed down, shattering a wheel. The post Thompson was tied to snapped and fell beside the cart. Somehow Thompson struggled out of his ropes and hobbled to one of the burned-out huts on the side of the road.

Heads down, we waited for a massive explosion. Cautiously I peeked over the wall, fully expecting to get a face full of debris when the barrels exploded, but nothing happened. When the cart was destroyed bugles sounded again, and the Mexican cannons stopped firing. I looked for smoke from a burning fuse somewhere among the barrels scattered near the dead horse.

"Sir, do you see any smoke?" I asked Travis as he stood looking through his telescope.

"No. Why would Santa Anna want to trick us into believing

he was sending a cart full of powder at us?" Travis said.

Alerted by distant gunfire coming from the north, I shouted, "It's a diversion!"

"Cavalry! Cavalry!" Someone shouted over the radio.

"Where? Who? How many cavalry?" I shouted at my radio.

"Coming over the hill from the northwest! About a hundred, riding fast."

"Ruiz, reinforce the center of the north wall!" I shouted.

"What is happening?" Travis shouted when he turned to look at the north wall.

Just as Ruiz ran down the steps, Carpenter shouted, *"Hold your fire! Hold your fire! Open the gate! Sarge, friendlies coming in the east entrance!"*

"Sir, riders coming in the east entrance," I told Travis.

Cavalry coming over the hill from the northwest! Carpenter shouted again.

"How many; what kind of cavalry?" I shouted at my radio.

About twenty-five Mexican cavalry chasing the friendlies!

"Open fire on the Mexican cavalry; rifles only! Secure the gate when the friendlies are in!"

When the Mexican cavalry were within range of the Alamo weapons, they opened fire.

"It's Fannin!" Travis shouted when he recognized the officer riding toward us.

"Aww, shit; it's Fannin," I mumbled. I was glad his men were here, but how would he react when he saw me? I was certain he wanted me, and to hell with reinforcing us.

"Colonel Travis, I don't think Fannin's here to help you."

Even twenty meters away, no one could help but notice the glaring shiner around his left eye.

When Fannin reined in his horse and dismounted, I

recognized Major Mitchell when he dismounted beside him. Most of Fannin's men dismounted as well, and moved toward the scaffold.

"He looks pissed," Sutter said from behind me. "I'll be nearby, just in case."

"Travis, I'm taking command of this garrison!" Fannin shouted as he climbed the stairs.

"You will not take my command!" Travis shouted back.

"This is my command now! Webber, you are coming with me!"

I came to the position of attention, and said, "No, sir, I will not."

"He will stay under my command!" Travis shouted, positioning himself between us.

"You insubordinate bastard, I'm your superior officer! Stand aside," Fannin said, drawing his pistol.

"Colonel Fannin! Colonel Fannin, I'm in command of this garrison!" Houston shouted from the balcony of the hospital.

When Fannin turned to see who had challenged his authority, Sutter tackled Fannin, and together they tumbled off the scaffold, landing on the men gathered at the bottom. The pistol went off, and men on both sides aimed rifles at each other.

"Hold fire! Hold fire!" Travis and Major Mitchell repeatedly shouted.

"Medic! Man down at the south gate," I shouted at my radio, but Taylor was already running toward us with his med pack in hand. I rushed down the stairs to help Sutter, who was arching his back in pain.

"Doc, over here! He's been shot," I shouted when Taylor arrived.

"I have him. What happened?" Taylor asked as he gently

rolled Sutter over to examine him.

"He tackled Fannin and they fell off the scaffold. Fannin fired his pistol at him."

After a brief exam, he said, "You're not shot, but you may have broken those ribs. Webber, take him to the hospital!"

"Are you a doctor?" someone asked Taylor. "Colonel Fannin has been shot."

"Colonel Fannin, did you hear me?" General Houston shouted.

"Someone get the general back in bed before he kills himself!" Taylor shouted as he started working on Fannin's foot.

"I'll do it. Sergeant Wright, you're in charge of the squad," I said as I got Sutter to his feet. Major Mitchell helped me walk Sutter to the hospital.

"Was that General Houston up there?" Mitchell asked.

"Yes, sir. He arrived yesterday afternoon. He was badly wounded by Mexican cavalry before he got in the gate."

"Sergeant Webber, be wary around Colonel Fannin. You were right about what Colonel Johnson would say when he returned from his patrol, but despite my reminder of what you told Fannin, he wouldn't leave. I reminded him time and again that you'd struck a superior officer, and you would get away with it. I also reminded him he's Travis's superior officer, and he could take command of the garrison to get you."

"You made him angry enough to leave? For good or bad, he's here with his men. Fannin will be carried to the hospital where he'll meet General Houston, who is in command of this garrison now."

"It should calm the situation, but not by much," Mitchell observed.

"Sir, I want you to know, I didn't plan any of this."

"He never does," Sutter strained to comment.

We slowly made our way up the stairs to the hospital, where we saw General Houston. I could see he was in pain, breathing heavily, leaning against a wall and pressing his forearm to his side.

"General Houston, Corporal Taylor said you must return to bed. Return to bed, sir!" I insisted as we gently deposited Sutter on a bunk.

"I must tell Fannin I'm in command of this garrison."

"Sir, Fannin's coming up here. Get back to bed," I ordered.

"What is wrong with Fannin?" Houston asked.

"Sir, he shot himself in the foot."

"He shot himself in the foot?" the general asked as his face melted into mirth when he tried to contain himself. His amusement was quickly replaced by intense pain when he was helped into bed by his guards.

When Doctor Pollard tried to help the general, I keyed my radio and shouted, "Taylor, get up here, now!"

Taylor burst into the hospital, pushed Pollard aside, and went to work on the general. After several minutes, Taylor had stabilized him again.

"General, you broke the seal around the bullet hole and your lung was collapsing again. You could've died before I got up here. Will you obey my instructions from now on?"

"Yes, Corporal Taylor," Houston said in a way that reinforced the true command structure.

Several men carried Fannin into the room, where Pollard ordered him to sit on a bunk. I had a perverse sense of satisfaction hearing Fannin yell when Pollard began cutting at his boot. I thought Fannin was yelling because his boot was being cut off, rather than from any pain he was in.

"Colonel Fannin, I've taken command of this garrison," General Houston said. "While I'm unable to fight with the rest of the men, Colonel Travis is in command, under my orders. How many men did you bring from Goliad?"

"I started with one hundred and fifty. I lost many of my men riding through over two thousand Mexican soldiers to get here. Webber will come back with me for punishment!"

"Colonel Fannin, remember who you're talking to," Houston said calmly. "Sergeant Webber told me what happened at Goliad, and it has been confirmed by Captain Dickinson and Sergeant Badillo. I will determine if Sergeant Webber's actions require additional punishment; you will not."

I was sure everyone picked up on the warning in Houston's calm voice. I figured it was a good idea to get away from Fannin's hateful gaze, so I excused myself and returned to the wall. I noted men were no longer crossing the bridge in either direction.

"Any changes?" I asked Sergeant Wright.

"Nope, they're just standing out there."

"How many do you see?"

"About five hundred. But that's not all of them, is it?" Wright asked as we watched the soldiers watching us.

"Fannin claims he rode through two thousand Mexicans to get here."

"Santa Anna has over three thousand men here? I think that could be right. You said Santa Anna left Mexico with about four thousand men. We killed and wounded over a thousand in two attacks. Even with General Urine arriving from the coast, he should have less than that."

"His name is Urrea, not urine," I stated. "If Urrea has arrived, Santa Anna should have about three thousand men left under his command, but we need confirmation. Ah, damn it! I almost forgot about Vicente Filisola, Santa Anna's second in command. He's located near San Felipe, but even if Santa Anna sent for him two days ago, it would take at least a week before Filisola could travel one hundred fifty miles and get here with the thousand men he has. I'll get with Travis and see who he can spare to recon the north."

"Since you and Sutter can't ride with your injuries, I'll go and radio back what I see," Wright volunteered.

"I want you to have backup. Don't leave until Travis tells me who can go with you."

***

When I arrived in the hospital, I said, "Colonel Travis, we need to confirm Colonel Fannin's report of two thousand Mexicans to our northwest. I'd like to send Sergeant Wright to take a look, but I want someone to ride with him. Who can you send?"

"How long will your patrol take?"

"Not more than an hour."

"You know Sergeant Badillo. Take him."

"Yes, sir."

I located Badillo and asked if he'd like to go on the patrol. He quickly agreed and said he'd get the horses ready.

"Sergeant Wright, I'm sending Sergeant Badillo with you. You'll find him in the corral getting the horses ready. When you're ready, I'll be waiting at the east entrance."

When they arrived ready to ride, I said, "Sergeant Wright, radio silence until you're on your way back. Ride northeast, and then swing west. No heroics; take a look and return. Got it?"

"Got it. What if I have to adapt—?"

"Just take a look and return. Open the gate!"

When they trotted out the entrance, I joined Carpenter, Ruiz, and Wallace on the north wall and watched my patrol ride quickly out of sight.

***

What should've taken an hour stretched into four without any word from Wright. I strained my eyes and ears, hoping to see them ride over the hill.

"Any word?" Sutter asked when he joined us on the wall.

"Nothing yet. How's your back?"

"Taylor said I was lucky nothing was broken."

"What were you thinking when you tackled Fannin?"

"Fannin pulled his pistol, and I thought he was going to shoot you."

"Maybe he was going to shoot Travis. Travis defied Fannin by not giving up his command, and Fannin was within his rights as the ranking officer."

"He shouldn't have tried to shoot anyone," Sutter stated. "I know you're going to stay here until Wright gets back, and I'm sure your helmet needs charging. Take mine; I just charged it. I'll charge yours and bring it back."

"Good idea. On your way, tell the squad to trade off and charge theirs. As long as the Mexican army is gathering out there, it's going to be a long night for everyone."

When Sutter started down the ramp, he put my helmet on and said "Damn Sarge, you've got a big head."

I didn't comment when I adjusted the headband in his helmet.

Chapter 11

Day Ten – Thursday March 3, 1836

Clear skies and a bright, nearly full moon allowed the Alamo defenders to see the area clearly while we waited hours in the deepening cold.

The soldiers stood in formation along the south road for most of the day, but just after sundown, wagonloads of wood were brought in and bonfires were lit behind the formations. They started talking loudly and laughing as they stood and warmed themselves. The north was as still and cold as the unburied dead lying on the ground.

"Anything, Sarge?" Sutter asked when he returned my recharged helmet.

"Nothing."

"I checked the walls. The east and west are clear, but there's a party going on along the south road."

"Does any of that activity fool you?" I asked.

"It's a distraction. I know this because you're here, watching the north."

"It's not the only reason why I'm here." I scanned the area

with my night vision goggles, checking their operation after Sutter had charged it.

"What looks like platoons of soldiers are crossing back and forth across the bridge."

"Are they withdrawing?" I asked hopefully.

"They've been standing out there all day. Maybe they're rotating platoons."

"Maybe they're taking a pee break. What time is it?"

"Zero one thirty. Sarge, even if he were captured, he would've said something."

"Unless he was out of range, and that annoys me," I said, fearing for Wright and Badillo.

"Even if we couldn't hear him, at least we would've heard shooting."

"Would we?"

"Sure, he would've defended himself…. That sounded like a grenade," Sutter stated when we heard an explosion in the distance.

"Damn it, Wright. Ruiz, keep your eyes and ears open. Sutter, go tell Carpenter to get ready. I'll get with Wallace."

While we were preparing for whatever would come at us, we heard another distant explosion, followed by bugles relaying messages from north to south.

"*Sarge?*" Someone asked over the radio.

"Maintain radio silence," I responded.

Sporadic musket fire in the distance had our undivided attention as we watched and listened.

"*This is Wright! We're coming over the north hill! Cavalry's right behind us!*" he shouted when he and Badillo appeared, riding fast toward the wall.

"Hold your fire! Open the gate!" I shouted and ran down the

ramp.

Mexican cavalry following behind them reined in and turned back when they realized they couldn't catch their quarry before they came into range of our cannons and rifles.

When Wright dismounted, I said "Sergeant Badillo, take the horses to the corral and report to Colonel Travis on the south wall. Sergeant Wright, I said take a look and return. What part of your instructions were unclear?"

"We spotted at least two thousand infantry and cavalry gathering in formation. We were going to return and report, but cavalry patrols came and went so fast, we couldn't move without being seen. It was hours before the patrols stopped, and the infantry began to move. I know I should've returned, but I took advantage of the situation and fired grenades on their massed formations," Wright reported.

"You were told to recon, not engage."

"When Snyder dropped his grenade on the Mexican right, you said Santa Anna got your message; our reach goes a long way. I took the initiative and extended our reach farther than any of them could've anticipated. Did I misunderstand you?" Wright asked.

"If you'd followed your instructions, we could've ridden out and dropped more than just two grenades on them. Now they're going to regroup, and we won't have another opportunity to catch them off guard."

"They were moving on our hidden position. I had to do something."

"It doesn't matter now. Take charge of the squad on the south wall. Move out."

Frequent, almost frantic sounding bugle calls traveled back and forth between Santa Anna's armies before I remembered our prisoner. I sent for him, and he was presented to us on the north wall with his hands tied behind him.

"Sutter, ask him what the bugles are saying."

"*¿Qué están diciendo las trompetas?*"

He listened for a bugle sequence to complete, and then said, "*Mantén la posición.*"

"Hold position."

"*Escuché otros mensajes. Uno dijo ataque, otro dijo que no ataque. ¿Puedo comer algo? Tengo hambre.*"

"What'd he say?"

"He claims he heard other messages. One said to attack, another said not to attack. He also said he's hungry," Sutter translated for me.

"Orders and counter orders are tracking back and forth between armies. If Santa Anna's dead, there may be a power struggle among his generals out there. I'll get with Travis and see what he wants to do. Keep an eye on things here and put the prisoner back in his cell. Untie him, and make sure he gets food and water."

When I climbed the stairs on the south wall, I said, "Barnes, what're they doing?"

"Looks like they're having a kegger."

"When was the last time you charged your equipment?"

"We all charged up about two hours ago. There's been movement in the huts on the right side of the road," Barnes said.

"Snipers?"

"I don't think so. There's just the one I can see, and when he changes positions, his hands look like they're empty."

"Where's he at now?"

"I lost sight of him two huts from the wall."

"Keep your eyes open and find him. Colonel Travis, I used

the prisoner to interpret the bugle calls we've been hearing. He claims one message said to attack, another said not to attack, and a third said to hold position. What do you think?"

"There's nothing we can do until morning. I want to parley with Santa Anna, and offer him an honorable withdrawal. Were the explosions I heard from your patrol?"

"Yes, sir. Sergeant Wright reports Colonel Fannin was right. There were about two thousand infantry and cavalry to our northwest. Since Sergeant Wright had to fire his grenades to escape, I suspect there's a lot fewer by now."

"Come with me," Travis said.

When we arrived in the hospital, General Houston was sitting in a chair next to the door of the balcony with Taylor hovering over him, arms crossed and looking unhappy. Fannin was seated on a bed with his foot bandaged, glaring at me while Travis spoke to them. I was relieved to get out from under Fannin's glare when I was beckoned to where Houston was seated.

"Yes, General?"

"You had a patrol out to the north. What did they see?"

I glanced at Travis before I spoke. "Sir, Colonel Fannin reported accurately. There were about two thousand infantry and cavalry."

"Were?"

"Yes, sir. Sergeant Wright fired two grenades at the infantry to evade capture."

"The grenades you use, are they as effective as a cannon?"

"Sir, a single grenade will kill everyone within five yards of impact." I pulled a grenade from my bandoleer and handed it to him.

"This small grenade will kill everyone within five yards?"

Yes, sir." A bugle sounded from Bexar again. "Excuse me, sir.

Sergeant Sutter, what's going on?"

"I'll ask the prisoner. Stand by."

"Sergeant Webber, what's happening?" Travis asked.

"Sir, I'm waiting for a report from Sergeant Sutter."

"Sarge, the prisoner said the bugle call is the order to advance."

"First Squad, prepare for attack! Colonel Travis, the order to attack has been given. I'm going to the north wall," I said, taking the grenade from Houston's hand.

"I'll be at the south," Travis stated, and we left the hospital together.

Cannons in Bexar suddenly opened fire with a ferocity and accuracy we hadn't experienced before. The bombardment was knocking holes in the parapets and walls. I surmised the heavy howitzers, expected to arrive by March seventh, had been ordered to reckless speed, and had arrived early.

"First Squad, remember your ammo. Use grenades on massed soldiers only; rifles on semi-automatic. Switch radios to VOX. Someone drop grenades on those cannons in town! Lock and load!"

"Grenade!" Two people shouted.

"Infantry to the northwest!" The radio shout got my attention as I ran up the ramp.

Under the bright moonlight, I didn't need night vision goggles to see soldiers advancing in tight formations from the northwest. When I turned my attention to the northwest corner, the reason for the platoons crossing the bridge into town became clear.

"Infantry advancing across the footbridge! Wallace, Ruiz, move to the northwest corner."

"Moving to the northwest corner."

"I'll cover the northeast corner," Sutter said.

"South wall, what's happening?"

"*Infantry advancing toward us in formation,*" Wright said, and fired a grenade.

The Mexican soldiers to my front shouted, "*Viva la Republica! Viva Santa Anna!*" and began running toward the wall.

When we fired grenades into the advancing infantry, I thought Santa Anna must be alive; if he were dead, they wouldn't have shouted for him. The battle-hardened Mexican infantry quickly closed the distance and threw themselves against the walls. They knew the closer to the walls they were, the less our cannons and rifles would deplete their numbers.

I was going to call for someone on the south wall to send a grenade over my head, hopefully to land close to the outside wall, when Sutter fired a grenade along the wall. It landed near the northwest corner, laying waste to infantry in that area. With my ears ringing from the explosion, I ran to the corner and sent a grenade along the wall in the opposite direction, raining destruction on the infantry close to Sutter's position.

Several times the Mexicans were driven back, but shouts and whipping from their officers quickly regrouped the men in front of us. The delay after each withdrawal gave us time to share what ammo we had left. Then the Mexican infantry obediently, fanatically surged forward. Again and again they kept coming; wave after wave, they kept coming; they kept coming. After each withdrawal I could see signs of weakness in their attack, because the cavalry was cutting down increasing numbers of fleeing soldiers. Each time the infantry surged forward, we were able to get them in an effective crossfire. We fired clip after clip into massed soldiers bunching up at the base of the wall, while our grenades exploded among the infantry farther out. I began to wonder if we were using our ammunition effectively enough, because men were pressed together so tightly, it looked like the dead were being propped up by the living as the mass of soldiers moved slightly side to side. I carefully picked my targets, aiming at those who looked around or those who tried to reload their muskets, and not at those who heads had flopped forward.

In the heartbeats between firing and being fired upon, there was no time to consider right from wrong. Terror in our minds and whispers of desperation in our hearts rose to screams in our throats as we reacted to being dead or alive from one breath to the next. The squad responded to the deafening noises and crippling fear as we were trained to do, but no amount of training could've prepared us for this. Lesser men would've taken one look and run for safety, but there were no lesser men on these walls. There was no safety; there was nowhere to run, because we all knew a gruesome death awaited us if our defense failed. I'd been in several firefights and lived to walk among the dead, but the scale of what I'd experienced in the past, even our last battle with the Mexicans, paled in comparison to the massive numbers of dead piling up in front of us. Despite their knowledge of what our weapons would do, they kept coming. If my three deserters were working with Santa Anna, and they had told him about our training and capabilities, he either ignored them or actually believed his men were like so many chickens; all expendable for victory. Even in the face of what they were familiar with—muskets, cannons loaded with nails, chopped up horseshoes, metal hinges, and iron junk of every sort turning them into giant shotguns clearing ever widening paths through their massed ranks—they kept coming. Grudgingly I had to admire these men as they threw themselves against the walls, clawing their way over their dead and wounded to get at us. As a band of brothers, we stood our ground with the Alamo defenders, firing round after round into the surging humanity massed at the base of the walls. They kept coming.

***

Slowly, it grew quiet. When I loaded another magazine into my rifle, I cautiously looked across the top of the parapet for infantry massing for another charge. Some were running away while others were hobbling, crawling, doing everything they could to save themselves. When I steeled myself enough to look over the top of the wall, the dead and dying were piled up against the wall so high, one soldier in the rictus of death was merely inches from my face. I was not a religious man, but I offered a small prayer when the gurgle of a death rattle finally brought peace to one unfortunate soul. I offered many small prayers for men on both sides, hoping it would be enough until a proper benediction could be given.

Despite the number of times I'd been in firefights, there was no getting used to it. No amount of training or experience that could steel my heart and numb my mind enough to prepare me for the bullet that will take my life. I didn't believe it was shameful or cowardly to ask for a bullet to instantly kill me. I didn't want to be the object of pity, existing in a life with a crippling disability. To put it simply, I didn't want to suffer like I'd seen too many do already.

I was tired; the type of tired that settled deep into my bones. Adrenalin had been sustaining me, but was now rapidly draining my strength. To keep from collapsing, I put my back against the parapet and slid down to my first rest since this nightmare began.

I had the duty, but I didn't want to do it; the roll call, not again. I sat with my back against the parapet and held my head in my hands. I didn't want to know—I just didn't.

"Sarge, are you all right?" Sutter asked.

I weakly waved a hand at him and sat quietly, alone.

"First Squad, listen up. This is Sutter. Sound off when your name is called. Wright."

"Here."

"Breckenridge."

"I'm okay."

"Barnes."

"Good, I'm good."

"Carpenter."

"Here."

"Ruiz."

"Here."

"Snyder."

"Still alive. I've been hit in the stomach again. I'm okay! I'm okay!"

"Wallace."

"Here."

Unexpectedly, I broke into silent tears when I heard that everyone was okay.

"First Squad, check yourselves. Does anyone need a medic?" Sutter asked.

"This is Taylor. I didn't hear from Webber."

"Webber's okay," Sutter reported.

"Not good enough! Bring him to the hospital. I want to examine him."

Several men got me to my feet and were trying to carry me, but I growled and grunted, shaking off the helping hands. My feet were moving like they were mired in wet concrete as I shuffled slowly across the scaffold. It was a lost cause when I tried to walk down a ramp. The incline was too much for my body to manage, and when my legs gave up, I went down.

"Medic!" was the last sound I heard.

***

The next thing I realized was a bright light finding its way to my eyes. When I turned my head to avoid its glare, I realized I was in the barracks. I tried to focus on a figure seated opposite to me.

"Doc, this is Sutter. He's awake."

"I'll be right there."

"What time is it?" I asked.

"Fifteen hundred hours."

"What; three in the afternoon? Why didn't you get me up?" I exclaimed and tried to get up, but found I was tied to my bunk.

"Sorry, Sarge, doctor's orders. He'll be here in a few minutes."

"Why am I tied up?" I said, struggling against my bindings.

"This time, I think I'll pass the buck and let Taylor explain," Sutter said candidly.

Taylor walked in and said, "Stop struggling. Until I evaluate you, you will remain where you are."

"What's going on?"

"Without moving your head, follow my finger with your eyes only."

"Not until you tell me why I'm tied up," I said, clamping my eyes shut.

"You will remain tied up until you cooperate, or I'll have as many men as necessary put you in the jail until you do. Your choice."

"Damn it, Doc, why the attitude?"

"I have wounded men who need me. Make a decision—jail or exam!"

With a frustrated sigh, I submitted to Taylor's order and opened my eyes.

"Was that so hard? Without moving your head, follow my

finger with your eyes only."

I should've known better than to argue with him, so I followed his instructions with barely enough enthusiasm to get the exam over with as quickly as possible. When he flicked his light in my eyes, I asked, "Is everything okay, like I know it is?"

"No. You show the most frequent symptoms of exhaustion, but you were also combative. Looks like you're suffering from a combination of exhaustion and the concussion."

"Are we back at that again?"

"I told you a concussion doesn't clear up in a day, but you're bouncing around like it's completely healed."

"Maybe I didn't get hit as hard as you think I did."

"I don't have the equipment to look inside your head to see the damage, so I have to assume the worst-case scenario. I know you've rested about ten hours, and I'm sure it's helped, so I'm putting you back on duty."

"Finally. Where's my rifle?"

"It's in the weapons rack."

"Sutter, why is my rifle not with me?"

"After you fell, we were trying to carry you to the hospital, but you were trying to punch everyone in sight, and we were concerned you might try to shoot us."

"I don't remember doing any of that."

"Now you know," Taylor said, and began untying the ropes while Sutter retrieved my rifle.

"What's the ammo situation?"

"I've redistributed the ammo in case of another attack."

"Come on, Sutter, we have work to do."

"I know you won't, but take it easy doing it," Taylor insisted.

***

The first thing I noticed was that there were few men on

the walls, and they weren't watching the area surrounding us. Most were either seated on the scaffolds, or lying beneath them. I walked to those nearest to me and saw they were sleeping. Cannons in Bexar were quiet, and none of our cannons were manned.

"Sutter, what's going on?"

"It's over. Travis had a talk with Santa Anna himself after sunrise, and they agreed to let what's left of his army return to Mexico after they've buried their dead. They agreed to begin burials on the south field tomorrow morning, but Travis thinks they'll be gone by then. We shot Santa Anna, because Travis said he was wounded."

"How many did we lose?"

"Among the garrison, fifty-one dead, seventy-nine wounded. We had one wounded. Snyder took another hit to his armor and was almost knocked off the tower."

"It's my fault. I left him exposed on the tower," I said.

"It was a good decision to leave him there. Actually, he's the unsung hero of the whole attack. He knew what he was doing up there, in the open, exposed to rifle fire with only his armor for protection. He had the best position to see in all directions, and was in radio contact with Taylor, who relayed messages to General Houston, who was seated on the hospital balcony. He shouted orders to Fannin, who had left the hospital and was hobbling around the compound, climbing ladders and ramps, directing people to where they were needed most. Houston was almost killed by a cannonball that hit near him, and now he's unconscious in the hospital." During his report, Sutter was looking around for something.

Slowly I walked to my former position on the north wall and stood, surveying the area in the bright light of day. Mexican dead were carpeted on the ground as far as my eyes could see, with barely a patch of bare earth anywhere between them. I already knew how high the dead were piled against the outside wall, so I didn't look down; not again.

"There's not enough hallowed ground on the planet to bury these men in," I whispered to myself.

"Travis wants to see you," Sutter suddenly said after looking around again.

"Why didn't you tell me sooner?"

"He's not going anywhere. He's in his office with a bayonet wound to his shoulder."

"They breached the south wall?"

"They came over the palisade after they took the cannons outside the gate. Travis jumped from the wall with most of his men and drove the Mexicans back, but not before he was bayoneted. Most of our losses were at the palisade."

"What about Crockett?"

"Wounded, but not seriously."

I noticed a few men were casually gathering and talking near Travis's headquarters when we walked toward it. Two men guarding the door opened it for us as we approached.

"Sir, how's your shoulder?" I asked Travis, who was writing at his desk.

"Corporal Taylor bandaged it. He had to set my arm because I broke it again during the fighting." He paused his writing only long enough to look at the fresh splint on his forearm.

"Sir, I hear you led the charge that saved us at the palisade."

"When they breached the palisade, David swung his musket like a club, and broke the stock over a Mexican's head. He liked that musket, and he's not happy about it."

That was a strange comment for him to make. He seemed

preoccupied with something.

"Sir, have we won?" I asked.

"We have." Travis didn't look up at me.

"Sir, I surrender myself under the conditions specified at my court martial." I placed my rifle on his desk next to a flintlock pistol.

"Sergeant Sutter, take him to the jail to begin serving his sentence."

Travis never looked up from his writing. He slid my rifle toward Sutter, and put his uninjured hand on the pistol.

"Yes, sir. Let's go, Sarge." Sutter recovered my rifle as he escorted me out.

When we left the office, I asked, "Do you know what's going on?"

"Look up," Sutter whispered.

"What?"

"Look up."

When I looked up, the distinctive double-click of a flintlock hammer cocked behind me. Before I could move, an explosive click-bang preceded an impact, like someone had hit me in the back with a bat.

"Medic! Webber's been shot in front of Travis's office!" Sutter shouted at his radio.

"Colonel Fannin, you will not move!" Travis said, cocking his pistol.

"I am in charge of this garrison, and I'll do what is necessary to maintain discipline!"

"You would commit murder to maintain discipline? You're unfit to command. You will be taken to the jail, where you will wait for a court-martial."

"I do not recognize your authority," Fannin sneered.

Travis quickly raised his pistol and struck Fannin solidly on his forehead.

"You will recognize my authority," Travis said to Fannin's unconscious body on the ground. "Sergeant Major Williamson, take Fannin to the jail. Free the other prisoner and escort him out the gate."

"Yes, sir. Give me a hand," Williamson said to the stunned men standing nearby.

"I have him! Sarge, where are you hit?" Taylor asked when he arrived.

"My back. Damn, it hurts."

"Sergeant Webber, I'm sorry for what happened to you, but it was necessary," Travis said apologetically. "Sergeant Sutter will explain. Corporal Taylor, you will take care of him. Will he recover?" Travis asked.

"Yes, sir. Our body armor protects us."

"So I've seen for myself. What do you need to see to his care?"

"I have everything I need, except his cooperation. Sutter, help me get him to his feet, and take him to the barracks. Colonel Travis, return to the hospital. You may have ripped out your stitches." Taylor pointed at fresh blood on Travis's shoulder. Travis nodded after he looked at his shoulder.

When I was seated on my bunk, Taylor and Sutter removed my armor and shirt.

"At least I know what to expect," I said.

"Yeah, and it's gonna hurt," Sutter said unsympathetically.

"Take a deep breath." Taylor pushed on a rapidly developing bruise with his thumb. "Did you feel any grinding in your back?"

I desperately wanted to unleash several choice words to accurately describe what I felt, but I limited my comment to a strained and simple, "No."

"Neither did I. Sit still while I tape you up."

"Sutter, I think you had something to do with why I was shot."

"I want you to know, I was totally against Travis's plan. When Fannin learned Houston was wounded again and unconscious, he announced he was taking command of the garrison. He went to Travis and had a discussion that could be heard across the compound. Then Fannin put Travis under guard in his own headquarters. After Fannin left, Major Mitchell told Travis that Fannin would shoot you at his first opportunity. Travis called me to his office and ordered me into silence. He asked me, again and again, if our body armor would protect us. I assured him it would, and reminded him about our wounds when Snyder and I were shot. Travis told me to send Williamson to his headquarters and then stay close to you, which is why you were under guard when I sat with you in the barracks, just in case Fannin would try to shoot you before we were ready. I was told to wait and watch for Major Mitchell to get Fannin into a position where he could shoot you near the headquarters in view of as many witnesses as possible. Like I said, I was against the plan, but I was ordered to go along with it."

"Before I was shot, why did you tell me to look up?"

"Even at close range, a flintlock pistol is inaccurate. The extended rim of our helmet protects the ears and neck, and by looking up, your neck was fully covered from the back."

While Sutter was telling the story, I couldn't describe what I was feeling, but whatever it was took the place of pain. For the first time in my life, I was truly afraid of what I might do.

"Barnes, bring him in," Sutter hurriedly said to his radio.

The door opened, and Thompson was led in with his hands tied behind his back.

"He's the one I saw in the huts last night," Barnes said, holding Thompson's arm.

Without comment, I stared at Thompson. The pain was returning while Taylor continued tending to my back.

"Sarge, please, I didn't want to join Santa Anna, but Sutter pushed me over the wall, and I had nowhere else to go. I wanted to come back so I could get my stuff and leave like you offered."

"Where's Hernández?"

"The last time I saw him, he was riding with Santa Anna when I was tied in the cart."

"Where's Sanchez?"

"He disappeared the first night we were in Santa Anna's headquarters. I haven't seen him since."

I stared long and hard at Thompson before I said, "Doc, do you have one of those pain pills?"

With bottle in hand, Taylor said, "Take one, and see me every four hours. Sutter, you're overdue."

"You bet I am."

"Thompson, if you expect to be welcomed back with open arms, I'm not going to make it that easy. Do you remember the promise I made to you?"

"No."

"I promised I'd let Travis decide what to do with you. Let's go see him."

"Sarge, you need to put your shirt on. Sutter, help him get dressed. If I'm needed, I'll be upstairs."

I don't think Taylor wanted to be a witness to Thompson's predicament.

The crowd that had gathered around Travis's headquarters to witness Fannin's attempt on my life had dispersed, as had the guards. When we entered Travis's headquarters, I said, "Sir, this is Corporal Thompson, one of my deserters. He's returned and—"

"And you expect me to punish him for his actions? He's your soldier. Do whatever you think is appropriate."

"But, sir, I can't court-martial him. I don't have the authority."

Travis sat back in his chair and waved his hand at me, listening and watching. I had tried to pass the buck to Travis, but he handed it back.

"Thompson, you know you've committed desertion and conspiracy. Tell me, what do you think I should do?"

"When I killed all those men on the road with my grenade, my worst nightmare came true."

"When you fired the grenade, what did you think would happen? Did you think it would explode into all kinds of colorful fireworks, and they would dance around, all happy about it? Here's your clue from our block of instructions on M203 grenade launcher: Kill radius of five meters!" I shouted, frustrated by his answer.

"Before Sutter pushed me over the wall, I was telling Hernández he wouldn't get any help from me, despite what we agreed to at the well. I was going to take your offer to leave, but Sutter and Hernández said they'd shoot me. What could I do?"

"You could've run to the gate and asked to be let in. Instead, you joined Santa Anna."

Thompson looked at Travis and me, then said, "I want to pack my stuff and go, like you offered."

"And so you shall. Sergeant Sutter, take him to the barracks and supervise while he packs."

"Can I have my M16?"

"What does a peaceful conscientious objector want with a rifle?"

"I have to protect myself out there!"

"If you want a rifle, there are plenty of muskets lying around. I'm sure the Mexicans won't mind if you take as many as you want."

"I don't know how to use a musket."

"Get with any of the men inside these the walls and ask them how to use it. Sergeant Sutter, give him a hand with that and get him out of the compound."

"What about never leaving anyone behind?" Thompson asked.

"You lied, because Sutter took ammo from you that you were going to drop to Hernández. You lied when you said Santa Anna killed Hernández. I don't know how many other times you lied, and I'm not going to ask. You abandoned us, now stay that way. Sutter, get him outta here!"

"Let's go!" Sutter ordered, pulling Thompson through the door.

After they left, Travis said, "You were lenient with him."

"There's no doubt his actions warrant a court-martial, but even if he were judged innocent, he'd never be trusted again. He's proven he won't fight, and we'd have to constantly watch him. Maybe someday he'll figure out why I let him go."

"Perhaps. Tomorrow morning, I want you and your men to enter Bexar and see if Santa Anna has gone. I know you and your men have the training to do this, and just in case he is still there, I know your armor will protect you. Tell me when you're done searching the town, and I'll bring my men in. Then, as payment, you and your men can have whatever you can find in his headquarters and on the bodies."

"Sir, looting's not legal, or ethical."

"It's not looting—it's battlefield prizes as long as you do not take anything from the townspeople, their homes, or the church."

"Yes sir; I'll inform the squad. Did you go to the hospital for your shoulder?"

"Not yet."

"Would you like me to escort you there?"

After receiving a look that told me to stop pestering him, I saluted Travis and left the room.

CHAPTER 12

DAY ELEVEN – FRIDAY MARCH 4, 1836

The morning had dawned clear and cold as I called a formation outside the barracks.

"Squad, Ah…Ten…Shun!"

"Lock and load!"

"At ease. Colonel Travis wants us to recon the town and see if Santa Anna is still there. If he's there, I have a promise to keep with him."

"Technically, he's a prisoner of war. You can piss in his face, but you can't hang him," Sutter said.

The reminder of my promise to Santa Anna brought laughter from the squad.

"If he's a prisoner, why isn't he in the jail?"

"The colonel was the last one to talk to him; you'll have to ask him."

"He belongs in our jail, so we'll bring him back, and then we're going out again to take whatever we want from Santa Anna's headquarters, and the bodies of his men."

"Sarge, that's looting," Wright observed.

"According to Colonel Travis, it's not. It's what he calls battlefield prizes, and I agree with him if we take from his headquarters and dead bodies only. We have to go into homes to look for any soldiers he left behind, so we'll use our urban operations training to clear the town. You know the drill—keep your eyes and ears open, watch for any armed soldiers who've been left as a rear guard, and don't shoot civilians."

"Santa Anna may have left his wounded. Should we bring Taylor?" Sutter asked.

"Good thought." I keyed my radio. "Taylor, we're going to recon Bexar. There may be wounded left behind."

"There's a lot of our wounded up here to tend to. If there are any in town, let me know and I'll follow."

"Roger that. Everyone switch your radios to VOX and move out."

Expecting a fight at any moment, we approached the bridge to Bexar, slipping and stumbling over bodies, trying to keep our footing.

"Sutter, despite what you said, I'm going to make Santa Anna bury these bodies, and then I'll hang him."

After running in pairs across the bridge, we spread out again, keeping low and watching for movement. We ran up on the cannon breastworks, but they were unmanned, except for the bodies of the men killed by our grenades. We set up and kicked in our first door, but only found bodies stacked like cordwood.

Looking around, I said, "There are too many buildings to clear. Split into teams of three. Spread out and kick in every door. I'll take the main street."

Carpenter and Ruiz had my back as we systematically checked every building through the center of town. We checked the tent where Santa Anna had his headquarters, and then went to the closed cathedral doors.

"There's lots of places to hide in here. Check high and low."

The heavy doors were unlocked, and we carefully pushed them open with our trained mindset they might be booby trapped. We peeked behind the doors and checked the overhead. Alerted by moaning, we found wounded men lying side by side across the floor and against the walls.

"Doc, we've found wounded in the cathedral!" I exclaimed.

"I'm on my way."

"Bring all the doctors you can spare. Find Travis and let him use your radio for a minute."

"Wilco."

"Sergeant Webber, what have you found?" Travis said over Taylor's radio.

"Sir, we're still checking the town, but it looks like Santa Anna's gone, and he left his wounded behind. We're continuing to search."

"Where are you?"

"Sir, I'll be in the cathedral. First Squad, continue your sweep."

"This is Sutter. We've reached the edge of town. We've checked out civilians on our sweep, and they say many wagons passed by here, heading south. We can see soldiers lying on the side of the road."

"Check out those nearest to you without going too far."

"Roger that."

"This is Wright. There's nothing but bodies everywhere we've looked. Judging from the amount of blood on the floors, they must've been alive when they were carried inside."

"Continue your sweep. If you find any survivors, report them to Corporal Taylor when he arrives. Then report to the cathedral."

When Travis rode in with about twenty men, he asked, "Sergeant Webber, any survivors?"

"Sir, there are several in the cathedral. I have Sergeant Sutter checking soldiers on the sides of the south road."

"This is Sutter. We've checked the men on the road. They're all dead. It looks like Santa Anna is dumping the recent dead on the road."

"Roger that. Sir, it looks like Santa Anna is heading south. He took the least seriously wounded with him and left the rest in town. Looks like he's dumping the recent dead along the side of the road instead of burying them."

"We'll continue the search. Take your prizes as we agreed. I'll send some men to follow Santa Anna and make sure he leaves," Travis said, when he accepted help dismounting his horse.

"Sir, Santa Anna doesn't know about the Declaration of Independence signed at the convention at the Washington-on-the-Brazos. You need him to take this knowledge back to Mexico, and make arrangements that he won't attack Texas again." Travis gave me one of the disbelieving looks I'd seen from him when we first arrived. "Tomorrow, a courier will inform you about the Declaration of Independence from Mexico. First Squad, we've been relieved. Meet at the cathedral."

While we waited for the rest of the squad to return, we searched Santa Anna's bed, and then the tent outside. Except for a few coins, little else of value was found.

When the rest of the squad arrived, I said, "Listen up. Travis said to take our battlefield prizes. Spread out and check the bodies, the tents, and sleeping areas."

"Where're you going, Sarge?" Sutter asked.

"I'm going to the cannons and check the bodies there. Then, I'll cross the bridge and check some of the bodies on my way back the Alamo."

"I'm coming with you."

It was a gruesome business searching the bodies, but after all we'd been through, it became easy after the first hour or so. We accumulated several coins found in the cartridge cases and pockets of the infantry, and even more from the few officers lying on the field.

When I had enough body searching, I was returning to the Alamo gate when I heard, *"Sarge, I found Hernández."*

"Where?" I turned to see Sutter waving his hands over his head. He was looking down at Hernández's body when I walked up.

"He was wearing his helmet, but not his armor. It looks like he took a round to his shoulder, and one to his chest," Sutter reported.

"First Squad, listen up. We've found Hernández. He's dead. If you can find where he was camped, recover his equipment. Keep your eyes open for Sanchez."

"Any eulogy for Hernández?" Sutter asked.

"If you feel the need, go ahead," I stated coldly, and then walked away.

"I guess someone will, eventually," Sutter commented, and followed behind me.

"Ah, shit!" A flash of guilt changed my mind. "We never leave anyone behind, not even our dead. First Squad, is Travis anywhere in your area?" I said to my radio.

"He's in Santa Anna's tent," Barnes stated.

"Get him and let him use your radio."

"Sergeant Webber?"

"Sir, are there any priests working in the cathedral yet?"

"The townspeople have not returned. Why do you ask?"

"We found one of my deserters on the field. We'd like to bury him."

"The cathedral uses a cemetery west of town. You can bury him there."

"Thank you, sir," I said over the radio. "Sutter, it looks like we'll have to walk back to town and find the cemetery. I'll go back to the truck and get the shovels. Meet me at the bridge."

"I'll get the horse over there, and let it carry the body," Sutter stated.

When we walked through town, the horse wasn't as cooperative as he could've been, and my cursing at the animal was not productive. I had planned for Sutter and I to bury Hernández alone, but the squad silently gathered around and helped calm the horse as we crossed another bridge to the cemetery. We picked a spot and took turns digging.

We were almost done when a priest walked to us and stood at the head of the grave. Some of the townspeople had also gathered and waited until we finished digging, and placed Hernández in. The priest recited a benediction in what sounded like Spanish, but I wasn't sure. When I looked at Sutter, he whispered, "Latin."

"Vamos a terminar el entierro para usted. ¿Cuál era el nombre de este hombre para su marcador de cabeza?" the priest asked.

"Su nombre era Manuel Hernández," Sutter replied, and handed him a coin.

"Gracias, señor. Que Dios vaya contigo."

"The townspeople will finish the burial for us. The priest wanted to know his name to make a head marker for Hernández. He also blessed us by asking God to go with us."

On our way back to the compound, we saw that the Alamo defenders had grown impatient waiting for Travis to give the order to collect their battlefield prizes. They had ridden out and recovered several cavalry horses grazing nearby. At first it confused me because I knew they already had their own horses. Then I realized a horse would be much more valuable in this time than the meager number of coins we'd found, which gave me an idea. In my mind, a thought that was long overdue action.

"First Squad, report to the Alamo," I said to my radio.

"What about the prizes Travis said we could have?"

"Get in here! Double time!"

***

"First Squad, fall in! Get your spacing. Squad, Ah…Ten… Shun!"

"Lock and load!"

"At ease. Did anyone find Hernández's rifle and armor?"

"I don't think we'll find them," Wright said. "Santa Anna probably has them."

"Agreed. Let's redistribute what ammo we have left."

When the clips were given out, I considered us fortunate because each of us had only four full clips left. I gave my last three grenades to Sutter, who then gave them to Wright.

"Gentlemen, I'm tired. It's not the kind of tired that goes away with a good night's sleep, or a three-day weekend. I've had my fill of bullets flying in my direction, and I count myself lucky to be wounded only once."

"Three times."

"You can't count the bullet in my back; you own that one," I said, still annoyed by Sutter's involvement.

"That's on Travis, not me. And what about your head wound?"

"Don't remind me. After what we've experienced over the past several days, I've decided I've had enough killing. I'm going to take myself up on my own offer and—"

"You can't quit!" Ruiz shouted over the sudden dissent

raised by the rest of the squad.

"At ease! I'm not quitting, I just can't carry on. Sergeant Sutter, front and center." Sutter took a single step forward. "Front and center, Sergeant."

"Sorry, Sarge—you're not going out there alone."

"I'm not afraid of the dark."

"I'm going with you. If you put me in charge, I'll put someone else in charge and follow you anyway," Sutter stated firmly, and stepped back.

"Sergeant Wright, front and center. As the next senior non-commissioned officer, I'm leaving you in charge of the squad. When Travis gets back, I'll inform him about our change of command. You'll report to him from now on. Are we good?"

"We're golden, Staff Sergeant."

"Roger that. Squad, Ah…Ten…Shun!"

"Lock and load!"

"Gentlemen, it's been an honor and a privilege serving with you. There are no finer soldiers anywhere, past, present, or future. My final order to all of you is: learn to use a musket. Sergeant Wright, take charge." I saluted him and walked to the barracks with Sutter in tow.

"What's the plan, Sarge?" Sutter asked when I rolled my sleeping bag and blanket.

"You heard me, I'm leaving."

"We're leaving, because I'm going with you." Sutter started packing with me.

"Why do you think it's necessary to go with me?"

"You have no idea where you're going, but I do. Like it or not, you're coming with me." Sutter grinned broadly at me, and said, "We'll need four horses."

"How many horses can you ride at a time?"

"One, but do you want to carry those heavy bags on your back when we ride?"

"Right. I'm sure there are plenty of spare horses by now."

"We'll need the additional horses that we can switch riding on, especially if one goes lame. He'll carry a lighter load. You finish packing for both of us, and I'll get the horses."

When I finished packing our bags, I went to see Taylor, who had returned to the hospital.

"I heard you're leaving. Where will you go?"

"I don't know. Sutter seems to have somewhere in mind, so I'll follow him for a change. I'm here to get a final change of bandages on my legs, and to get some of those pills for my back. I'll be bouncing around on a horse, so I'm sure I'll need them for a while."

"Here, take the bottle. Sutter will need them, too. That's all there is, so go easy with them. I can't change your bandages because I'm out. As you can imagine, there's been a run on them over the past few days. Take this antibiotic cream and use it when the bandages fall off."

"We could use a doctor wherever we're going. Why don't you come with us?"

"No, I'm needed here. There are too many wounded to care for, and these doctors are finally learning from me."

"Are you learning from them?"

"Of course I am."

"Corporal Taylor, it's been a pleasure, and an occasional pain in the ass," I said with a smile, and offered my hand. He took it and firmly held it for a while before letting go.

I was going to speak with General Houston, but he was still unconscious. I waved to Taylor before walking out the door.

I saw Travis ride in through the gate and enter his headquarters with some of his officers, so I followed them in.

"Sir, Sergeant Webber reports," I said with a salute.

"Sergeant Webber, I'm glad you're here. Are you ready to begin your sentence?"

That took me by surprise. It looked like our departure was going to be delayed.

"Yes, sir," I said, and placed my rifle on his desk.

"This is an honorable man," Travis said to the gathered men. "For what you and your men have done here, I've decided to release you from your sentence." Travis stood and handed my rifle to me.

Sergeant Major Williamson didn't look happy, but he didn't protest the decision. On second thought, Williamson never looked happy.

"Sir, Sergeant Sutter and I will be leaving. We've had our own change of command, and Sergeant Wright is now in charge of the squad. I've told him to report to you when he settles in. He's a good man, and you won't have any trouble with him, like you did with me."

"You've proven your knowledge of the future again, but you have the date wrong. A courier arrived this afternoon from the Washington-on-the-Brazos, and they have declared independence from Mexico. I'll send the courier back with a message of what happened here, and I'll mention you and your men highly in my report. I'm truly sorry to see you leave." Travis stood, offering his hand. I gently squeezed it, considering it had the splint attached.

"Farewell, gentlemen." I stood at attention and saluted. It was remarkable to me that every man in the room, including Sergeant Major Williamson, returned my salute.

I went to the barracks to pick up our bags, but they were

gone. Sutter, holding the four horses packed and ready to travel, saw me through the open door and shouted, "Come on, Sarge, let's go!"

"What're you looking at?" I said to the horse when Sutter handed me the reins. "I'm going to need a block of instructions on how to manage these things."

"I know all about horses, and I'll teach you on the way. No long goodbyes. Let's go."

When we mounted and rode toward the gate, First Squad was standing in formation on one side of the gate. Crockett was standing on the opposite side with the men he still had alive. I heard Sutter groan when we approached.

"Squad, Ah…Ten…Shun!" Sergeant Wright shouted from the front of the squad.

"Lock and load!"

"Present…arms!"

I saluted the squad as we rode past. David and his men fired their muskets into the air, raising cheers from everyone inside the walls.

"I was hoping to avoid a sendoff," Sutter said. "Now I feel guilty about leaving."

"I'm concerned about the squad. I really shouldn't leave them."

"Wright's a good man," Sutter stated confidently. "He'll take care of them."

With neither of us willing to talk any further, we rode in silence toward the south. When the Alamo faded from sight behind us, Sutter turned us west and we rode until sunset, when we decided to stop and set up camp.

***

"We're going to die in this time, aren't we?" Sutter asked,

poking the fire with a stick.

"I hoped we'd be returned to our time after the battle was over, but it didn't happen. If it's not too early to ask, where're we going?"

"San Francisco."

"San Francisco? Does it exist yet?"

"It was founded by Spanish colonists in 1776, so it should be a fairly large port city by now."

"Why are we going there?"

"We need supplies. Then we're going to the American River, to a place where the town of Coloma will be located."

"I'll bet it's not there yet."

"Nope."

"Why are you being evasive?"

Sutter looked around before he said, "Ever heard of a place called Sutter's Mill?"

"Sure, everybody knows it's where the California gold rush started…hey, wait a minute."

"How about listening to some history for a change."

"I'm all ears."

"My great, great, and I think great again grandfather was Captain Johann Sutter. In 1847, he contracted with James Marshall to build a sawmill on the American River. In 1848, the sawmill was almost completed when Marshall found a nugget of gold."

"Johann Sutter didn't discover the gold?"

"Not according to history. They tried to keep it a secret, but word got out, and a year later the gold rush began. We'll be there twelve years before it happens, and there's enough gold to make us rich, even in this time."

"Now I know why you spend your leave with your dad in California."

"My dad has a spot where my brothers and I go. Floods carry sediment to a bend in the river, and between the four of us, we pan about three hundred dollars' worth of gold every time we go. We usually spend it at a local bar and restaurant."

"You get that much gold this long after the gold rush is over?"

"In the future, there will be more than enough for my brothers and I to pan for."

"Where we're going, wouldn't it be called El Dorado?"

"El Dorado's a metaphor for a place where riches are easily and quickly accumulated, and we're going to make ourselves very rich, very quickly—so yeah, we're going to El Dorado."

***

The sun had just gone down when a tall, gaunt man rode toward our camp.

"Greetings, strangers. My name is…Sam. Can I join your camp for the night?"

"Sure, join us. I'm Nick Sutter, this is Elliot Webber."

I was going to protest the intrusion, but Sam said, "There's safety in numbers, don't you agree?"

When Sam was warming his hands by the fire, he somehow looked familiar to me, but I couldn't place where I'd seen him.

"Where are you going?" Sutter asked Sam.

"I am going to San Antonio de Bexar to join a fight going on there."

"The battle's over," Sutter said. "Santa Anna was defeated the day before yesterday, and he's going back to Mexico with his tail tucked between his legs."

"Oh. I so much wanted to be there."

"You might consider going somewhere else," I said. "Bodies are lying all over the place, and they'll need people to help bury them."

"Can you tell me about the battle?"

"I'm not a good story teller," I said. "You could get the details from the men we left behind. I'll give you the names to ask for."

"Sarge, what about the notes you've been writing? Let Sam read them."

I had to dig into my bag for the papers I'd borrowed from Travis's office when he wasn't looking. Sam must've been a speed reader, because he finished reading in about fifteen minutes.

"Interesting; and I missed all of it," Sam said, clicking his tongue. "Do you know what the Library of Congress is?"

"It's the largest library in the country, or will be someday," I said. "Lieutenant Walker likes to go there on leave to research the Civil War."

"He's as interested in the Battle of Gettysburg as you are in the Alamo," Sutter stated. "The difference is, we've been there and done that."

"And we could've died there. In case you've forgotten, we lost Hernández and Sanchez!" I stated caustically.

"We don't know about Sanchez! For all we know, he ran off before it all started!"

"Forgive me," Sam interrupted. "I am not one to get in the middle of a conversation, but I have a good friend who is in charge of the Library of Congress. Can I take this to him? I am certain he would like to have a record of the battle."

"Give it to him, Sarge," Sutter stated. "You'd enjoy knowing that you sent an accurate, updated history of the Battle of the Alamo to where they could read about it in the future."

"I suppose it's not going to do me any good if I keep it. Go ahead, take it to your friend."

"Thank you. His name is John Meehan, and he has the grand title of Librarian of Congress. As I recall, he is the fourth librarian in charge of the entire library. The next time I'm back east, I will personally give this to him."

***

The next morning, Sam had disappeared. Only his horse remained as evidence he had been there.

EPILOGUE

We'd been on West Range Road for about twenty minutes when I said, "Looks like fog ahead. Slow down before we get to it." When we started slowing, I looked at the rear-view mirror and said, "Watch out for the speeder behind us. Damn, he's coming up fast. Give that maniac all the room he wants."

"Yes, Staff Sergeant," Corporal Barnes said.

It seemed as if the fog was backing up before us when the maniac driver caught up with our truck. He frantically blew his horn and pulled sharply in front of us. When both vehicles had stopped on the shoulder of the road, I recognized Lieutenant Walker, in his civilian clothes, when he jumped from his car with briefcase in hand.

"Is there a problem, sir?" I asked when I left the truck and saluted the platoon leader.

"Stand fast, Staff Sergeant Webber!" Walker said, opened his briefcase, and brought out a thick stack of paper. "Read this."

"Now, sir?"

"Yes, now!"

"Staff Sergeant Webber does not need to read what he wrote."

When a tall, gaunt man strode from the fog, I noticed the fog couldn't have been natural because it had sharply defined borders as it ominously surrounded us, like a dome.

"You!" Walker exclaimed.

"Call me Librarian. I will give everyone their memories from the experiment I sent them on."

A ring of fog, like a halo, appeared around the heads of the squad. Everyone was frozen in place when miniature lightning bolts flashed from the halo and struck the heads of the squad members. It took only a few seconds before the halos dissipated, and everyone was silent while we sorted out the memories planted in our heads. When I caught up with the memories of what I had done, I realized there were some things I wished I'd done differently, but I had accomplished what I needed to do. With our superior firepower, the Alamo had been saved. I wished we hadn't had to kill so many men, even one of our own, but we'd adapted to an impossible situation and won. But—we didn't kill anyone, I thought. I was so confused when I realized I hadn't actually killed anyone.

As if he was reading my mind, Librarian smiled at me, and then said, "It will sort itself out."

"Why did you do this here, now?" Walker asked, gesturing around him.

"As I stated, it was an experiment. Would you like me to share my observations?" Librarian asked.

"Please do," Walker stated.

"My species does not have an authoritative hierarchy, so I go on my own research to gather information on what you might call leadership styles and their interactions. I was able to observe Staff Sergeant Webber's actions, and reactions to the lack of compatible, trained, upper echelon leadership from your time.

My most important observation was how the soldiers from this moment in your history adapted to the fluidity of any particular moment in their past. It was extraordinary in comparison to my observations of other soldiers of the past. I was able to watch how your history unfolded after Staff Sergeant Webber and his men changed it. The comparison between histories, before and after my experiment, was interesting, but not remarkably so."

"And I know why. There was nothing strategic about the Alamo. Colonel Travis should've abandoned the Alamo, as he was ordered to, and joined General Houston. Failing that, General Santa Anna should've bypassed the Alamo and engaged General Houston. Houston would've had to retreat to the Mississippi, and the protection of the army garrison stationed there."

"What you extrapolate from your written history was not part of my experiment. I enjoyed your interactions with those in your First Squad and the Alamo defenders. Sacrifice is a new concept to my species. I will have to dwell on what I observed," Librarian said thoughtfully.

"Lieutenant Walker, how can you have printed what I supposedly wrote, when I haven't done it?" I said, holding out the papers in my hand toward him.

"This area surrounding us is what you might define as a time milieu," Librarian stated, gesturing to the fog.

Looking around, I hoped someone else would ask the obvious question. It didn't happen.

"Okay, what's a milieu?"

"It's a physical setting in which something occurs," Walker said.

"I control time within this milieu, and in this moment, time has been suspended. Staff Sergeant Webber, you are correct. Because you have not traveled to your year 1836, what you have done does not exist outside this milieu."

"If you control time, why didn't you just drop us off before we left?" I asked.

"Since your limited intelligence cannot possibly grasp how this milieu operates, it is enough for you to know that you had to be physically stopped before you reentered the milieu. First Lieutenant Walker accomplished that when I suggested he do so when he was at the Library of Congress. If I were to release this milieu now, the paper record of what you have done would remain, but it would be blank."

"Because it was printed on paper from this time?" Walker suggested.

"It would be blank because it is based upon events which have not occurred outside this milieu," Librarian corrected. "Biological memories would remain unless I remove them."

"What about the original document I saw in the restricted archive?" Walker asked.

"It has disappeared with no memory or record of its existence. Outside this milieu, history as you know it has not changed. Within this milieu, no one knows you are here. You are outside what you know as normal time."

"We're in limbo?" Walker asked.

"A crossroads, from where I can go anywhere, to any time."

"If I could go on one of your research experiments, could I choose where to go?" Walker asked.

"What?" I exclaimed. "Sir, I've got a head full of crap I didn't do, and you think I'm going somewhere else to do it all over again? Hell no!"

"At ease, Staff Sergeant!"

"Lieutenant Walker, I know where you want to go, but you are aware of my experiment and the parameters of it. It would taint the results."

"You have the ability to put memories into minds. Can you take them out?" Walker asked.

"When an experiment has concluded, I remove the accumulated memories before I release a milieu and allow everyone to go on with their lives without interference," Librarian stated.

"What's the point? I'd like to update the history of the Alamo," I said.

"If he were to leave your memories intact, and you were to relate corrections as you've experienced them, you'd have to give your references. What would you say; I saw them in a dream? You'd be discredited in a heartbeat," Lieutenant Walker stated with some disdain.

"You are correct," Librarian agreed.

"Since you control time and memories, can you send me on one of your experiments where I can choose to go?" Walker asked.

"I know where you want to go, and why. I am unaccustomed to repeating experiments with the same people as the last, although another experiment with these men could be interesting."

The fog that seemed to be held at bay swiftly and silently flowed in. Arching electrostatic shocks began jumping from every surface.

"Hernández, Sanchez, get back here!" Sutter shouted when they jumped from the truck and disappeared in the thickening fog.

When I turned to run after the insubordinate pair, a bolt of lightning arced from the truck bumper. As if by a massive hand, I was hurled backward through the air, landing hard on my back and sliding to a stop at Librarian's feet.

When I tried to get up, the fog snuggled tightly around everything and everyone. Sounds were rendered silent. The headlights on the truck dimmed in the fog flowing in on us as I desperately clung to my consciousness that was reluctantly slipping away.

About the Author

Having been born on December 24 created an important life lesson; choose wisely, the best is not always the largest. I followed a family tradition of military service, and despite my tours in Vietnam and Desert Storm, I continued to pursue my favorite activity of reading science fiction. I am a late starter to writing and have found writing as enjoyable as reading. I write the type of science fiction I like to read: believable, without incredibly ridiculous situations that suddenly appear to solve all the character's problems.

Made in the USA
Monee, IL
01 February 2020

21152258R00173